SILVIA'S
ROSE

BOOKS BY
JERRY S. EICHER

THE ADAMS COUNTY TRILOGY
Rebecca's Promise
Rebecca's Return
Rebecca's Choice

THE BEILER SISTERS
Holding a Tender Heart
Seeing Your Face Again
Finding Love at Home

EMMA RABER'S DAUGHTER
Katie Opens Her Heart
Katie's Journey to Love
Katie's Forever Promise

FIELDS OF HOME
Missing Your Smile
Following Your Heart
Where Love Grows

HANNAH'S HEART
A Dream for Hannah
A Hope for Hannah
A Baby for Hannah

LAND OF PROMISE
Miriam's Secret
A Blessing for Miriam
Miriam and the Stranger

LITTLE VALLEY
A Wedding Quilt for Ella
Ella's Wish
Ella Finds Love Again

THE ST. LAWRENCE COUNTY AMISH
A Heart Once Broken
Until I Love Again
Always Close to Home

PEACE IN THE VALLEY
Silvia's Rose
Phoebe's Gift
Mary's Home

STANDALONES
My Amish Childhood
The Amish Family Cookbook
(with Tina Eicher)

SILVIA'S ROSE

JERRY S. EICHER

HARVEST HOUSE PUBLISHERS
EUGENE, OREGON

Cover by Garborg Design Works

Cover Image © Dean Fikar, volgariver, pellinni / Bigstock

The author is represented by MacGregor Literary, Inc.

SILVIA'S ROSE
Copyright © 2017 by Jerry S. Eicher
Published by Harvest House Publishers
Eugene, Oregon 97402
www.harvesthousepublishers.com

ISBN 978-0-7369-6930-7 (pbk.)
ISBN 978-0-7369-6931-4 (eBook)

Library of Congress Cataloging-in-Publication Data
Names: Eicher, Jerry S., author.
Title: Silvia's rose / Jerry S. Eicher.
Description: Eugene, Oregon : Harvest House Publishers, [2017] | Series:
    Peace in the valley ; 1
Identifiers: LCCN 2017006752 (print) | LCCN 2017010984 (ebook) | ISBN
    9780736969307 (paperback) | ISBN 9780736969314 (ebook)
Subjects: LCSH: Amish—Fiction. | BISAC: FICTION / Christian / Romance. |
    GSAFD: Christian fiction. | Love stories.
Classification: LCC PS3605.I34 S55 2017 (print) | LCC PS3605.I34 (ebook) |
    DDC 813/.6—dc23
LC record available at https://lccn.loc.gov/2017006752

Printed in the United States of America

17 18 19 20 21 22 23 24 25 / LB-GL / 10 9 8 7 6 5 4 3 2 1

ONE

Esther Stoltzfus stepped off the front porch of the small house on Fords Bush Road and looked out over the peaceful valley. A gentle April breeze wafted down from the Adirondack foothills and moved across her face. She reached up to brush a few stray hairs back under her *kapp*. What a *wunderbah* home this would make for her and little Diana. They both needed a fresh start, and a place to fully heal after Lonnie's passing.

A smile filled Esther's face. How right she had been in her decision. Months ago she had made the arrangements to purchase this place through the King family, who lived a few hundred yards down Fords Bush Road. *Mamm* and *Daett* had traveled up with her from Lancaster County and were now busy unloading the U-Haul with help from most of the Amish community's adults.

Esther took another long look across the vista to the north. What a change this place was from the flat farmlands of Lancaster County. For a moment her breath caught. It seemed almost too much change—but surely she could handle it. Had not the Lord forced change on her with Lonnie's passing two years ago?

That tragic time had changed her life in ways she hadn't planned, but she had survived. The Lord's will was always the best—no matter how hard it seemed in the day of trouble. The Lord used change to teach lessons that were needed. Esther hoped she had thoroughly learned what the Lord sought to teach her through that time of sorrow.

When the idea for a move occurred to her, she had embraced the possibility willingly. Perhaps here she would find again what she had lost. Her husband had been ordained a minister two years after their wedding, and she had flourished in the role of a minister's wife for two more years before the Lord took Lonnie. *Yah*, the Lord gave and the Lord took away, and surely this move was the Lord's giving again. She was sure of that. She would become part of the Amish community here in the valley, as she had been in Lancaster County—a solid part of a tradition that was more than five hundred years old.

How she had loved Lonnie and his kind and gentle ways. He had been exactly the husband she had wanted: steady, dependable, and faithful to the Lord. They had been given one daughter, little Diana, before Lonnie passed. Now the time had come to move on.

Her instincts were also right about Isaiah Mast. The handsome widower had stopped by a few minutes earlier and given her a brief smile. True, they didn't have a dating relationship or even an understanding, nor had Isaiah asked her to move to the valley. She had merely followed her heart, sensing that Isaiah might be the right kind of man. The kind of man she could trust. And Isaiah wouldn't think her bold or out of her place in making this move. He, like she, would see the hand of the Lord at work.

A smile continued to play on Esther's face. She shouldn't linger while the others finished unloading the last of the boxes. The heavy pieces of furniture were already in the house, and most of the men had gone home to do their chores. *Daett* had walked down the road with John King to help where he could, and later everyone would return for supper. Afterward, the women would make a final check to make sure Esther was settled in and comfortable. In the meantime, she needed a few moments to collect her thoughts.

The small community had already wrapped warm arms around her and made her feel at home. Esther lifted her head for one last look before she walked around the U-Haul to gather two small boxes into her arms and head back toward the house. As she passed several of the women on their way out, she received tender smiles. Many of the community's women would think her presumptuous if they knew of her plans, but that was because they didn't understand yet. Esther was not given to passionate emotions. She was a simple woman, and she knew what she wanted. This move was in the Lord's will, and so would be her eventual marriage to Isaiah Mast if all went as she hoped.

Ahead of her, *Mamm* put her hands on her hips and scolded, "Where have you been, daughter? You vanished into thin air."

"I was just catching my breath," Esther told her. "They'll understand."

Mamm's face softened. "You're braver than I am, that's all I can say. Moving to a new community by yourself and with a small daughter too."

"It's what I want, *Mamm*. Surely you can see how welcoming everyone is, just as we knew they would be."

"On that I agree." *Mamm* gave Esther a sharp look. "But you haven't told me the whole truth, have you? What is the real reason for your move? Is it Isaiah Mast? I noticed he paid you some attention when he was here earlier."

Esther hid her grin as another woman passed by on her way for more boxes. "Not here, *Mamm*. I'll tell you later."

Her mother merely huffed and joined the others in heading for the U-Haul as Esther made her way around the piled boxes in the living room.

Bishop Willis's *frau*, Beth, had just put away some coffee mugs in the kitchen and turned to take the two small boxes from Esther's arms. She smiled and asked, "How do you think you'll like it here?"

Esther returned the smile. "I was just looking around when I was outside. Everything is so beautiful and so different from Lancaster County. I'll like it a lot. The change will be nice. A fresh start and all."

"*Yah*, a fresh start." Beth's face grew sober. "We all mourned with you when we heard of Lonnie's passing. And now we'll stand with you as your life begins again."

"Thank you," Esther replied. "Lonnie's death wasn't how I expected life to turn out, but the Lord leads us into uncomfortable places in accordance with His will. He makes *goot* things out of bad. That's what I'm hoping will happen here in the valley."

"We all move on in different ways, I suppose," Beth allowed. "Your way might be to find what you once had and settle in again. Is that what you're thinking?"

Esther nodded. She might as well admit the truth to the bishop's *frau*. She should be blushing with such a bold confession, but she was no longer a starry-eyed teenager. "Lonnie was a steady and faithful husband," Esther whispered. "We would have loved each other all the days of our lives if the Lord had not made other plans."

"*Yah*, I understand." Beth comforted her with a quick pat on the arm. "The ways of the Lord are hard to understand sometimes, but life moves on and you're moving on with it. That's the way of our people." She paused and leaned closer. "Is there anything I can do to help? You know, we have quite a handsome widower in the community. Minister Isaiah Mast is much in need of a *frau*. Word has it that he's one reason you're settling here."

Esther laughed softly. "Isaiah has not said anything to give me such a hope."

Beth's eyebrows went up. "But you do have an interest, then? This is *goot*."

Esther opened a box and didn't answer.

Beth gave her a quick glance before she continued. "Did you know of Isaiah from when he lived in Lancaster County?"

Esther hesitated. "We knew each other from a distance during our *rumspringa*, but Isaiah lived in another district."

The bishop's wife nodded and seemed satisfied.

The front door slammed, and Esther turned to see five-year-old Diana enter with two little girls by her side. They were obviously close to the same age, and they had already begun a solid friendship. Esther opened her arms, and Diana flew into her mother's embrace for a hug.

"I see you have new friends." Esther knelt to offer her hand to the other two. They bashfully demurred and dropped their gazes. "You're not going to shake my hand?" Esther teased. "Who are these pretty little girls?"

"Betty and Mary," Diana announced without further explanation, hurrying off with the two in tow.

Both women laughed.

"Looks like the men are coming back," Beth observed, glancing through the kitchen window. "There's Joseph Zook walking up from his greenhouse. Have you met him yet? He lives down the road a bit, so I suppose you'll be seeing a lot of each other. He mourns his own sorrow. He too needs a *frau*."

"No, I haven't met him," Esther demurred. Surely Beth didn't expect her to consider another choice besides Isaiah. "What was his loss?"

"His *frau*, Silvia. She was an *Englisha* girl who dropped in out of nowhere and ended up marrying Joseph. We never knew her, though. He moved here from Southern Lancaster County after her death. He won't talk much about her, and none of us knows the circumstances well."

"I'm sorry to hear that. That kind of loss is never easy."

After a moment when neither woman spoke, Esther told her, "Well, I'd best go out for more boxes."

"Where do you want these dishes?" Beth called after her.

"Just put them on the top shelf." Esther waved her hand in the general direction of the upper cupboards.

"I can do that." Beth gave her a smile. "When you see Joseph, be sure and speak a few words to him. Help us draw him out of his shell."

Esther nodded and continued on. Was Beth expecting Esther to resume the duties of a minister's *frau* even *before* she wed Isaiah? Showing kindness to a hurting man was something she could do. The ease with which Beth accepted Esther's place in the community took her breath away. She hadn't even had a date with Isaiah yet. What further sign did she need that the Lord's hand was in this move?

Her steady and ordinary ways had been rewarded. She did not need fancy notions about love at first sight, pounding hearts, and all of those other *Englisha* ideas to be happy with another husband.

After she stepped through the front door, she greeted the women who were clustered at the bottom of the porch steps. "Thank you all for helping. I so appreciate it!"

One of them was Dorrine King, who lived just down the road.

As Esther passed by, Dorrine turned to give her a smile and a quick squeeze on her arm. "You're welcome."

When Esther approached the U-Haul, she saw it was empty except for one large box. The man Beth had referred to as Joseph Zook was bent over, his back turned to her, as he lifted the box. His arm muscles rippled as he heaved it upward. His beard came well down his chest, and his eyes above the box were a blaze of blue. He wasn't handsome like Isaiah, but he wasn't bad to look at either. Esther noticed as he turned to face her that his left leg was twisted. He stopped short, apparently startled by her appearance in front of him.

"You must be Joseph," she said with a warm smile. "Beth just told me you are my neighbor. Shall I take that?" She held out her arms.

He gazed at her for a moment. "It's okay. I can manage." His look shifted down to his leg, and pain flashed across his face. Esther's eyes were drawn there too.

He shrugged. "My leg got caught in a pulley when I was small. It's never been the same, but I get around."

"I didn't mean to stare..." she began. Was that the right thing to say? "I'm sorry. I just thought..."

He tried to smile. "Think nothing of it." He lifted the heavy box even higher, as if to emphasize the point. He moved past her, his limp not as pronounced as she had expected it to be.

"Hello, Joseph," the women by the porch steps said as he passed.

Joseph nodded but didn't pause. One of the women held the front door open for him.

Esther pulled herself up into the truck and began to gather up the debris.

Dorrine and another woman hoisted themselves up into the

truck as well. "I'll do this," Dorrine said. "There's plenty for you to do inside."

Esther didn't attempt a protest. As she turned to leave them, Dorrine told her, "Esther, you remember my cousin Arlene, don't you? She has been staying with us this winter."

"Hi, Arlene," Esther offered in greeting, and Arlene nodded in return.

"It was nice of you to say a few words to Joseph. He lives right across the road from us, and we've all been trying to draw him out of the dream world he lives in," Dorrine said. "And Arlene has taken a fancy to the man. So far she hasn't been successful in drawing his interest, but we keep hoping."

"I'm trying. I really am." Arlene declared. "I've been working for him in his greenhouse, but he is so strange! He thinks about nothing but his roses. He even talks to them. The poor man has to be brought back to the real world. With the Lord's help, I hope to accomplish the task. He has so many needs, and I know he's lonely living down there with his son, Ben. He moved here to escape his sorrow when his *frau*, Silvia, died."

"Well, I hope you succeed," Esther told her. "Joseph seems like a nice enough man."

"So you will help?" Dorrine asked.

"I don't know how I could." Esther forced a laugh. "The heart of a man is the Lord's territory, but if there's anything I can do, I surely will."

Dorrine smiled at her. "That's kind of you to say. But I guess you are a minister's *frau*."

"I *was*," Esther corrected.

"Ah, of course." Dorrine's gaze dropped. "We were sorry to hear of your loss. How hard it must be to lose a husband so young."

"It is," Esther agreed. "But the Lord helps us in our sorrows."

"You are very brave to move all the way to the valley by yourself," Dorrine told her.

"Maybe." Esther allowed.

She wasn't exactly brave, just practical. But that was for another conversation. "I'll be seeing both of you, then, in the days ahead." She turned to hurry back into the house as Arlene took the broom and began to sweep the truck.

TWO

Two hours later Esther sat at her dining room table as dusk fell outside the small house. The men had set up her table, and the women had draped it with a white linen cloth. Beth had supervised the supper preparations, and now Esther's plate was loaded with potatoes, gravy, sliced ham, coleslaw, green beans, and a well-buttered, fluffy roll. Diana was perched beside her on the bench, with smaller portions on her plate.

"This is *goot* eating," Diana declared, beaming up first at Esther and then at her grandmother, who sat on the other side of her.

"*Yah*, it is," Esther agreed.

"This is such a decent community," *Mamm* said. "They sure have been a big help with this move."

The clatter of silverware and soft voices filled the kitchen, reaching into the living room, where the overflow crowd was also eating the evening meal.

"I want some more," Diana piped up.

"You do?" Esther glanced downward. Her daughter's plate was indeed empty of everything, except for a few green beans. "You must have worked up quite an appetite, dear heart." Esther dipped out a small spoonful of potatoes beside the green beans before slathering it with gravy. Diana dove in without hesitation.

"You women have outdone yourselves," Esther told Dorrine, who sat beside her.

Dorrine's husband, John, must have overheard, because he leaned over the table to say, "Our women have all brought the finest cooking skills of Lancaster County with them. You've not moved out to the sticks."

"John," Dorrine chided.

Esther joined in their laughter. "I'm quite happy here already," she assured them.

"So what brings you here to our valley?" John asked.

"Well, for one, it's a beautiful place with very nice people. Also, it's a fresh start for Diana and me."

"Sometimes getting away after a tragedy is wise," John agreed. "We certainly want to welcome you to the community. If you need anything, Dorrine is at home all day, and I'm usually close by out in the fields."

"I'll keep that in mind." Esther gave him a gracious smile. "Thanks again for the help you've already given. I'll try not to be a nuisance to my neighbors."

"I'm sure you won't be," Dorrine said as one of the children pulled on her elbow and demanded her attention.

Esther turned to check on Diana. Her plate was empty again.

"Now I'm ready for dessert," Diana announced.

"Not so loudly," Esther said softly. "It's coming soon."

As if on cue, Beth appeared with pecan pies. The offering was greeted with cheers from the men, who proceeded to take large pieces before they passed the pies. Shoofly and apple pies were brought out next, but neither of those was as popular as the pecan.

Clearly pecan pies carried the day in this community. Esther would have to remember that when she baked for community events.

After the pies had been eaten and a prayer of thanks offered by Bishop Willis, Esther began to gather up the plates. But Beth wouldn't hear of it and shooed her away. "You go rest. We'll take care of the dishes. I'm sure you're exhausted."

"I am," Esther admitted. "But I do want to help."

"There will be plenty of opportunities for that later," Beth said, taking Esther by the elbow and leading her into the living room. The men had found seats, and several of the women with smaller children to tend were also there, chatting happily.

Deacon Daniel's *frau*, Sadie, jumped up and offered Esther her chair. Esther stifled her protest. They wanted to serve her tonight, and the gesture was appropriate.

"Thank you," she told Sadie as she took the seat. Beth had vanished back into the kitchen.

Isaiah was sitting across the room from her and looked up to offer a smile. Esther returned the greeting, and the conversation buzzed around them again. Now that she had a better look at him, Isaiah appeared not unlike what she remembered from her *rumspringa* days. Maybe he had put on a little weight, but what man didn't after his wedding date? Especially if the marriage was a happy one. Her Lonnie had put on a few pounds after they said the vows.

Esther continued to sneak glances in his direction. He had to notice, she was sure, but he pretended otherwise. The man's arms and shoulders were sculptured by a lifetime of fieldwork, and his skin was lightly tanned for this early in the year. He obviously spent most of his time outdoors. He wasn't handsome in a dashing sort of way, but neither had Lonnie been. That was fine. She didn't want flash and glitter in a husband.

Isaiah caught her glance the next time and smiled. When she held his gaze for a second, he got up from his seat to come across the room. "Care if I sit beside you?" he asked. "I have to catch up on all the Lancaster County news."

"Of course not." Esther added her warmest smile.

There was a flurry of seat switching as the women adjusted to the change. Several of them exchanged sly looks and pleased grins. Beth wasn't the only woman glad to see the community's single minister moving off of his limb.

"I didn't mean to cause all that," Isaiah objected.

"We'll remember the favor you owe us the next time you catch us breaking the *Ordnung*," one of the women teased.

Ripples of laugher went around the room, and Esther joined in. None of this surprised her. Isaiah was a decent man. They were well matched in so many ways. What else explained his ease around her and his willingness to make such a public display of his interest in her? Everyone would know that this was more than catching up on Lancaster news.

"So!" Isaiah said, once he was settled in his seat. "You drove in today with your *mamm* and *daett*?"

"*Yah*, and our hired driver's wife followed us in the family car. The two are at a motel for the night, and they will take *Mamm* and *Daett* home tomorrow."

"I see," he said. "It's *goot* to have your parents along for the move, I'm sure."

"*Yah*, it is," she agreed.

"So how are things going in Lancaster County? Do they have as much rain as we do?"

"It was bright and sunny all the way here," she chirped. "And the same yesterday at home. So..."

"Ah...Lancaster County," he mused. "I get lonesome for the homeland sometimes, stuck as we are all the way up here in the shadow of the Adirondacks."

"But it's beautiful here," Esther protested.

"Tell him!" several voices chorused.

Isaiah chuckled. "I'm just teasing. There's nothing like riling up the locals with comparisons to where we came from. Really, I love this part of the country. I wouldn't want to live anywhere else. I hope you soon feel the same."

"I'm sure I will."

"Do you need help around the place in the next day or so?" he asked. "We have several single men who would jump at the chance of helping a pretty young widow settle in."

Laughter rippled again.

"How about offering yourself there, Isaiah?" one of the men asked.

"I guess I could get on my knees and beg her for a date." Isaiah winked at Esther. "I doubt if she would dare turn down my charms in such a public place."

"Then you'd better take your chance while you have it, Isaiah." One of the women spoke up. "After tonight they'll be lining Esther's front porch with marriage proposals, to say nothing of Sunday evening dates."

This produced hoots and hollers all around the living room.

Beth stuck her head out of the kitchen doorway. "What's going on?"

"Just teasing Isaiah," someone said. Beth withdrew with a smile on her face.

"We are a happy community," Isaiah told Esther after the ruckus died down. "I hope you feel quite welcome."

"I'm sure I will," Esther said.

"So how are you really doing? Even though it's been awhile since Lonnie passed, the grief must remain."

"*Yah*, it does. And you? You know what I went through from a husband's perspective."

"This is true. The Lord gives and the Lord takes, but blessed be His name."

A comfortable silence settled between them.

Then he looked up to ask with a grin, "No lining the front porch with marriage proposals while you lived in Lancaster County?"

"No." She lowered her head.

"So you're free," Isaiah mused, more statement than question.

Esther smiled encouragingly at him. She hadn't expected this quick action from her old friend, but neither did she complain.

Isaiah glanced over to Diana. "You have a daughter, I see. I thought I remembered that, but I wasn't sure."

"*Yah*, Diana. Did you never..."

A cloud drifted across his face. "The Lord didn't bless us with *kinner*."

"I'm sorry. It does make it easier if they leave something behind for us who have to stay."

"Well said. You are a wise woman, Esther."

Her face flamed for the first time.

"Are you preaching the woman a sermon over there, Isaiah?" one of the men hollered across the room. "She's blushing like a rose."

"No. We're just remembering what the Lord has given and what the Lord has taken." The room fell silent, and Isaiah leaned closer to Esther. "I didn't mean to embarrass you with that compliment."

"It's okay," she told him. "You did no wrong. The Lord's ways are close to my heart. To have you speak such words of praise touched me deeply."

Isaiah nodded and smiled.

"Is that the proposal we've been waiting for?" one of the men hollered again.

Isaiah chuckled. "I was choosing my words carefully, that's all."

"Putting them together just right, I suppose," the man added. "Why don't we get such care for our Sunday morning sermons?"

Laughter filled the room again, and Isaiah shook his head. "You people are hopeless, but I'm glad I can supply such amusement for you on this fine evening."

One of the women leaned toward Esther. "I hope this talk isn't bothering you."

"Not in the least," Esther assured her. "Laughter is *goot* for the soul, and this way I get to see if Isaiah has a sense of humor."

Hoots filled the room, and Isaiah raised his eyebrows.

"The woman can give back better than she gets," someone said.

"I see burning pain all the way down to your toes, Isaiah," another man chimed in. "You should have made your marriage proposal earlier, before the woman discovered your real character."

"Behave yourself for once," Isaiah shot back.

"I *am*," the man said, and the chuckles continued.

Isaiah sat beside her without much comment, apparently lost in thought or listening to the chatter. She didn't dare look at him again. She had been bold enough for one evening.

"Well, I'd best be going," he finally said. "It's been *goot* catching up on things. We'll have to do this again."

Esther gave him her warmest smile. "I would like nothing better, Isaiah."

He smiled at her in return and then moved across the room to hold a whispered conversation with one of the men before leaving. Esther watched his broad shoulders as he went out the door and into the dusk.

With Isaiah gone, Esther noticed Joseph Zook's absence. He must have left early with his son. She didn't remember seeing them after supper, but she hadn't been keeping track of them.

Joseph would have been welcome to stay. She didn't want him to feel left out. Maybe in the future she would have a chance to make him feel welcome. A man living alone in a house with his son could not be a *goot* thing. It might be nice if Joseph would return Arlene's attentions. If the relationship progressed to marriage, that would surely help Joseph's standing and acceptance in the community. Though new to the valley, perhaps she could help Joseph move on and overcome his sorrow.

All around the room people began to stand and make their way over to offer their best wishes.

"Glad you moved into the area, Esther."

"Hope you get settled in without too many adjustments."

"Be sure to let us know if you need anything."

"May the Lord bless you for coming to the valley," several said, their handshakes firm and their smiles sincere.

"I believe we'll be very happy here," she assured them.

Once things had quieted down, Dorrine asked with a giggle, "Did you have a *goot* time?"

"I had a wonderful evening," Esther replied.

"I saw Minister Isaiah spending time with you," Dorrine said with a smile. "And teasing you too. Everyone likes you already, Esther."

"I don't know about that," she objected. "They seemed more taken with him than with me."

"That they are," Dorrine agreed, "but they were taken with you as well. I'm so glad you're here and that we're neighbors. We'll get along splendidly."

"I think so too."

As Dorrine and John left, Diana, *Mamm*, and *Daett* joined Esther on the porch to watch the buggies leave. The stars were bright above them, and off in the distance, the lights in the Adirondacks added their own twinkle. Below them long streams of headlights flowed like water on the turnpike.

Esther ruffled her daughter's hair. "So Diana, what do you think? Do you like it here?"

"*Yah*, I do," her little voice replied.

"I love it too," Esther spoke into the night.

Daett and *Mamm* whispered something to each other, but she knew them well enough to know that they were agreeing perfectly with her.

THREE

The following Saturday afternoon found a wisp of distant clouds moving across the sky from the north. The sun's warmth filled Esther's small house and banished the last of the morning chill. *Daett* and *Mamm* had left early on Wednesday morning for the drive back to Lancaster County, and the peace of the community had settled over Esther and Diana in the days since.

"Thank You, dear Lord," Esther whispered, as footsteps came up the front porch. They were followed by a gentle knock. Esther stepped away from the stove and her pan of hot chocolate and headed to the front door, where Dorrine was standing on the porch with a bright smile on her face. "*Goot* afternoon, Esther."

"How *goot* to see you, Dorrine." Esther opened her arms for a hug.

A moment later Dorrine took a step backward. "I saw Diana playing in the yard. She's such a sweet little girl."

"Thank you. That's kind of you to say."

Dorrine picked up the bag she had set on the porch floor. "A little gift. Tomatoes from Joseph's greenhouse."

Esther reached for them. "It's a bit early for them, isn't it?"

"*Yah*, but he has a green thumb, and with Arlene helping him almost every day, there's plenty of produce. She brought us two bags this size, which is much more than we can eat."

"Well, isn't that great," Esther gushed, sneaking a peek into the bag. "These look wonderful. He is obviously a *goot* gardener."

"That he is. Arlene will be making a decent catch if she can ever capture his attention." Dorrine sighed. "Jospeh is so bashful and withdrawn, though, that I despair at times. How he managed to get married the first time is beyond me. On top of that, Arlene's not the best with men."

Esther clucked her tongue and held the door wide open. "Would you like to come in? I'm not completely unpacked yet, but I finished Saturday morning cleaning an hour ago."

"Settling into a new place takes time," Dorrine comforted her. She followed Esther inside with a worried look. "Arlene troubles me. Maybe I'm making a mistake by giving her hope that pursuing Joseph will result in a happy ending for her. Maybe he has his back up, sensing that we've set our minds to making the relationship happen. John says we need to hang in there awhile longer, and eventually Joseph will see the light of day. But Jospeh hasn't seemed to notice Arlene in a romantic way so far, and I wonder if Arlene might better spend her time looking for a husband in some other community."

Esther motioned toward a kitchen chair. "I'm sorry you're worried for her, but I bet Arlene will make headway with Joseph soon. She's a lovely young woman, and she obviously cares for him. He just hasn't seen that yet. Would you like some hot chocolate? I have some about ready on the stove."

"I would love some." Dorrine beamed.

Esther poured the hot cocoa into mugs and took a chair across from her guest.

Dorrine stirred her cup for a moment and then looked up at

Esther. "I have a favor to ask, since you seem to have hope for our venture. If it's not too much trouble, would you mind visiting Joseph with me? Maybe if you and I team up, we can point him in her direction."

Esther laughed. "I'd love to help, but I don't know what I can do. My guess is that Joseph needs time yet before he'll be interested in another woman, and that doesn't happen overnight."

Dorrine frowned. "I think you underestimate yourself, Esther. What an encouragement you have been to me this morning already, and you might be surprised by how much Joseph has changed since you arrived. When he was here for your moving day, I saw him smiling and laughing for the first time in many months. I think it was because of your influence."

Esther laughed. "Mine? Oh, I doubt that. Besides, did you notice that he left early? No, I can't imagine I was the one who made him so cheerful."

"Oh, but you did!" Dorrine insisted. "It's your personality, Esther. I haven't seen Minister Isaiah have such a *goot* time before, either. Everyone enjoyed your company so much. I know I did."

"That's very kind of you to say, but—"

"No protests." Dorrine waved her hand about. "I know you want to help, and you can do Arlene a lot of *goot* if you draw Joseph out of his sorrow. I've tried talking with him, but I don't get anywhere. He might open up to you."

Before Esther could answer, another knock came on the door.

"See how popular you are?" Dorrine said, laughing.

Esther laughed along with her, but she sobered quickly when she opened the front door. "Joseph! Well, this is a surprise. What can I do for you?"

He held out a paper bag. "I'm overflowing with tomatoes down at the greenhouse, so I thought I'd bring you some. I'll have lettuce heads next week if the weather helps them along. That is, if you want some."

"I would love some!" Esther said cheerfully, taking the offered bag. "But now that I'm settled in, I'll have to get my own garden going. I have the perfect spot picked out."

He lowered his head. "That's *goot*, but please know that you're welcome to use a corner of my greenhouse if you prefer. That would keep you from having to deal with the elements."

"Thank you, Joseph. That is a very kind offer. I'll have to think about that. Would you like to step inside?"

He hesitated. "I should be getting back."

Esther held the door open wide. "Please. Dorrine's here. You're welcome to join us for a cup of hot chocolate."

He peered cautiously around the edge of the door.

"She won't bite," Esther teased.

He grinned and followed her inside.

"Have a seat." Esther pulled out another chair at the kitchen table. She poured the last of the hot chocolate from the pan and set the mug in front of Joseph.

Dorrine hadn't said a word yet.

"Don't you two know each other?" Esther teased.

They both laughed.

"I thought so." Esther grinned at the both of them. What a lovely day already, full of fresh produce and kind neighbors who wanted her to feel welcome.

Joseph took a sip of his hot chocolate and turned to Dorrine. "I was just telling Esther that she's welcome to use a little corner of my greenhouse for her garden if she wishes. There's no sense in tilling more soil here when I have everything down there ready to go."

"That's nice of you to offer," Dorrine said with a smile. "I'm sure Esther will appreciate your generosity."

He settled back in his chair. "That's what neighbors are for."

"I'm glad to hear that," Esther told him. "But we noticed you left early the other night. I hope we didn't scare you off."

"No." Joseph grinned. "I wanted to attend a lecture down at the community hall in Fort Plain on plant diseases. But I doubt you are interested in hearing about such things."

"I'm quite interested," Esther corrected him. "Not that I garden to the extent that you do, but it sounds like useful knowledge. Was there anything special I need to know?"

"I'm listening too," Dorrine piped up. "I don't know much about gardening either, but I'm sure it's important information."

Joseph took another sip of hot chocolate. "It seems that the experts are learning more all the time about how plants repel disease if they're raised in healthy ground. On the other hand, if the soil becomes weak and robbed of nutrients, plants can contract diseases." He paused in thought. "It's almost as if they despair and wish for death. Isn't that interesting?"

Esther and Dorrine exchanged a glance as Joseph continued. "So instead of depending on sprays and chemicals, the best preventive measure against disease is the quality of the soil. We must always make sure that the nutrients are there." Joseph paused again with a ghost of a smile. "I'm not a minister, but it seems to me that has a *goot* spiritual application. We can fight off the temptations of the world when they appear in our lives, or we can nurture a vibrant relationship with the Lord and so fend off many temptations before they take root in us."

"That is quite interesting," Esther agreed. "No wonder you're such an expert at growing vegetables. Such knowledge and insight!"

"*Yah*, that *is* interesting," Dorrine seconded. "Have you shared this information with Arlene yet?"

"She is very helpful around the greenhouse, but I don't think she has much interest in soil conditions. But I'm not complaining. We had plenty of produce to sell at the market this morning." Joseph gulped down the last of his hot chocolate and stood to his feet.

"You don't have to leave yet," Esther told him.

Joseph smiled sheepishly. "I have work to do. I hope you enjoy the tomatoes. And I hope you'll take me up on my offer to start a small garden in my greenhouse. I'd be happy to watch over your plants and give you any advice I think will be helpful."

"I accept," Esther said, following Joseph to the door. "I'll come down next week. Thank you so much for the tomatoes...and the kind offer."

"You're welcome." He tipped his hat and was gone. Esther watched him walk across the lawn with his limp. She hadn't noticed it in the house, but she hadn't been looking for it. Maybe his limp was more pronounced when he moved fast or was nervous. When he paused near the gate, Diana ran up to him. Joseph bent down and engaged the girl in what appeared to be an animated conversation. She had something in her hand, and Joseph took it from her. A praying mantis, from what Esther could see. The creature crawled up Joseph's arm, and as he moved closer to the fence, the creature jumped onto the rail above the rosebushes. The two followed its progress, their heads close together. Esther smiled and returned to the kitchen.

Dorrine was drinking from her mug, but she put it down when Esther came in the room. "That was awesome! You drew the heart right out of the man in minutes—maybe even seconds. Joseph opened up to you like a sunflower following the sun. I'm going to tell Arlene what her problem is. She has to show more interest in gardening to draw information out of him the way you do. He obviously likes to talk about his work. Maybe I can get a gardening magazine for Arlene to read so she'll have something to talk about

with Joseph. Imagine. Preventive measures for plant diseases. I do
declare. And the spiritual lesson he drew from his gardening knowledge? Why, Joseph almost sounded like a minister, talking about
the temptations of the world and how to deal with them. I—"

"Whoa there!" Esther said, laughing.

"I have never seen anything like it," Dorrine continued, unde-
terred. "I knew you would be a blessing to all of us the minute you
got here. Arlene could learn a lot from you."

"I'm glad if I can help," Esther tried again. "But—"

"I knew you could reach him, Esther. I just knew it." Dorrine
took another sip of chocolate as she fanned herself. "I hope you
take him up on his offer. You should try to influence Joseph every
chance you get."

"What if Joseph gets fancy ideas about me? Not that I would
want him to."

Dorrine huffed. "I wouldn't be surprised if he does, but Joseph
knows you're as good as taken. That was plain enough to see the
other night, and what chance does he have against Isaiah Mast? I
mean, you're not going to—"

"No, I'm not," Esther interrupted. "So I guess there's no harm in
it. Joseph seems sensible enough, and—"

"*Goot*! I know this will work. Arlene will be so happy."

"Well, I wish her the best in her pursuit," Esther said, taking
Joseph's cup to the sink. "Now, the question is, what am I going to
do with all of these tomatoes?"

Dorrine laughed. "Joseph apparently didn't see my bag, even
though it was sitting there in plain sight. That's the kind of thing
a man doesn't see, even when he's holding forth on fancy ways to
fight plant diseases. I suggest you make ketchup."

And with that, Dorrine bounded to her feet and gave Esther a
hug. "Thank you for the hot chocolate and the marvelous insights,

but I must be going. Arlene's probably home by now and busying herself with early supper preparations."

"Maybe you should invite Joseph over for a meal sometime," Esther suggested. "Get him used to family again. Maybe that's part of his problem."

"That's a brilliant idea. We'll have you and Diana come too. That way Joseph won't feel we're obviously matchmaking."

"He might talk all evening about plant diseases."

"And if you're there, that won't be a problem," Dorrine said as she bustled out of the house. She tossed a goodbye wave over her shoulder.

Diana ran along with Dorrine to the end of the driveway before turning back. Esther watched from the living room window as her new friend made her way down Fords Bush Road, hurrying as fast as she could.

Life would be both interesting and enjoyable in the community, Esther decided. Thank the Lord her own world would continue on its calm and steady way even amid the storms of life. That was all she asked of the Lord. That and the chance to see Isaiah again at the church services tomorrow. He would definitely make a worthy husband. There was no question about that.

FOUR

On Sunday morning, Esther chose her dark blue dress from the closet rack. She placed the pins carefully and checked the results in the mirror. She could have chosen a more risqué color, perhaps a lighter green, but the dark blue would make a better first impression. In the mirror stood a properly demure Amish woman who wouldn't lose the ground she had gained with Isaiah on Tuesday evening.

Life would begin again here in the valley, and eventually—if all went according to plan—she would be a minister's *frau* again, leading the district's women with her example more than her words. Even in her *rumspringa*, not one fancy *Englisha* dress had hung in her closet. Life had always been a time of preparation for the duty that lay ahead, and nothing about that destiny had changed with Lonnie's death.

With one more satisfied glance in the mirror, Esther went down to the kitchen to find Diana with her empty bowl in front of her. "I'm ready to change, *Mamm*," Diana sang out.

Esther gave the girl a quick hug and patted her back, "Off you go, then. I'll be right in to help you finish."

The girl scampered away, and Esther rinsed the oatmeal from

the bowl and utensils and set them on the counter. She normally washed dishes only once a day, but that might change once she wed Isaiah and more *kinner* were added to the family. *Kinner* were a great blessing from the Lord, and a home should be full of them, even if the dishes needed washing after each meal.

Esther left the kitchen and entered the bedroom to help Diana dress. Bent on one knee in front of the girl, Esther set the *kapp* on Diana's small head before she pushed the pins in.

Diana wiggled and objected, "One pin is *goot* enough, *Mamm.*"

"We have to keep your *kapp* straight," Esther instructed her. "And watch where you play after the service so you don't bang your head against anything."

"I'm always careful," Diana protested. "You know how I look after playing outside. I'm clean and proper, and nothing is dirty."

"*Yah*, you're a dear, sweetheart." Esther planted a kiss on Diana's head. "I'm glad you're looking forward to this Sunday."

"Oh, I am!" Diana declared. "Mary and Betty will be there."

Esther gave her another kiss. "By the way, what did Joseph say to you yesterday as he was leaving?"

Diana's face glowed. "He knows all about praying mantises, *Mamm*! He said there are many thousands of different kinds, and they jump out of the bushes to catch things. Did you know that?"

"No, I certainly didn't."

"And the woman mantis eats the man mantis. Did you know that?"

"Joseph told you *that*?" Esther gasped.

"*Yah*, but I'm not sure what he meant."

"I guess he means the one eats the other," Esther blurted out. "But what a horrible thing to tell a little girl."

"Joseph knows a lot of interesting things like that," Diana said proudly.

"What else did he tell you?"

Diana shrugged. "Well, some of the mantises can change colors depending on what they sit on. Isn't that great?"

"*Yah*, it is, but I want you to forget about the eating thing."

"People don't do that, do they?" Diana peered up at her *mamm*. "Eat each other?"

"Certainly not! Of course people don't eat each other."

Esther hustled her daughter out the bedroom door. They collected their shawls in the living room before heading toward their small barn. Diana watched from a corner as Esther harnessed their horse, Biscuit, and led him outside to the buggy.

"You can practice holding up the shafts," Esther told Diana.

Anything to wash images of praying mantises eating each other from a little mind, Esther huffed in silence. All her sympathies for Joseph had vanished into thin air. He had no sense! But he did have a son to raise and no *frau* in the house. Esther took a deep breath and calmed herself. Joseph may have been careless with what he said to her daughter, but he had obviously meant no harm.

Esther gave Diana a bright smile as the little girl attempted to heave upward on the shafts. They didn't lift more than an inch off the ground. "That was a *goot* try, sweetheart. You'll soon be big enough to pick them up all by yourself."

Diana sighed and stepped back as Esther settled Biscuit under the shafts. Moments later, Diana's face brightened. The girl pointed toward the split rail fence. "Joseph said our roses should bloom this week."

"Oh, he did?" Esther managed to keep the edge out of her voice as she fastened the tugs.

"*Yah!*" Diana declared. "He said I should come out and sniff the roses early in the morning. That's when they smell the best. I want to do that, *Mamm*. Can I?"

"I don't see why not," Esther agreed. She helped Diana up into the buggy.

"We should keep a blanket on the ground to keep the bush warm," Diana continued. "The flowers bloom longer that way."

"Joseph told you all this?"

"*Yah, Mamm.* He knows a lot of things."

"It appears so." Esther clucked to Biscuit, and they trotted out of the lane to turn south on Fords Bush Road.

"When can I see Joseph again?" Diana asked, her face peering toward the greenhouse as they trotted past.

Esther paused before answering. There was no reason to sow suspicion in Diana's heart about Joseph. Instead, she motioned toward the Kings' driveway. "Look. There are John and Dorrine with their three children. They're almost ready to set out too."

Diana leaned out of the buggy to wave, and the whole King family waved back. Esther smiled and joined in.

Thankfully, Diana was distracted from her obsession with Joseph Zook, but clearly he had made quite an impression on her young mind. Esther was sure Joseph had meant no harm with his adult talk, but she would steer Diana clear of him when they had supper with the Kings later in the week.

"I saw Arlene with them too," Diana sang out, still looking back after her vigorous waving. "Joseph said I can come help him at his greenhouse. He says Arlene doesn't know much about gardening."

"Really?" Esther tried to stay calm. Why would the man have said such a thing about Arlene? "I'm sure Joseph is a very smart man, but you needn't accept everything he says. In fact, I think you should try to think about something else now."

Diana settled back in the buggy and concentrated.

Esther changed her mind. "Forget I said that, Diana. You may talk about whatever you want."

Diana chattered away, thankfully about little nothings for the rest of the trip while Esther's mind continued to replay what Joseph had said. Insects eating one another. Such a serious topic for a little girl. Where was the man's good sense? Well, one thing was sure. Diana needed a *daett*. There was no question about that. A good practical man...like Isaiah.

Esther sighed. She must think more kindly of Joseph. It wouldn't do any good to harbor ill feelings toward him, especially after she had promised Dorrine to help steer him and Arlene together. After all, Joseph hadn't told Diana anything false. It was just a little inappropriate for her age. And even then, it hadn't upset her, and she'd been able to follow the conversation and repeat much of it to her mother. Maybe Joseph had noticed that Diana was a smart and curious little girl and had responded accordingly.

Esther pulled back on the reins as they approached Abram and Emma Troyer's place on Florien Road, where the service would be held. She drove past the end of the sidewalk and parked alongside the other buggies near the barn, where the men had gathered. One man's form detached itself from the group and came toward them.

Esther kept her gaze away from him until she had climbed down from the buggy and reached back to help Diana. She turned to face Isaiah, who was standing near Biscuit's head. "*Goot* morning. What is this, curbside service?"

Isaiah chuckled. "We can't have our newcomers thinking the community has no manners. So I had to see to your horse myself."

"All of you have been very kind to us," she replied.

He grinned and began to unhitch the gelding. "What's your horse's name?"

"Biscuit."

"That's quite *Englisha*."

"Lonnie named her."

"And a *goot* name it is."

Esther stopped short at the sight of Joseph descending from his buggy at the other end of the line.

Isaiah followed her glance. "Joseph's a little late today. He's usually the first one to the service."

"Maybe he can't wait to hear your sermon," Esther teased.

Isaiah laughed heartily. "I doubt that. Joseph's a deep thinker. I'm more on the practical side."

"I'm sure the practical has its value. Like helping me unhitch. I thank you very much."

Isaiah grinned from ear to ear. "I hope you'll allow me to help you after the service as well."

"I'd welcome that, Isaiah. And I'll be listening closely to your sermon today."

"I'll make sure it's a very special one, then," he said with a wink over his shoulder as he led Biscuit toward the barn.

She almost had a date with the man on her first Sunday in the community. Most women would probably have pounding hearts about now, but she felt only thanks for the Lord's goodness. Lonnie's loss had not been easy, but Isaiah's interest and kindness would help her heal.

Esther took Diana's hand as they crossed the lawn to enter the mudroom. She left their shawls there and entered the kitchen. Beth Willis was the first to greet her with a kiss on the cheek, followed by the other women. Esther took her place in the line of married women and waited until the time came for the service to begin. She found a seat on the bench, and Diana nestled in beside her.

The first song was given out and led by a man with a strong voice. Esther relaxed and joined in the joyous music. She lifted her eyes from the page to watch as the ministers left for their morning meeting upstairs. Isaiah had his head properly bowed in the line of men who moved up the steps. This was so like home in Lancaster County. The singing, the congregation, the feel of the black leather songbook in her hands. These people were her people.

Esther sang with all her heart until the ministers returned and the sermons began. Isaiah stood first, which was what she had hoped. Not that she planned to judge the man, but she needed to hear a *goot* sermon like the ones Lonnie used to give. Isaiah would give one, she was sure.

Esther closed her eyes as Isaiah began to speak, and the sound brought tears to her eyes. This wasn't Lonnie's voice, but in other ways they were so similar.

"The Lord God is our God," Isaiah said. "He reigns among His people this morning. The Lord is high above the earth. He lives in the heavens, and looks down upon His people. We are like the dust under our own feet to the Lord, yet He has compassion and mercy upon such feeble creatures. Are we not frail and given to great weakness? We cry when we feel pain. We sorrow and wonder what the Lord is about. Yet His ways are higher than our ways. As the heavens are high above the earth, so is the Lord's thoughts above our thoughts and His path above ours. Let us take courage this morning and seek the Lord while He may be found. Trouble lies everywhere in this world, both on the left hand and on the right. Tribulation is always near to both the sinner and the saint, yet there is also laughter in our mouths and joy in our hearts. Much more so to the people of God than to those who follow their own way. I say, blessed be the name of Lord, and blessed be the work of His hands."

"*Yah*, blessed be the work of His hands," Esther whispered. She opened her eyes.

Isaiah was standing near the far wall of the living room, his gaze fixed on the congregation as he spoke. The man didn't thunder or preach doom and gloom. He didn't pace about the way some preachers did. Isaiah said each word as if he meant it. There was no great profundity—unless simplicity was profound. Isaiah's every gesture spoke of his stability, of his commonness, of his faithfulness in the smallest manner to the Lord. This was what she wanted, what she was.

She had come home.

FIVE

On Monday morning, Isaiah Mast pushed his straw hat back on his forehead as he tracked the smooth flight of the small plane coming in to land on the airfield behind his farm. A hand waved from the cramped cabin window, and Isaiah lifted his own hand in greeting. The plane banked and disappeared from sight behind the line of trees, its wheels a mere hundred feet from the ground.

"Someone's out joyriding," Isaiah muttered, though a smile played on his face. He turned and entered his barn to begin his after-breakfast chores.

His smile continued as he thought of Esther Stoltzfus's face yesterday at the Sunday service. How like this *Englisha* plane she was. She had flown in from Lancaster County with her daughter and had landed smoothly in the community. But that was where the similarities ended. Esther was a woman of the Lord. She followed His ways in such a practical and down-to-earth manner. Never had he thought to find a woman to replace Mandy, but here she was right in front of him. Esther was exactly what he needed in a *frau*.

Isaiah's smile flickered. His interest in Esther during their *rumspringa* had been brief, mostly because she wasn't in his district and

Mandy had been. It had been easier to find a *frau* close by, so he had done so without regret. Mandy was the right woman for him back then, just as he suspected Esther was the woman for him now.

Isaiah grabbed a fork from its hook on the wall and attacked the muck in the first horse stall. Truth was, he needed a *frau* in the house again, a fact he hadn't been ready to face until recently. But here Esther was, and the door was as open as the need was apparent. His marriage to Esther would fulfill not only the needs of his heart, but also those of the community. A minister without a *frau* was a question mark in many ways. Stability came from marriage and the care a man could give his family.

Mandy had given him no *kinner*, while Esther had borne Lonnie a child. They would begin life together as a family. He wouldn't have thought to visit Lancaster County in search of her, so it was *goot* that Esther had moved to the valley—likely in pursuit of him. He didn't hold that against her. The move simply demonstrated her fine spirit. Esther must have remembered their encounters and connection from their *rumspringa* days and believed he would be a suitable husband for her now.

He didn't think she was wrong in that assumption. He was a good match for her, and she was a good match for him. The other single woman in the community at present was Dorrine King's cousin Arlene, and she only had eyes for Joseph Zook—which was just as well. Isaiah had no interest in Arlene. From the looks of things, Joseph hardly knew Arlene existed, yet it was obvious that Arlene was in pursuit. Isaiah couldn't imagine Esther being that way. One hint from him that the path was blocked, and Esther would turn around. That was why he had gone out of his way to show her that she was both welcome in the community and that her interest in him was not in vain.

Esther was no dreamer, and neither was he. Women who had

stars in their eyes caused men headaches with their romantic notions. This younger generation of girls seemed to pick up more *Englisha* ideas all the time, but not much could be done about such problems. He could warn of the dangers in his sermons, but the subject was a touchy one. How did one, for example, persuade Arlene that her cause was hopeless? Even a gentle rebuke could produce waves of tears and bring widespread recriminations from other single women. Whispers would abound, all about ministers who were hard-hearted and cruel when it came to young girls' dreams.

Better to allow the young women to entertain their hopes. They would learn soon enough that life was more than romance. Love was best expressed in duty, in hardship, and in faithfulness to the Lord's will. Farm life wasn't easy, and that hadn't changed much over the years. The *Englisha* thought they could circumvent the Lord's ways with all their fancy schemes and equipment, but in the end a man must still earn his living by the sweat of his brow. When a man's *frau* stood beside him, that was love. That was what he wanted.

Isaiah threw the last of the muck into the wheelbarrow and headed for the back of the barn, where his manure spreader was parked. He ran the wheel up a narrow plank and tipped the contents into the spreader. Once he had accumulated a full load, he would run the spreader over his hayfields. Some farmers piled the daily muck on the ground and later loaded the pile onto the spreader when they had free time during the winter months, but he was not of that mind. The extra effort expended to load the manure twice was senseless. With the spreader full, all it took was a quick trip after lunchtime when the team was already harnessed. Before long, the job was done.

Isaiah returned to the next stall and continued his work. Perhaps when he was finished he should find a reason to call on Esther.

But for what? If he had been faster on his feet, he would have asked her yesterday if she had anything that needed repair around her place, but one didn't speak of such things on the Lord's day. Better a trip made on the grounds that there was always work that could be done. That's how a practical mind worked, and Esther was, above all, practical. She would appreciate the gesture, and their relationship would continue to grow.

He could ask her for a formal date this coming Sunday evening. It wasn't too soon to do so. Their relationship was already on a fast track. They were treating each other as if they were old friends, but even more, it seemed presumed that they belonged together—which they did. She had accepted his confirmation of her interest in him with stoic grace. In a similar situation, a young, romantically inclined woman would have fluttered her eyelashes and exclaimed over every interest he expressed in her—as if the world had never seen the courtship of a man and a woman before.

Isaiah grinned. He could just see Arlene's reaction if Joseph ever asked her home from the hymn singing. Likely the woman would pass out on the spot and need cold water splashed on her face to revive. Isaiah laughed out loud as he finished mucking the stall. He emptied the wheelbarrow and returned to spread straw liberally on the clean floor.

With the strings hung on the barn wall, Isaiah whistled for his driving horse, Echo. The horse lifted his head in the barnyard and trotted over. Isaiah led Echo inside and tossed on the harness. He fastened the straps and had Echo outside and hitched to the buggy minutes later. Isaiah glanced toward the empty house before he climbed into the buggy.

Isaiah glanced toward the heavens. "You have indeed blessed me with the prospect of a *goot frau* again. Thank You."

He settled on the buggy seat, and Echo trotted out of the lane to turn north toward Highway 5. From here, the main road ran above the valley floor between Little Falls and Fort Plain. The small airport lay on the right near the stop sign on Highway 5. As he passed, he noticed the airplane he saw earlier parked near a hangar with its engines idling. Isaiah clucked to Echo, his gaze fixed on the plane's sleek outline for a few more seconds. An *Englisha* airplane was a fancy thing, but so was simplicity itself. Esther was like that. She was a beautiful woman who displayed her grace as the Lord intended. Simplicity brought its own reward if one had the patience. Look how much grief he had saved himself since Mandy had passed. He could have worn himself out in a search for a *frau*, driving from community to community. He could have agonized over his loss or dreamed of stars in the sky. Instead, he had trusted in the Lord, and the Lord had provided.

Isaiah held tight to the reins as Echo trotted west on Highway 5. The traffic wasn't heavy this morning, but the tourists who frequented the area weren't used to seeing buggies on the road. One must always keep a sharp eye out for trouble, but a simple life gave one that time. Amid the rush of modern life, the virtue of carefulness could often be lost.

He would be careful in his relationship with Esther in the months ahead. He already knew Esther's past, and she knew his. They had neither hidden secrets nor troubled families. All was calm on the surface, as all was calm beneath the waves. If trouble arrived it would most likely appear from the outside, as the death of their spouses had encroached upon both of their lives. Hopefully neither of them would have to suffer through that valley again. The Lord gave and the Lord took, but the Lord didn't place burdens too heavy to bear on one's shoulders. Unless Isaiah was wrong, he and Esther would be blessed for many years to come. They would grow old together with their *kinner* gathered around them.

"Whoa there," Isaiah called out to Echo. They pulled left at Fords Bush Road and into Esther's driveway.

The front door burst open, and little Diana raced out to meet him. Isaiah hopped down from the buggy as Esther appeared in the doorway.

"*Goot* morning," he hollered to Esther. He bent down on one knee to greet Diana, who came to a panting halt in front of him.

"Are you Isaiah?" she asked as she peered up at him.

"That I am. And you are Diana."

"Yep. So why are you here?"

Isaiah laughed. "I need to talk with your *mamm* about some things."

"There she is." Diana waved toward the house, as if Isaiah needed directions.

He got up from his knee and smiled down at her. "I'll tie up my horse. His name is Echo. Then I'll be right in."

"I'll wait for you. I like the name Echo."

"You do? Well, I'm glad."

"Do you know anything about roses?" she asked, pointing toward the fence.

"Ah," he said. "Let's see. Roses are red, and violets are blue. Sugar is sweet, and so are you."

Diana giggled. "You're funny, but Joseph told me all about roses. They are supposed to bloom this week. Don't you think so?"

"I guess we'll have to wait and see," he allowed as he secured Echo to the hitching post.

"Come on." She tugged on his hand. "Let's see if you can smell them before they bloom. Joseph said these roses will give off the sweetest scent."

Isaiah waved toward Esther, who was still on the front porch, as he allowed Diana to lead him. The little one could prattle away.

There was no question about that. "When was Joseph here?" he asked.

"Saturday afternoon, when he brought *Mamm* a bag of tomatoes. *Mamm* doesn't have a garden yet. Dorrine was also here." Diana smiled up at him. "Joseph told me all about roses and praying mantises."

"Really? I guess I'm not surprised. Joseph is a smart man."

"Oh, he is," Diana agreed. She knelt in front of the still-closed rose blossom and motioned with her hand. "Come closer and smell. I think Joseph will be right."

Isaiah glanced toward the front porch again before he got on his knees. Esther gave him a shrug of her shoulders and an *I'm-sorry-about-this* sort of look. He managed to smile. Esther didn't need to feel bad. Diana was obviously an energetic child who needed a *daett*. She would calm down with proper training.

"Sniff," Diana ordered.

Isaiah complied.

"Smells *goot*, right?"

Isaiah winked at her. "I'm sure all roses smell *wunderbah* once they blossom." Then, turning to look at Esther on the porch, he told her, "And now, little one, I must speak to your *mamm*."

Diana jumped to her feet and led the way to the front door.

"*Goot* morning," Esther cooed. "What a pleasant surprise."

Isaiah stepped up on the porch before he answered. "Diana was just showing me the roses that are supposed to bloom soon."

"*Ach*, that's all she thinks about since Joseph told her it would happen this week. Do you have time to come in?" Esther's face was aglow.

"*Yah*, I do," he replied. "If you have some work I can tackle. I wouldn't want to keep you otherwise."

"Ah...let's see," Esther mused. "The sink in the small bathroom is stopped up. I planned to address the problem myself, but if you're here and willing, so am I. I'm sure you can do a much faster and better job than I can."

"That's what I'm here for," Isaiah said with a smile. "I didn't bring my plumbing tools, though."

"I have a little toolbox I use." She winced. "Not a manly sort of thing, but it has what you'll need to open drains, I'm thinking."

"I suppose that will work," Isaiah allowed as Esther held the door open wide.

She hurried off but returned with her toolbox. He followed her down the hall and into the small bathroom.

"Here it is." She set down the toolbox and moved aside.

Isaiah positioned himself in front of the small vanity and placed pressure on the trap fitting, which moved easily enough. "Shouldn't be anything to it," he told her. "Maybe a small bucket to catch the water from the pipe."

She handed him the wastebasket, which was clean once she removed the plastic bag. He smiled up at her, and Esther lowered her head. Her meekness was the Lord's blessing—shown again so clearly, as if he needed any further confirmation.

"*Yah*, you could have done this yourself easily enough," he told her as he emptied the contents of the plugged trap into the wastebasket.

"I suppose so, but it's a joy to have a man around the house for a few hours. Would you like to stay for lunch? It's a little early, but you can sweep the upstairs if you feel the need to occupy your hands."

They laughed together as he fastened the trap again. "Maybe I'll pass on the sweeping and the lunch, much as I hate to. I should be in the fields back home. I'm the only one there to tend to things. May I take a rain check?"

"You're welcome anytime, Isaiah. I can even make supper for you once or twice a week if you wish. I'm sure bachelor cooking has grown old by now."

"*Yah*, it has," he agreed. "I like that idea a lot, so I'll take you up on the offer. Maybe on Friday night, then? Shall I come over after chores?"

"That would please me greatly," she said, following him to the front door.

He tipped his hat, and she stayed on the front porch as he climbed in the buggy and drove out of the lane with a quick good-bye wave over his shoulder

SIX

That afternoon, Joseph placed the pot with a single rose on a shelf before he drew a long breath over the blossom. The fragrance held a tangy smell of orange, mellowed by the scent of wild meadows with a hint of the deep, dark night. Truly, this was the rose of his dreams, the one he had worked toward creating with Silvia while she was alive. The small greenhouse behind the cabin where they had lived had been filled with seeds and roses. Silvia had worked beside him constantly after their wedding. Their joy had known no bounds once Ben was born and their family was complete.

Joseph brushed the backs of his fingers over the explosion of tender rose petals, the colors flowing into a deeper orange toward the center. This rose was the closest he had ever come to anything on this earth that reminded him of Silvia. It somehow caught the essence of her smile and the beauty of her soul. She had left this tribute to the love she had given him so freely.

There would never be another Silvia—no hand so tender, no laugh so dear, no woman who could move him so deeply. This simply was a fact, and nothing could be done about it. He didn't mourn anymore what the Lord had taken. He was thankful that Silvia had been allowed to share the remaining years of her life with him—three short years after their wedding. He, the crippled Joseph Zook, had known more happiness than he had ever dared hope for. And Silvia had left him a son, a handsome son, who would never walk lame through life as Joseph did.

Silvia had taught him all he knew about roses and had opened up the secrets of a world he would never have known if not for her. *Yah*, Silvia was not from his people. She had come from the other world, showing up out of the blue to rent the little cabin in the woods. He was convinced she had come from God as a gift to him. For that he would be ever thankful.

Silvia had been *Englisha*. She had arrived from where he never dreamed of going. He was a man of the community, and *rumspringa* had been only a word, a time spent without real temptations. There had never been a question as to whether he would remain in the community or jump the fence as some did.

When Silvia appeared, he dared not gaze upon her beauty. That she had noticed him was too much. That she had spoken to him took his breath away. That the Lord had allowed such a woman to stand at his side and say the sacred wedding vows was something he would never understand. It was as if it had all been a dream. That she had been taken from him in death was not the surprise. That she had existed at all was the amazement of his life.

And now this rose, a new hybrid grown with Silvia's counsel and instructions, had been taken by her father to the Pageant of Roses Garden, where the seeds would be grown and studied. For three years Joseph had waited. This October was the date for the final testing. Silvia's father would be there, and he would send the news on whether the rose had won an All-American Rose Selection award. There was no money involved, but that was okay. The award would bear record to the greatness of the woman who had been its inspiration. If the brilliance of Silvia's Rose in the faraway

Englisha rose gardens of California was half of what his own plants displayed, then winning the contest was no problem.

Silvia would be rememembered properly. He was sure of that, as in deep down certain. The woman he had married had been educated in *Englisha* schools, but she had left her world shortly after she received her cancer diagnosis. She had moved to an Amish community to find peace before her illness took her. They had fallen in love and married. To the end, Silvia was the one who had given the most. She had argued this was not true, that he had loved her the best, but he had known better. Even at the end, he had taken his beloved wife in his arms on her deathbed, and she was the one who held him close.

Joseph bent low over the rose blossoms and closed his eyes. He jerked his head up when Arlene yelped behind him, "Joseph! There you are!"

His lame foot slammed against the greenhouse wall, and for a moment the pain stole his breath. He bent over to rub his leg with both hands.

"What were you doing?" Arlene demanded. "I've been looking everywhere for you."

"I was here," he said. "With my rose, this…" He stopped.

Her laugh was loud. "Your rose? What's so special about it?"

A ghost of a smile crept past his pain. "Can't you tell? Can't you see the difference?"

Arlene bent close. "I don't know. It looks like a rose, smells like a rose, and it's pretty. But then, all roses are pretty."

He studied her for a moment. "Yes, but by crossing one species of rose with others, a new species can be created."

Arlene's face flamed for a second. "Roses are roses. They're not like cows and horses, which are alive."

"A rose is very much alive," Joseph told her. "That's a new hybrid you're looking at, and, therefore, since I was the one who did the cross-pollination, I got to name the rose, and—"

"What's cross-pollination?"

"That's when you cross two different plant varieties. In this case, roses."

She had a blank look on her face.

"You don't understand," he said with a sigh.

Arlene's face turned into a pout. "I don't know why you always have to run me down, Joseph. It's not as if you're so high and mighty with your lame foot. There's no need for you to put on airs."

"I was trying to explain, Arlene," he protested. "I'm not putting on airs."

"Yes, you are," she insisted. "You probably even named this rose that you claim is your own."

He hesitated.

"See? That's what I mean. How would someone like you know how to come up with a brand-new rose? If there even *is* such a thing, which I doubt. A rose is a rose, yet here you are claiming you have made a new one, daring to give it a name."

When he remained silent, Arlene hesitated for a moment. "So what did you name this supposedly new rose?"

His gaze was fixed on her face.

"Don't stare at me, Joseph, as if you don't know me. I'm here for you when no one else is. Can't you see that?"

"The name is Silvia's Rose."

She gasped. "That was your *frau's* name."

"*Yah*, so what's surprising about that?"

"Why would you name a rose after your *frau?*"

"Just forget it, Arlene. I will say no more about this."

"But you're thinking it," she retorted. She followed his halting steps as he turned and walked away. "That's not *goot* for you, Joseph.

Imaginations are the devil's workshop. You know that. What would be practical is if you grew things that would sell well at the produce market on Saturdays. You are *goot* at growing things, and I'm *goot* at knowing what will sell. You know you grew way too many tomatoes this season. Why don't you let me decide what we plant, and then you can grow them? Your obsession with this rose ought to show you how much help you really need."

"*Yah*, I do need help," he allowed. "And this is why I keep you around. And *yah*, you are *goot* at planning…but you're wrong about the rose. Silvia's Rose will make more money than any of my produce ever will."

She said nothing, her face filled with disbelief.

Joseph shrugged. "So what do you suggest we do about the produce, then?"

"That's better," she said, pulling a pencil and tablet from her apron. "I've kept careful track these past two Saturdays of what sold at the market. I took stock of everyone's stands and how much they sold."

"You did all that?"

Her face reproached him. "I care about you, Joseph, and about Ben and the business. You could double your income with a little planning. And you shouldn't have offered ground in the greenhouse for Esther's garden. We need all of that space."

"You don't want Esther down here, do you?"

"No, I don't. For one thing, we really do need the space. For another, Esther is promised to Isaiah, and you shouldn't be tempted by her."

He laughed heartily. "I think we can spare the space for Esther's garden. As for her tempting me, that's not going to happen."

"How can you be so sure?"

He hung his head for a moment. "I've been in love once, Arlene. I don't expect the same gift from the Lord twice."

Arlene rolled her eyes. "Such talk is foolishness. You must not mourn for what has been. I didn't know Silvia, and certainly you must have loved her, but don't let her death continue to turn that love into bitterness. You need to get past your sense of loss so you can see what God has provided for your future."

Joseph sighed. "Enough. We had best get to work," he said with a forced smile.

"Joseph, please don't turn your heart away from me. Don't be angry. I want only what is best for you and Ben. Can't you believe that, or at least give me a chance? Neither of us is getting any younger. Please let me help you."

"You are helping me. Draw up your list of what we should plant this week, and I'll start laying out the new beds."

She brightened considerably at his words.

"Oh," he continued, "I'm going to try another kind of rose this year. Would you like to help me with that?"

Her face flushed red. "That's a most awful thing to ask me! No, I won't be entertaining your fantasies. We don't have time or energy for that."

"Okay. I'll do it myself." He turned and limped away.

She caught up to him. "I didn't mean anything by that, Joseph. I wasn't trying to be cruel, just honest with you."

He paused. "Write up your list of what we need to plant and then bring it to the back greenhouse. We really must get started, Arlene."

"Fine. I can do that," she said, hurrying away.

Joseph sighed. He backtracked and lowered his head over the rose again. This was where he had been interrupted.

"You will win, Silvia," he whispered. "You will charm all of them."

SEVEN

The late Wednesday evening sun had dipped below the horizon as Esther and Diana walked hand in hand down Fords Bush Road. A hush had fallen over the valley, broken only by the call of distant ravens and the occasional *Englisha* automobile on Highway 5. Diana was unusually silent and subdued, the skip in her step gone.

Esther reached down to tickle her daughter's chin. "What's wrong, sweetheart? You're not yourself tonight. Don't you want to eat supper with the Kings?"

"I'd rather be going to Joseph's house. And I'm tired."

Esther paused to bend down and gather Diana in her arms. "Are you homesick for Lancaster County? Is that the problem?"

Diana buried her face in Esther's shoulder.

"I know it's hard for you. I miss some things about Lancaster County too, but this is our home now. We'll have a nice dinner with our new friends. Joseph will be there, and then on Friday evening Isaiah is coming to our house for supper. That will be a happy time, don't you think?"

"He doesn't like my roses," Diana muttered. "He wouldn't even smell them."

"I'm sure that's not true," Esther told her. "Maybe Isaiah just doesn't know you that well yet."

Diana didn't appear convinced.

Esther released her, and they continued down the road. Moments later Esther's arm jerked as Diana came to a halt. "What now, sweetheart?"

"I'm going back for a rose since Joseph will be there. I want him to smell how *wunderbah* they are. The first one bloomed this morning."

"But if we cut the bloom, the smell won't be as *goot* for Joseph. Let's just leave the rose there, and you can show Isaiah on Friday."

Diana pouted but gave in, and the walk resumed. Perhaps she really shouldn't be this jumpy about Joseph. He meant no harm with his talk of roses and praying mantises. So what if Diana was fascinated with him? Esther was not a jealous person, and neither was Isaiah.

She stopped and let go of Diana's hand. "I've changed my mind, dear. Go pick your rose for Joseph. There will more by Friday evening that you can show to Isaiah."

Diana squealed and raced up the road, her bonnet strings flying behind her. Esther watched the girl go, a smile playing on her face. She had made the right decision, the kind she should have made earlier in the day by going down to see Joseph about beginning a garden. She had blamed the delay on her busyness, but that wasn't the whole truth. Isaiah would be able to hold his own with Joseph when it came to Diana's affections. Joseph would be wounded deeply if he even knew of her fears. She must leave them behind and comfort Joseph this evening if she could. They did, after all, share similar losses of the heart.

Esther bent on her knee to meet Diana, who came back on the run with a rose stem held between her fingers.

"Let me smell it first," Esther said once Diana came to a panting halt.

Her daughter held the bloom close, and Esther took a long sniff. "That is a *wunderbah* smell."

Diana beamed. "I broke the stem off long enough to have a place to hold it."

"You are a wise girl." Esther smiled and stood.

Diana danced a few steps. "Joseph will love my blossom."

"I'm sure he will," Esther agreed. "And I hope you and Joseph have a *goot* time, but other people will be there too. Remember that it's not *goot* manners to pay more attention to the guests than one does to the hostess."

"Who's the hostess?"

"Dorrine. Her husband, their children, and their cousin Arlene will also eat with us."

"That's a lot of people. I'll talk to all of them after I talk to Joseph."

"It's too bad Dorrine doesn't have little girls." Esther brushed Diana's cheek with her fingertips. "You could play with them."

"Will Betty and Mary be there?"

"Not tonight, sweetheart. You can see them on Sunday at the service. Maybe you can play in the house with Dorrine's dolls. She's sure to have some."

Diana appeared skeptical and clutched the rose stem in her hand. As they turned into the Kings' driveway, Dorrine threw open the front door and greeted them with a hearty, "*Goot* evening, you two!"

"*Goot* evening!" Esther returned the greeting and nudged Diana, who echoed her *mamm*'s words.

Once they were inside the house, Dorrine knelt to hug Diana. "What have you here?"

"A rose for Joseph." Diana held the stem aloft in triumph.

"She had to do a little begging before I let her bring the rose along," Esther explained. "Joseph had a chat with Diana last week and predicted the blooming. This is proof he was right."

Dorrine flashed a frown to Esther. "Joseph is quite taken with roses. Arlene came home in tears on Monday after an argument with him. Poor girl. It seems that she can't do anything right with that man, and she tries so hard."

"That's too bad," Esther said sympathetically.

Dorrine grimaced. "I do agree that Joseph is impossible. Arlene is so ready to step in and mother that poor boy of his, but Joseph is lost in his own world and can't see a thing beyond his flowers. I despair at times."

"Maybe Arlene should move on to greener pastures, as you've suggested."

Dorrine's frown grew. "That's part of the problem. According to her, there aren't any."

"What are greener pastures?" Diana asked.

Esther patted her daughter on the head. "Run outside and play a little while, dear. This is adult talk."

"Do you have any dolls?" Diana asked, peering up at Dorrine.

"I'm sorry, but I don't. Maybe I can find—"

Dorrine stopped when Joseph and Ben appeared in the living room window, making their way across the road. Diana noticed them and ran outside to race across the lawn.

Esther, watching through the window, held her breath until Diana stopped short of the road and waited in the Kings' yard.

"*Kinner*, they are a burden and a joy." Dorrine smiled. "But come, have a seat while Arlene and I put the final touches on supper. We have corn and mashed potatoes tonight with the best gravy recipe we could dig out of our family history. Joseph showed a real interest in that menu the last time we had him here, so we have redoubled our efforts. The way to a man's heart is through his stomach. Perhaps the problem is a matter of finding the right recipe?"

Esther waited before she turned away from the window. Joseph was taking the rose Diana handed to him. He seemed to sniff the flower deeply as the little girl leaped around in front of him. Ben stood by with a grin on his face.

"She's quite taken with him, isn't she?" Dorrine murmured.

"And he with her," Esther added.

"Maybe we ought to have Diana give Arlene lessons in what charms the man's heart?"

Esther chuckled. "Like what? Bringing him roses?"

"Men," Dorrine grumbled. "They're impossible sometimes."

Esther didn't protest. Dorrine turned to lead the way into the kitchen, where Arlene was standing at the stove, stirring the contents of a large pot.

"Well, there you are," Arlene said. "I wondered what had happened to you."

"We were keeping an eye on Diana," Esther told her. "Can I help with something?"

"You can take a chair and sit," Dorrine ordered. "We're almost done."

"Did you bring any Lancaster County recipes with you?" Arlene asked, her face hopeful. "I might need some to try and win some attention from Joseph."

Esther hid her smile. "I didn't, but it looks like Diana uses only roses. Have you tried those?"

Arlene frowned. "You wouldn't believe the horrible discussion I had with Joseph on Monday. I even told him that if you keep a garden in the greenhouse...well, he might be tempted to...something more than a friendship."

"Arlene!" Dorrine chided. "How could you?"

Arlene fanned her face with a dish towel. "I know. I feel awful about it. I know there's nothing romantic between the two of you, Esther, but the idea must have come from the outrageous things the man was saying. Joseph believes he brought a new rose into existence, which everyone knows only the Lord can do. I never dreamed how full of himself he is."

"People come up with different hybrids," Esther told her. "I don't know how it's done, though. Maybe that's what Joseph was trying to say."

Arlene turned back to her pot. "I hope you're not supporting Joseph in his fantasy. The point is, no one can make new roses. A rose is a rose. I know there are different colors, but it's still a rose."

Esther cleared her throat. "Maybe part of the problem is getting into arguments with him. Can you avoid exchanging harsh words?"

Arlene opened her mouth to speak, but just then the front door slammed, and voices drifted in from the living room.

Arlene whispered, " I trust he'll like my supper—and I'll keep my mouth shut about roses."

"I think that's probably a good idea," Esther agreed.

Dorrine excused herself and hurried into the living room.

"On another matter," Arlene began, "I see that you have Isaiah's attention sewn up. How did you do that so quickly?"

"We knew each other from a few years back," Esther told her, "so it's not as though we were strangers."

Arlene didn't answer as Dorrine escorted the men and Diana into the kitchen. Joseph greeted Esther and Arlene, and then he, Ben, and John pulled out chairs and took their seats. Esther pulled out a chair for Diana, one with a pillow on the seat to act as a booster for the little girl. Dorrine brought the food to the table and seated herself. Arlene did the same after a brief glance at Joseph.

"Let us pray," John said. He lead out in a short prayer of thanks.

After the "Amen," Dorrine and Arlene passed the bowls of hot food.

"What have you been doing with yourself?" John asked Esther. "I saw Isaiah's buggy at your house on Monday, but all has been quiet since then."

Esther gave him a soft smile before she answered. "*Yah*, Isaiah stopped by to offer help, and I put him to work fixing the drain in the bathroom."

"That shouldn't have been too difficult."

"I must not have worked him too hard," Esther agreed. "He's coming back for supper on Friday evening."

John chuckled. "I'm glad to see you two getting along. Minister Isaiah has been a widower long enough. It's not *goot* for a man to be alone, according to what the Lord spoke in the garden all those years ago. Things have not changed since then. A man needs a *frau* in the house."

Esther nodded. "I'm glad the Lord's blessing seems to be upon my move to the valley and upon Isaiah's interest in me. We both have sorrowed, and now the Lord is choosing to bless us, for which we are very grateful."

"That's well spoken." John appeared solemn. "And what about you, Joseph? Has the Lord been blessing you lately?"

Joseph lowered his head to say, "Not in that way, no."

John added quickly, "I'm sorry if I offended you. I was only trying to tease. I'm sure there's someone out there who would fill the empty place in your home."

"Perhaps," Joseph allowed, and then he turned toward Esther. "You didn't know my *frau*, Silvia, did you?"

"No, but I'm sure she was a worthy woman. She came from the *Englisha, yah*? What a story that must be."

A hint of a smile played on Joseph's face. "There is a story. Silvia came from the other side of the fence, but she was a lovely woman, not unlike an angel who flew in by the hand of the Lord. I knew about her illness before we wed, but Silvia loved me deeply." Joseph dropped his gaze for a moment. "And I loved her with all my heart."

"That's beautiful," Esther said, her mind racing. There was more to this, she was sure, but no one said anything. Perhaps the subject was better left alone for now. "I heard that you create new rose lines," she finally added.

Joseph gave Arlene a quick look. "That I do."

"Have you had any success?"

"*Yah*, I have. But I should find out just how great the success has been this October."

"Oh?" Esther leaned forward in her chair. "What's so special about October?"

He hesitated. "Maybe I can show you the rose sometime when you come over."

"I would love that."

"I showed Joseph my rose," Diana piped up. "He said it smelled very *goot*."

"I'm glad he liked your rose," Esther said, smiling gently at Joseph. "All roses are worthy of praise."

Joseph's head jerked up. "You don't think all roses are the same, do you, Esther?"

"No," she answered, careful to avoid Arlene's eyes. "Sometime you'll have to tell me more about your dabbling in hybridizing. It all sounds very interesting."

A smile grew on Joseph's face as John spoke up. "If I may interrupt these rose stories, what I'm interested in is Joseph's plans for the produce market. Will there be room for poor farmers like us to sneak in a few products?"

Joseph joined in the laughter this time. "You can talk with Arlene about that. She's making all our plans for the produce. I'm sure we'll be working it out so that it fits in with the community's needs. The Lord has given Ben and me plenty of food to eat and a house to live in. There's no reason to be greedy."

"That's true," John agreed, and the smiles returned to Dorrine's and Arlene's faces.

Esther listened to the conversation flow around her. She would have to look into this rose project of Joseph's soon. From what she could tell, more was there than what readily met the eye.

EIGHT

On Friday morning, with Diana's hand in hers, Esther pushed open the door of the round-framed greenhouse and called out, "Hello? Anybody around?"

"*Yah*, I'm coming," Joseph called from somewhere in the back.

"It's Esther and Diana," Esther called back.

They waited as Joseph's hesitant step came toward them. As he drew nearer, Diana ran up to him with her face aglow. "Can I see your special rose? The one you told me about?"

Joseph bent low to give her a quick hug. "You can if your *mamm* doesn't object. She's probably anxious to get started with her garden."

"That's okay," Esther told him. "I should have been here earlier, but I had to make preparations for supper tonight."

"Minister Isaiah?" Joseph teased with a twinkle in his eye.

Esther laughed. "So you do notice things other than praying mantises and roses?"

He chuckled. "I suppose so, but I do get a little caught up in my own world."

"I wasn't trying to correct you or scold you," Esther assured him. "Although, about the praying mantis..."

He nodded. "I'm sorry, Esther. I shouldn't have shared something like that with a child as young as your daughter. I got a little carried away and forgot her age."

"It's okay. I have to confess I was a little upset at first, but children know how to handle things like that better than we think they can."

"Can we see the rose now?" Diana asked, tugging on Joseph's sleeve.

He looked to Esther. "Do you want to come along too?"

"Certainly." Esther didn't hesitate. "I told you Wednesday evening I wanted to see what you are doing."

He seemed pleased and led the way to the adjoining greenhouse. "Where's Arlene?"

Joseph didn't pause in his shuffle. "She's busy in the back gathering up the produce we will take to the market tomorrow."

"Maybe I should help with the work rather than start on my garden spot this afternoon," Esther suggested.

"That's kind of you, but it's already late in the season, and everyone needs a little garden to tinker with."

"I want my garden planted with nothing but roses," Diana piped up.

Joseph laughed. "See there? Out of the mouths of babes comes wisdom."

Esther joined in his laughter. Joseph's shuffle soon came to a stop by a line of rose pots stretching along a wide shelf.

"Here it is," Joseph declared, reaching for the tallest pot. "My very own precious rose." He brought it down to Diana's level. "Smell deeply, little one."

Diana closed her eyes and took a long sniff.

"What do you think?" Joseph bent close to listen for the answer.

"It is..." Diana slowly opened her eyes. "It is very sweet and *wunderbah*," she said dreamily.

"Ah, that's *goot*! Take another sniff before I put the rose back."

Diana complied, her face rapturous.

"It is called Silvia's Rose," Joseph told her. "A sign of the Lord's blessing on my life with its beautiful and heavenly smell."

"So this is your hybrid?" Esther asked.

He set the pot on the shelf and turned to face her. "It is, but perhaps we had best not say more about that. For some, it's a sensitive subject."

"That would be Arlene?"

"*Yah*."

"I would like to know the full story if you don't mind."

His gaze drifted to her daughter, and Esther turned to say, "Diana, why don't you run back to where Arlene is working to see if you can help her? I'll call you if I need help in the garden."

Diana took another quick glance at the rose before she skipped off.

Joseph watched the small form retreat from sight before he spoke. "The story began a long time ago, when Silvia showed up in our district. I told you the basics the other evening—of her being *Englisha*, and of her beauty. I soon learned that though she was in remission from cancer, she felt her time was short. I couldn't believe she desired my attentions, let alone my love, but that was how it was. She joined the community, and we dated, and we were wed. I don't have to tell you how deeply we loved each other, and how taken I was with her." He glanced down at his lame foot. "Maybe suffering draws people together? I don't know."

"Did she tell you of her background in the *Englisha* world?" Esther asked.

Joseph's grin was wry. "You make it sound as if she were a fleeing murderer. Silvia was not like that. Her parents had divorced when she was young, and she was shuffled around between their homes. She never told me much about her growing up years, but the illness made her walk away from it all. I do know that Silvia's great love in life was gardening, or horticulture, as she called it. She had what the *Englisha* call a PhD."

"*Yah*, the *Englisha* give that as one of the highest degrees, I'm thinking."

"Something like that." Joseph nodded. "Silvia had a doctorate in horticulture from Oregon State University. She taught me everything I know about roses, and most of what I know about gardening." His voice caught. "Silvia had connections through her father, who submitted the seeds after Silvia's death. Three years I have waited while the rose is grown at the Pageant of Roses Garden, and they study the results. I call it Silvia's Rose, the beautiful expression of the woman I loved. The judging is this October." Joseph turned to look back at the white-and-orange blossoms.

"So you hope to win something with this rose?"

"*Yah*, an award for Silvia's sake. She deserves the best."

"I understand."

"*Yah*, I believe you do," he said with a smile. "But I'm not surprised. You're different, Esther. I knew that the first time I saw your daughter."

"But I'm not different," she protested. "I'm ordinary and boring."

"Perhaps. But I've known the heart and love of a great woman, and yours is like hers."

"Stop that, Joseph Zook," she scolded. "You'll have me blushing like a teenager."

He grinned. "I doubt that. I'm the one who is common and ordinary. But come, we must see to your garden."

As they made their way to the garden space he had set aside for her, Esther asked, "Have you told others in the community the story of Silvia's Rose?"

"No. They've never asked. I did say a little to Arlene this week, and she reacted the way I expected people would."

Esther quickened her steps. "But what if you win this award, Joseph? You know that could bring attention to you and the community."

He paused. "I would do anything for Silvia, Esther. She wanted this win for me. I pray the Lord will grant her this honor." Joseph turned toward some empty ground in front of them. "Now, back to gardening. All of this is yours to plant. Once Arlene adjusts her list with what is selling best on Saturday, we'll be doing our own planting. In the meantime, put in what you want. I tilled the earth this morning. I think I've done enough for what you need. There are seeds on the rack over there. Help yourself."

"But I can't just take this space for nothing, Joseph," Esther protested. "I must pay for this."

He grinned. "I'm glad to help you and Isaiah with your new start in life. Next year you'll likely have your own garden at his place."

"I suppose so," Esther allowed.

"Let it be my way of making it up to you for telling your daughter about praying mantises eating each other after their nuptials. I really am sorry about that. I don't know what I was thinking."

"It can happen, I guess." She managed to smile.

"You mean the female eating the male?"

Esther gasped. "Joseph!"

"I'm teasing."

"You know it's not like that. Surely you learned that from Silvia."

A smile played on his face. "I was thinking of Arlene."

Esther clamped her hand over her mouth to stifle an outburst of laugher.

He laughed along with her. "She has a wound somewhere in her life, but that's another subject. Do you need anything else before I go help Arlene?"

"I'm fine," she told him. "Thank you."

He moved off with his steady shuffle. Maybe Joseph was right. She hadn't thought of that angle. What was Arlene's home life like? She hardly knew the family. But Arlene did love Joseph in her own way, and he did need a *frau*. Now that she knew of Joseph's deep love for his former *frau*, Esther would have to pray that love could grow in Joseph's heart for Arlene, though that might be difficult with the romantic ideas Joseph carried about marriage.

Esther made a face. The two had a long journey ahead of them, but stranger things had happened. Maybe Joseph could be persuaded to lend Arlene a helping hand. Love was above all practical and safe, and it should fit into everyday life. That was how the Lord made things. Roses didn't always fit too well. They had seemed to work for Joseph in his first marriage, but maybe it was time he learned to walk with his feet on the ground.

That's how she, Esther Stoltzfus, planned to live her life. She had moved all the way from Lancaster County for the purpose of becoming Isaiah's wife, and look how things were working out. Quite well, and roses were not needed.

Esther found a string and two small stakes to set up the line. With a hoe she scraped a gouge into the earth along the string line. She found a tablet and pencil on an upper shelf and drew a rough diagram of her plot. She dribbled the seeds in the open earth and covered them—carrots, lettuce, tomatoes, green beans, celery, peas. She wrote each one down and worked for more than an hour, one row followed by another until she had planted all the produce she wanted.

"Looks like you're doing okay," Joseph said from a few feet away. Esther jumped, and Joseph laughed. "Sorry, I didn't mean to sneak up on you."

"It's okay." Esther caught her breath. "Any advice from the expert?"

He grinned. "No, it looks fine. Besides, you grew up with gardening, and it's not my business to clutter your brain with information."

"But I want to know," she insisted.

"I'll take care of things from here," he assured her. "All you have to do is keep the weeds pulled. That I don't do."

"Offering me a spot here in your greenhouse is very kind of you, Joseph. I'm grateful."

"I'm glad to help. Now, don't you have to get home and prepare supper for Minister Isaiah?"

"I have plenty of time. Can't I help you with something?"

"Well, if you don't mind, you could run some boxes out to the wagon for me? I don't want to impose, but with my foot, the hardest part of getting produce to the market is loading it up."

"I'd be glad to," she said without hesitation. She put up her hoe and tablet and followed Joseph across the greenhouse. He didn't pause until they arrived where Arlene was working with Diana, who chattered beside her.

"I'm helping, *Mamm*!"

"That's *goot*, sweetheart," Esther replied, gathering up two boxes from the pile that were waiting to be loaded in the wagon. When she returned for more boxes, Joseph was gone.

Observing Arlene's silence and cool demeanor, Esther told her,

"Don't give up yet, Arlene. Joseph told me some of the story of his life. I'm beginning to see why the two of you are having trouble. My advice is that you should also try to get to know more about him and why he does some of the things he does. It may help you change your attitude toward him. Joseph does have a tender heart, and the man could help you."

"And how can he help me?" Arlene whispered as Joseph reappeared again.

"I'll tell you later," Esther whispered back as she picked up a large basket for a trip to the wagon. Joseph was still there when she came back, and Arlene looked ready to burst with impatience. This time Arlene picked up a box of her own and followed Esther to the wagon.

"You'd best be telling me right away, Esther. What did you mean about him helping me?"

Esther turned to face Arlene. "The bottom line is that you have to stop knocking his roses. Joseph has a tender side that manifests itself in unusual ways, but scorning them isn't going to help you win his heart. The man has much to offer. You should learn from him."

"That's it?" Arlene huffed. "I was hoping you would offer a way for me to pull him away from his fantasy life with the roses and his dead *frau*." Arlene whirled about and hurried ahead of Esther back into the greenhouse.

Joseph looked up when they joined him again. Arlene ignored him and went back to her work. Esther gathered up her daughter for the walk home.

"Thanks for your help," Joseph called after her.

"Thank you for the garden space," she called back with a smile.

He knew much more than was obvious about the science of

roses, which was the first lesson Arlene should learn—but she seemed incapable of accepting Joseph as he was. Joseph had been given a very special gift from the Lord, one that few people experienced, but the dangers were also obvious. How could he settle the second time for a *frau* who needed him without the glory of roses to light their way?

NINE

A late evening hush hung over the valley as Esther heard Isaiah's buggy pulling into her driveway. She shook her white apron twice to shed the bread crumbs before she hurried to the front door. Isaiah wouldn't expect a woman to be all fancied up in her Sunday clothing when he arrived for a Friday evening supper. An apron-clad one was fine—especially if the food was good—and, if she had to say so herself, she had a delicious supper ready.

Esther opened the front door and waved as Isaiah came to a halt beside the hitching post. She could have run out to meet him beside his buggy, but that was how starstruck teenagers acted. Isaiah might think she was gloating over her easy conquest of him, which wasn't true. They were like two streams that had come together in their proper place. *Yah*, she had been the one who brought about the meeting, but Isaiah had played his part. His readiness to move their relationship forward meant that she had read the Lord's will correctly with her move to the valley.

Esther waved again to Isaiah, who was busy tying up his horse. As she waited, Diana appeared around the corner of the house at a fast run and didn't slow down until she came to a halt in front of Isaiah's buggy. She began chattering away as Isaiah bent down to listen, and moments later he threw back his head in laughter. Diana giggled, and Isaiah took the girl's hand. The two ambled toward the house, their attention focused on each other.

"I helped Joseph and Arlene all morning while *Mamm* was working on her garden," Diana was saying as they came within earshot. "Isn't that true, *Mamm*?"

"That's right," Esther agreed with a smile.

Isaiah tickled the girl's chin. "I wasn't doubting you, Diana."

Diana peered up at him. "Are you staying for supper?"

"Yep!" Isaiah proclaimed. "If your *mamm* will let me."

Diana grinned, and Esther told her, "Run along now. There's still light enough for you to play outside. I'll call you when we're ready to eat."

"I want to ask one more thing," Diana declared. "Joseph said that even if flowers look the same, they don't all smell the same. Do you think that's true, Isaiah?"

"Ah..." Isaiah appeared puzzled.

"I smelled my roses when we came home from Joseph's place." Diana waved her small hand toward the fence. "And I can't tell any difference. Would you see if Joseph is right, Isaiah? Come smell them."

Isaiah shrugged and winked at Esther. "I'm afraid I don't know anything about roses—"

"But you can smell," Diana insisted.

"I think I'll wait to smell the delicious supper your *mamm* has prepared for us."

"Okay." Diana gave in with a sigh. Then she perked up. "But why do praying mantises eat each other? That's what Joseph said they do."

Esther gasped. "Why are you bringing that up again, Diana?"

"Well, you won't tell me, and Joseph won't either. I asked him this morning."

Isaiah turned his head to hide his laughter, his beard jiggling despite his efforts.

"Joseph shouldn't have told you those things in the first place," Esther told her. "He's sorry now. You're just a little girl, and he feels bad about it. He told me so himself. Now, please forget about praying mantises eating each other."

"But I want to know," Diana insisted, standing her ground.

Esther squatted down and took her daughter's hands in hers. "Sweetheart, the Lord made people and insects differently. People don't do things insects do. I wish Joseph hadn't told you this."

Diana puckered her face. "I like him, *Mamm*. He makes me feel big and important."

Esther wrapped her arms around her daughter's thin shoulders. "You're certainly growing every day. Run now and play. I'll call you when supper's ready."

"Won't Isaiah sniff my roses?" Diana tried once more, looking up at him plaintively.

"Sure, why not." Isaiah was sober faced now. He took Diana's hand and allowed her to lead him to the rail fence. Together they bent over one bloom and the next one, and then the one after that. Esther strained to hear the conversation between them.

"Is there a difference?" Diana looked up hopefully.

"Hmm...I think maybe only the bees can tell the difference."

"I can't tell either, but thank you for smelling them with me."

"Anytime," Isaiah said, smiling as he watched the small figure disappear around the edge of the house.

He walked back to Esther, who waited for him on the porch. "It looks as if your daughter is fascinated with Joseph."

"You can say that again."

"And what about you?"

"Isaiah, you shame me with that question. I didn't come all the way from Lancaster County with Joseph Zook on my mind!"

Isaiah grinned slyly. "Aha. So you're confessing your real reason for moving to the valley from Lancaster County?"

"You just want to see me blush, but I'm not the blushing type. If you want to talk plainly, we will. I've done nothing I am ashamed of. *Yah*, I came partly because of you—as you surely know."

"I'm just teasing. Now can I come in? All this rose sniffing has exhausted me."

Esther suppressed a smile. "I didn't expect to see the day that Isaiah Mast would be on his knees in front of roses. Or concerned about Joseph and me...as if there was anything to be concerned about. Shame on you."

"Well, Joseph is a man who needs a *frau*, just like me. You can't expect me not to take notice. Especially when he offers you a spot in his greenhouse for your garden."

She tried to change the subject. "That was a fine answer you gave Diana. Where did you come up with that? About the bees being able to tell the difference?"

"Maybe I have a few inspirations from time to time."

"I know you do, Isaiah, but that was *goot*. I wouldn't have known how to explain it."

"I guess we could have walked down and asked Joseph."

Esther gave him a sharp glance. "I think I know you well enough, Isaiah Mast, to hear irritation in your voice."

"You sounded irate a moment ago yourself, yet you planted your garden this morning in the man's greenhouse."

"That is true," Esther agreed. She held the front door open wide. "I'm becoming a bundle of contradictions."

"All because of Joseph?"

"Maybe if you heard the story about his *frau*, you would understand him better. Or do you already know?"

Isaiah flopped down on the couch. "I can't say that I have. The man comes from Lancaster County. People down there are kind of secretive, and Silvia passed before Joseph moved here with Ben."

"Well, it's a touching story." Esther gave him a warm smile. "But enough about Joseph."

"Okay, but the way the talk is going, I thought maybe he was coming for supper."

Esther rolled her eyes before heading for the kitchen. Isaiah rose and followed her.

"Have a chair," she offered. "Supper's just about ready."

He took a deep breath. "I like the smells in here much more than I do the ones by the rail fence."

"I thought you looked cute down on your knees sniffing the roses."

"You'll have me blushing soon," he said with a smile. "But in all seriousness, your lives seem quite wrapped up in Joseph's all of a sudden. Every time I come around, that's all Diana speaks of. Now with this garden, you'll be seeing a lot of him."

"I didn't plan this," she protested. "Dorrine asked me to help her connect Arlene with Joseph. Now I've ended up with your questioning the situation. That's not helpful." She brought a platter of pot roast to the table and awaited his inspection.

Isaiah leaned forward with a look of rapture on his face. "Now *that's* definitely better than the smell of roses."

"Glad you like it," she said with a soft smile.

Next, she went to the stove and brought back a bowl of mashed potatoes. Making one more trip, she said, "And here's the gravy." She set the boat on a hot pad in front of him.

Isaiah lowered his head until his beard touched the edge of the table. He took several deep sniffs before exclaiming, "What more could a man want on a spring evening than a supper like this served by a *wunderbah* woman like you, Esther? How long has it been since I've had this kind of meal?" He pretended to tick off numbers on his fingers. "I had begun to forget."

"You haven't been that bad off. I'm sure your *mamm* and your sisters see to it that you're invited to the family gatherings—and often enough, I'm thinking."

"That they do," he said. "But this is still very special. I want to make that clear, even if I didn't bring you any roses."

Esther gasped. "Roses! Why would you bring roses? That can't be another reference to Joseph."

Isaiah shrugged. "With all this talk of roses and Joseph, I just thought—"

"Well, you thought wrong. I don't need roses."

Isaiah studied her for a moment. "What is going on, Esther?"

"Nothing is going on," she said as she brought a bowl of corn to the table.

Isaiah drew the dish close before he looked up. "When a woman says nothing is going on, that means there usually is. That's what I learned from living around my sisters with all their emotional ups and downs. But I didn't think you were into drama, Esther. Mandy was a simple woman, you know." He smiled up at her. "I like simplicity. So what is this 'nothing'?"

She let out a breath. "It really is nothing. If I seem a bit off, maybe you can attribute it to the move and settling in a new community. I'm so thankful for folks like the Kings. They've been *wunderbah* to Diana and me. They had us down for supper on Wednesday evening with—" Esther stopped abruptly and grabbed the salad.

"With Joseph," Isaiah finished for her.

"*Yah*. Arlene is interested in him, and the Kings thought including him in the mix would help move that relationship along."

"I see," he said. "Sounds like drama to me."

"Not really," she insisted, "although I do plan to talk with Arlene about how she can improve her approach to Joseph. I had some ideas this afternoon, which I haven't fully explained to Arlene. He has a tender side to him that I didn't expect, and his story of his *frau* really touched me, and..."

"And?"

"You don't want to hear more about roses or Joseph. Besides, we need to eat. I'll go get Diana."

Esther scurried to the front door and called out, "Diana, time for supper."

Dusk had almost fallen, and the little girl appeared at once from around the corner of the house to follow Esther back into the kitchen.

"There you are," Isaiah said to Diana. "What were you doing out there?"

"I was playing in my little doll playhouse under the oak tree."

"Oh," he said. "Is it a pretend playhouse?"

"*Yah*." A look of delight filled Diana's face. "Joseph let me make a big playhouse out of boxes today at the greenhouse. He said I could make more when I come down again and *Mamm* works on her garden."

"So you had lots of fun today?" Isaiah asked.

"*Yah*, I did," Diana said. "But I wish Joseph or the King family had some girls to play with."

"That's too bad." Isaiah hid a smile. With that, he bowed his head, and Esther and Diana did likewise as he offered thanks. Esther tried to keep her thoughts on Isaiah's words, but her mind was racing.

Things were not going well. Isaiah's impressions of her were all the wrong ones. Thankfully, she had avoided the story about Silvia's Rose and the award Joseph hoped to win.

Isaiah finished the prayer with a solid, "Amen," and fixed his gaze on the food. Esther passed the dishes to him, and he helped himself to generous portions.

"I hope everything tastes okay," she ventured.

"If it tastes as good as it smells, it'll be more than okay," Isaiah replied, buttering a piece of warm bread fresh from the oven. With a wide smile he spread on a thick layer of blackberry jam. "I think I'll have to come back here more often."

"You're welcome anytime," she told him with a warm smile.

Isaiah chuckled. "Maybe we can make this our regular Friday night date. Perhaps we could do this instead of a more traditional courtship, since we've both been wed before."

"I agree," she said without hesitation. "That is a *wunderbah* idea."

"And this is *wunderbah* nourishing," he said, taking a big bite from the slab of jam-coated bread.

TEN

The following Tuesday afternoon, Esther held Diana's hand as they strolled down Fords Bush Road to Joseph's greenhouse.

"Can I make a playhouse again today?" Diana begged.

"You had best leave those big boxes alone, sweetheart. What if they come crashing down on your head? Anyway, I don't think Joseph is home this afternoon. Your imaginary dollhouse in the backyard is all you need."

"I want to play with Joseph's boxes. They make the best playhouse," Diana whined.

"Well, you'll just have to wait until Joseph is home."

That wait would be awhile if Esther had anything to say about it. She could easily avoid Joseph if she kept a sharp eye out and only visited the greenhouse while he was away. The plan had worked to perfection today. Joseph and Ben had driven out of their driveway right after lunch, and she had left the dishes in the sink in her rush to get on the road. She was going to try to keep Diana away from Joseph as much as she could without it being too noticeable. There would be too many questions in Diana's young mind if they cut off all communication, and a cold shoulder to a neighbor would be terribly impolite.

Isaiah had said nothing more about Joseph last week after supper, and because she was in no danger of falling for Joseph, there was no sense in acting as if he were a real threat. Yet why was she on pins and needles when it came to him? There was no reason at all. With a little guidance, Diana's heart would soon be drawn to Isaiah's steady and predictable ways. Her heart was already there.

Esther quickened her steps but stopped short when the Kings' front door slammed and Dorrine hurried across her front lawn.

"*Goot* afternoon," Dorrine sang out. "Headed down to your garden patch, I'm guessing."

"*Yah*, that's the plan."

"I think Joseph just left." Dorrine leaned over the front gate. "This would be the perfect time for a chat with Arlene about...well, you know what. You have such a way with Joseph, and Arlene could learn so much from you."

"Well, I'll try," Esther told her. "But Joseph is not what I'm used to in men, so maybe I don't have much to say. The man has some high ideals."

"That's foolishness!" Dorrine dismissed the objection with a quick wave. "You have Isaiah eating out of your hand in the short time you've been here. Why, his face practically glowed at this past Sunday meeting. I haven't seen the man so happy since before Mandy passed."

"You have to remember that Isaiah and I have known each other from way back," Esther reminded her. "That's why it seems like the Lord has brought us together without much fuss."

"You undersell yourself, Esther!" Dorrine said, reaching down to brush a few stray hairs out of Diana's face. "How is my little darling today?"

"We're going to play with Joseph's boxes," Diana announced.

"You are?" Dorrine raised her eyebrows.

"Well, that's Diana's plan," Esther said. "I want her to wait on the playhouse building until Joseph is back, but I hope to be out of there before he returns."

"Oh?" Dorrine raised her eyebrows.

Esther forced a laugh. "I'll tell you later." She pointed down at Diana.

"What, *Mamm*?" Diana asked, peering upward.

"You weren't supposed to see that."

Dorrine chuckled. "They have eyes everywhere, *kinner* do." She bent down to Diana's level. "Does Joseph fascinate you?"

"What's that mean?"

"You like him, don't you?"

Diana glowed. "*Yah*! He tells me lots of things."

"Some things you shouldn't know," Esther muttered.

"Really? Like what?" Dorrine asked.

"Praying mantises—"

"Sweetie, why don't you run on in and help Arlene?" Esther interrupted.

As Diana scurried off, Dorrine said, "She's such a dear little girl. If the Lord should see fit to bless my life with such a gift, I would never get off my knees for giving thanks."

Esther smiled. "I pray your wish will be granted soon. Am I correct in thinking..."

Dorrine blushed. "How did you know? Well, never mind. Would you pray that I might have such a blessing?"

"If the Lord wills it," Esther agreed.

"*Yah*, to that we must always submit." Dorrine sighed. "But what else was Joseph telling Diana that was so out of line?"

"All about praying mantises and the female's habit of eating the male after their..."

Dorrine giggled. "Joseph is strange, but what a thing to say! No wonder you're upset. Did you chastise him?"

"I tried, but he's so innocent...and with his lame leg and all... But he did apologize on his own. I don't think he always knows what his words do, and there is Arlene..."

Dorrine nodded. "I know. The comparison could cross a man's mind. I have tried to speak to Arlene about the way she talks to Joseph, but on the other hand, those Southern Lancaster County people are all a little strange. Usually that end of the county stays pretty much put where they were born."

"So there's the problem, but let me say that Joseph does have a kind heart. He told me more about Silvia."

"Well, she's gone now, and he needs to accept that and consider settling down with Arlene if only for Ben's sake. So anything you do to help things along would be greatly appreciated."

"I'll do what I can," Esther told her. "Now I'd best be going, or Joseph will be back before I even get started."

"Don't avoid him," Dorrine advised. "The more you're around him, the better it will be for both Arlene and Joseph. A woman's influence on a man can be *wunderbah* even when they aren't married." Dorrine winked before hurrying back across her front yard.

Esther continued to the greenhouse. Dorrine's words had comforted her, in a way. As for Joseph, what he had gone through must have touched his heart at great depths. What man in his condition wouldn't be moved deeply if a *frau* like Silvia had loved him with all her heart? Silvia had likely done that out of gratitude for Joseph's tender care through her illness.

So why shouldn't her heart be moved by the story? She was sure Isaiah would feel the same way if he took the time to listen to the tale. Isaiah shouldn't worry that Joseph would change her. There was no danger in that. She was the same ordinary person she had always been, even if she could feel for Joseph and what he had gone through.

Esther entered the greenhouse and headed toward her small patch of ground in the back. It was too soon to expect the seeds to have sprouted, even with Joseph's green thumb. Still, she figured she would find some weeding to do. Sure enough, short blades of some weeds had already begun to appear. She found a hoe hung on the wall. She was grateful that Joseph made things easy for her. He indeed had a tender heart. Arlene was foolish not to handle him with care instead of abrasiveness. Joseph was a man who could feel deeply, which meant he could be easily wounded. Likely that was why Arlene had yet to experience success in her relationship with him.

Half an hour later, satisfied with her work, Esther went in search of Diana and Arlene. She found them in a far area of the adjoined greenhouses, where Diana was playing with some empty boxes. Seeing her *mamm*, Diana cried out, "Look at my playhouse! Arlene let me use these smaller boxes, and they're even better!"

Esther squatted down to peer inside the makeshift shelter. "It's very nice, sweetheart. You have a lively imagination." She blew Diana a kiss and got up to join Arlene at the bench, which ran along the side of the greenhouse.

Arlene gave Esther a wry look. "Your daughter is quite taken with Joseph. Maybe I ought to claim Diana as my own until he changes his mind about me."

Esther laughed. "I don't think that would help."

"No doubt Diana is helping you to charm Isaiah."

"It's not Diana who can help you with Joseph. It's *you*, Arlene. You would win him over easily if you simply changed your attitude toward him. You could certainly be more respectful than you are. That's what men want—respect."

"But he says such crazy things!"

"Like what?"

"I already told you. That he creates roses! What man would say such a thing? And he smells them all the time with this strange look on his face." Arlene threw her hands upward in exasperation.

"Arlene." Esther sighed. "Are you sure you should even try to win Joseph's affections if you feel that way about him?"

Arlene set down the pot she was working with and looked sorrowfully at Esther. "You're saying that because with me out of the way, you can move in on him."

Esther gasped. "How could you think of such a thing? You need to wake up to reality. I'm *not* trying to steal Joseph. I'm seeing Isaiah, but I do have to speak with Joseph from time to time. And I've heard his story, so I know what I'm saying is the truth. If you want to wed the man, you have to love him."

"But I do!" Arlene insisted. "And even with him being lame. He's still well able to supply for his *kinner*—if the Lord should choose to give us any." Arlene blushed and rushed on. "Joseph would be exactly what a husband should be if he wasn't so crazy. But that can be fixed—and I think you can help me. If you're really not after him, then you can prove it by helping me. You could talk to him. He might listen to you. He sure won't hear what I'm saying."

"I've been trying to tell you that Joseph isn't the problem. *You* are."

"How can you say that, Esther?" Arlene practically shouted. "All I want is a steady, normal life full of the *goot* things of the community—like home, *kinner*, and a husband who can provide for our growing family. Don't you want these things yourself?"

"*Yah*, of course. I had them with Lonnie, and I expect my relationship with Isaiah will be blessed in the same way."

"And I want the same from Joseph. Are you going to help me or not?"

"Arlene, honestly, I can't help you right now. You have to change your attitude. You're not going to change a man who is..."

"Strange?"

Esther tried again. "No, not strange...but *special*. He's had unusual experiences in life. His lameness, his great love for Silvia, and his loss of her love. Those things would be hard for anyone to bear and at the same time to leave behind him."

"I don't understand a word you're saying," Arlene declared, shaking her head. "None of us is more special than anyone else. Isn't that what the community believes? Isn't that what Isaiah believes? Now, if Isaiah believes such a thing, why are you saying otherwise?"

"Because I think Joseph is special in his own way, and I'm not disagreeing with anyone by saying that. Another thing you should consider is that perhaps Joseph has something you need. You could benefit greatly from his tenderness and soft heart. Perhaps there is something in your life that..."

"Stop talking foolishness," Arlene snapped. "It's not me who needs changing."

Esther attempted a smile. "I'm not trying to argue with you, Arlene. Really, I'm not."

"I guess you and I just don't see eye to eye." Arlene jerked her head as if for emphasis.

Esther sighed again. "I'm sorry we're not agreeing. In the meantime, I think I'd better go."

Arlene said nothing to stop her from leaving.

ELEVEN

Early the following Friday evening, Isaiah clucked to Echo as they trotted briskly toward Deacon Daniel's home. The sun had been out in full strength since dawn, and the temperature had crept up into the upper seventies. Summer was around the corner. The whole valley would blossom with life, and the long winter would be forgotten. The seasons were all blessed of the Lord, yet Esther had chosen a *goot* time to arrive in the community—the spring.

Any courtship should begin in the spring. He had taken Mandy home from the hymn singing for the first time on such a day back in Lancaster County. Courting was best begun when the Lord awakened the earth, and marriages were best sealed with the sacred vows in the fall with the winter's snow lying near at hand. Marriage was a practical thing, undergirded by a deep trust in the Lord's ways.

He had been blessed once with a *frau* who walked with him in faith, and now it seemed the Lord had chosen to bless him a second time with Esther. They could begin their marriage this fall in the full confidence that their love would stand the test of time, and live through the winter of life. They had both already walked that road to its ultimate sorrow, yet found the Lord sufficient. *Yah*, He was even sufficient enough to give again what He had chosen to take away.

"Whoa there," Isaiah called to Echo as he turned into Daniel's driveway. Isaiah parked beside the barn and hopped down to look around. There was no sign of the deacon, but at this time in the evening Daniel would be in the barn. Isaiah found the tie rope beneath the buggy seat and secured Echo to the ring on the sidewall.

Isaiah pushed open the barn door and entered the whitewashed interior. Daniel ran a tidy operation with his 120-acre dairy farm on the rim above the valley floor. Fresh signs of the evening's milking shift were everywhere, with wisps of grain on the floor in front of the stanchions. The floors were still wet from their washing down between milking shifts. Few could match the deacon when it came to business or in his duties as a deacon.

"Howdy there," Isaiah called out, and a muffled call came from the back of the barn.

Daniel's bearded face appeared and broke into a smile. "Isaiah, it's you. Why didn't you come for the first milking? That's when you were needed."

Isaiah laughed and joined in the teasing. "You know how well my *daett* taught me to avoid work."

They laughed together and Daniel stroked his beard. "So what brings you out tonight? Shouldn't you be at Esther's place for supper?"

Isaiah grinned. "I'm headed that way, but I gave myself a little extra time to stop in and chat."

"And timed just right to avoid the milking?"

"That's what my *daett* taught me."

The two laughed again. "Well, you seem to get along fine with Esther," Daniel told him. "You can't have trouble there, I'm thinking."

"Who says there's trouble?"

"She seems well matched for you, as Mandy was," the deacon continued. "The Lord has blessed you."

"*Yah*, He has." Isaiah hung his head for a moment. "I'm not one to complain, or to think that I can't handle what is my responsibility, but in this matter I think I should ask for help."

Daniel appeared befuddled. "What could be wrong? Sure, Esther might have been a little forward in making the move to the valley on her own, assuming you were open to her advances."

"You do have a sharp eye," Isaiah muttered.

"I'm not blind, you know," Daniel said with a chuckle. "But Esther knew you from your *rumspringa* days, and you knew her, so there's nothing wrong with any of this. You *should* be beating a trail over to her house on Friday nights." Daniel smiled. "By the way, I like that plan. It's mature and practical, unlike some of these youngsters and their dates on Sunday evenings. Here you get to sample the woman's cooking skills and make sure she passes the test."

The two laughed again and Isaiah told him, "I'm sure glad you agree with me."

"So that's all you want? My agreement? My blessing?"

Isaiah raised his head. "No, there's more. It's about Joseph Zook. What do you know about the man?"

Daniel wrinkled his face. "Well, you know he keeps pretty much to himself. He comes from Southern Lancaster County, and he has suffered what you have suffered—the loss of a woman he loved."

Isaiah nodded. "But other than his grief, there's nothing wrong with him?"

"Not that I know of. He keeps the *Ordnung* to a T, and he makes no trouble in the district. He pretty much stays in that greenhouse of his, but there's nothing wrong with that."

"Nothing about roses, then?"

"Roses? I know he grows them. What do you mean?"

"I don't know. I keep hearing about his roses over at Esther's place. Her daughter, Diana, is constantly speaking of them. Esther doesn't say much, but Joseph does have a thing with roses, doesn't he?"

"*Yah*, I guess he does now that I think about it." Daniel stroked his beard again. "But what's wrong with roses, Isaiah? I expect he makes a decent income from the sale of his roses at the produce market. The *Englisha* like such things, even though they aren't really appropriate for our people."

"That's just it," Isaiah replied. "There seems to be nothing wrong with roses, and yet there *is* something wrong somewhere. Could you ask around, perhaps? There's some story about his former *frau*, who was *Englisha*, I believe. Esther began to tell me but then stopped. She seemed sensitive, even touchy, about the subject."

Daniel grinned. "You're not thinking he's competing for Esther's affections with his roses, are you?"

Isaiah snorted. "Not in the least. Esther is not his type. Nor is he hers. She's much too practical, but I'd like for Esther to stay that way. That's why I need to know what Joseph's story is."

"Well, then." Daniel nodded. "Let's begin with Joseph's *frau*, Silvia. Surely you're aware of what happened there?"

Isaiah shook his head.

"Well, as I understand it, Joseph's life with Silvia was quite touching. She showed up suddenly from the *Englisha* world as a single woman, young and *goot* looking, if I'm allowed to say that. Silvia was clearly devoted to the man, which made for many questions. But it all became clear after their wedding, and Silvia admitted to everyone that she had fled to the community to find peace from her fight with cancer—or rather to make peace with her coming death. She told everyone she was estranged from her parents, who had

divorced when she was a child. This didn't hinder Joseph's appreciation for Silvia's affections, and she seemed to need and want his
love. Joseph helped to bring healing between Silvia and her father,
I think. So the Lord provided, I guess, for both sides, and now that
Silvia is gone, Joseph has become a bit of a dreamer. You can't blame
him, can you?"

"I guess not," Isaiah allowed. "But the roses?"

"Well, Silvia had an *Englisha* degree in horticulture. She taught
Joseph a lot of what he knows about gardening."

"And roses, apparently."

"And roses," Daniel echoed. "Are you happy now?"

"I guess I should be..."

"But you're not?"

"Let's just say I suspect there's more to it."

"You could ask Esther. She might know."

"And you don't think that's a problem?"

"Now we're back to Joseph trampling on your territory. Are you
sure you want to go there, Isaiah?"

He sighed. "I wish Joseph had left well enough alone, or that
Esther had the sense to stay away from him. But she's new in the
area, and she's become involved in trying to help out with Arlene's
attempt to snare Joseph's affections."

Daniel slapped Isaiah on the back. "Cheer up, my friend. You're
acting like a starry-eyed teenager."

"That's what worries me," Isaiah said, beginning to move out of
the barn.

The deacon followed him. "Isaiah, maybe you're looking for
another Mandy, but no two women are alike. This is Esther. If she's
the one, you need to accept her as Esther, not as Mandy all over again."

"But I don't want them to be different. Mandy was a *wunderbah
frau*, and Esther fits the bill. Things should stay like that."

Daniel shrugged. "You know what they say. No two flowers smell alike."

Isaiah stopped in his tracks. "Who says that?"

"I don't know. I guess I heard it somewhere."

Isaiah forced a laugh. "I'd better go or I'll miss my delicious supper." He untied Echo and climbed into his buggy. With a wave to the deacon, he trotted Echo out of the driveway.

"Confound it," Isaiah muttered. "Where did the man hear about flowers that don't smell the same?"

He had come up with the brilliant answer for Diana about the bees the other week, but everyone knew that all flowers smelled alike to humans. He should have challenged the deacon for listening to such things. But what could he say? He was the one who had brought up the subject of roses, and Daniel hadn't seen him by the rail fence on his knees in front of Esther's flowers. That was an embarrassment better left alone. He had already fallen low in his pursuit of Esther's affections, but how did one disappoint a child who wanted to smell roses? Diana might have been reduced to tears by his refusal to spare himself a little humiliation.

Isaiah groaned as Echo trotted west on Oldick Road. Maybe a *goot* supper at Esther's place would restore his spirits. He should have left Joseph and his stories alone, but he hadn't been able to resist that either. If Esther was going to be his *frau* by this fall's wedding season, he needed to know what affected her life.

"Whoa there," Isaiah hollered to Echo as they came to the stop sign at Fords Bush Road. With no traffic in either direction, Isaiah jiggled the reins and turned Echo north. A moment later he pulled into Esther's driveway. The front door burst open, and Diana raced out to greet him. He came to a stop and hopped down from the buggy step.

"*Goot* evening, Diana." He bent down to give the girl a hug. "It's so nice to see you."

"Today I got to make a playhouse in Joseph's greenhouse out of boxes again," she exclaimed, her face aglow. "It was the best playhouse I ever made."

"I'm glad it was." He tried to smile. "Let me tie up Echo, and then we can go on in the house."

"I'm playing in the backyard until suppertime," she told him. "I'll be imagining that all of Joseph's boxes are there for my *wunderbah* playhouse."

"You do that," he said as Diana raced around the corner of the house.

Isaiah whirled about when Esther spoke from a few feet away. "I'm sorry she always talks about Joseph whenever you come."

"It's okay," he assured her. "You can't control the girl's fascination with the man, as long as her mother doesn't feel the same way."

"Isaiah, please," Esther said. "I'm just a common woman, and a simple one."

"I'm glad to hear you say that," he said, tying Echo to the hitching post.

Esther stayed near him, her gaze downcast.

Isaiah turned to face her. "You never did finish that story about Joseph's roses."

"Please, Isaiah." She lifted her face to him. "Can't we just eat supper and ignore Joseph for the evening? I don't want to think about his roses or about him. I'll tell you the story sometime, but not tonight."

"Well, would you happen to have pecan pie for dessert?" he asked with a grin.

Her face lit up. "*Yah*, of course. I know how you love pecan pie."

"That'll make the evening perfect, then. That, and to see your smile."

She lowered her head. "Are you trying to make me blush?"

"I wouldn't dream of it, Esther. A woman who can cook a supper like you can doesn't need to blush."

"Oh, Isaiah," she said, reaching for his hand. She fell in beside him for the walk to the house.

TWELVE

A week later as the morning light streamed over the greenhouses, Joseph held the hose in one hand and brushed cobwebs away from the rose petals with the other. Spiders had no respect for sacred places, but their busyness was an admirable trait—at least in the Lord's eyes. The Holy Scriptures commended the spider because she worked with her hands and did so even in king's houses. But in his opinion, this rose was held in higher esteem than the homes of kings.

"Silvia's Rose." Joseph bent close to whisper a prayer. "May the Lord's blessing be upon you as His blessing was upon my beloved *frau.*"

"What are you muttering about again?" Arlene's sharp voice caused Joseph to jump. The spray from the garden hose flew skyward for a second before he pointed the nozzle back to its proper place.

"You're always talking to your roses," Arlene continued. "Don't you have anything better to do?"

"Talking to plants helps them grow."

Arlene snorted. "That's nothing but an old wives' tale. I thought you would know better."

"Apparently I don't," he said, moving the flow of water onto another plant.

"Don't you want to improve yourself, Joseph? I mean, most men want their lives to be normal instead of strange. Here you are talking to roses! Who does that?"

"Well, for one, a German professor named Gustav Fechner. In his 1848 book *Nanna*, he proposed the theory that plants can benefit from human conversation."

"Who?"

"Then there's Rich Marini from Penn State's horticulture department, who says there's evidence that plants respond to sound."

Arlene wrinkled up her face. "You are very strange, Joseph. Who are these people?"

"*Englisha* researchers. It's not old wives' tales, Arlene. Maybe you are the one who should learn a thing or two."

Anger showed on her face. "How can you believe what the *Englisha* say? You know they make things up, like evolution and all that stuff about the world taking millions of years to be created—all while we know that the Lord spoke the world into existence in a moment of time. How can you change a plant by talking to it? That's almost as bad as thinking you can create new roses."

Joseph smiled. "I water the plant, and that changes it. Talking is another form of watering...in a sense."

"Listen to yourself just...talking nonsense," Arlene sputtered. "No one else in the community believes that plants can be made to grow by talking to them."

"They grow *better*," he corrected with another smile. "Now, how are we coming with the Saturday market preparations?"

Arlene seemed to simmer down a bit. "I've begun to pack the cabbages, but if you'd come help me instead of talking to your roses, I wouldn't be so far behind. With all the extra money my plan will bring in, you should be grateful—and in this case, you could express gratitude by helping me. Can you understand that much, Joseph?"

He grinned. "Maybe if you say it real slow, I can."

"You're laughing at me," she chided. "While I'm the one who should laugh at you for your silliness."

"I'm not complaining. I don't mind people laughing at me."

"Silly man. Even that attitude is unnormal."

"I don't think that's a word, Arlene."

"Stop correcting me!" she shrieked. "That is a word. *Yah*! *Un*-normal. Why wouldn't it be? My *mamm* used it, and *Daett* does too, and that goes for *Dawdy* as well."

"If you say so."

"Well, at least you're correctable. I just wish you didn't have to be corrected so much."

He laughed. "You know you don't *have* to correct me, don't you, Arlene?"

"Then who else would, Joseph? You and Ben live all by yourselves in that big, old house. Poor Ben is not much more than skin and bones, and I'm not the only one who thinks so. You need a *frau*."

He hid his smile. "And you're volunteering?"

She turned red. "You know that's not decent, Joseph."

"Forget it, Arlene." He turned off the water. "I'm ready to help you now."

"Well, it's about time."

As they walked, he continued. "I do thank you for coming up with the plan for our produce. I think you did a *goot* job."

Her face burst into a glow. "Why, thank you. I didn't think you'd ever say a kind thing about me. Esther even suggested that I should try to be more...well, forget about that. She was obviously wrong."

Joseph chuckled. "Esther thinks you should be more accepting of me. Is that it?"

"*Yah*! How did you know? She thinks I should try and understand your crazy talk about roses, but how can I do that? I'll never talk to roses to make them grow faster. My *mamm* taught me—"

"*Yah*, I know."

He came to an abrupt halt by the cabbages, and with care he harvested each one slowly. He lowered them gently into crates scattered along the edge of the patch. Arlene joined him a row away, muttering to herself.

"So what do you want from a young man who decides to court you?" Joseph asked. "Are you expecting him to take you home from the hymn singings on Sunday evenings?"

"Joseph!" Arlene gasped. "You know I'm not looking for just any young man to court me."

He laughed. "Okay, fair enough. So what if *I* wanted to court you? What should I do in that case?"

Arlene abruptly stopped moving. "You would do this, Joseph?"

"I'm not saying I would, but as you pointed out, I don't have a *frau* and Ben needs a *mamm*. How much work would I have to put into this courting business with you?"

The words came out in a rush. "You wouldn't have to put anything in. I don't need anything fancy. Nothing at all."

"No taking you home from the hymn singing, then?"

"That's not necessary," she assured him.

"I don't have to talk to you like I talk to my roses?"

Tears formed at the edges of her eyes. "You're teasing me. You're saying this only to laugh at me because I corrected you."

"Arlene." He sighed. "I'm not laughing at you. I'm serious. But you need to know I don't want a *frau* who's always trying to change me."

"In that case, you don't have to change one bit," she declared.

He twisted off several more heads of cabbage.

"Joseph, please," she begged. "Don't ignore me. I can't stand that."

He straightened his back. "I don't know how to say this so that you will understand. There will never be another Silvia. Is that okay with you?."

"Are you actually saying you might want me as your *frau*, Joseph?" She struggled to compose herself.

"Esther has got me to thinking," he admitted. "I really do need to move on with my life, so maybe we could make it work. Perhaps we can arrive at an agreement and see how it goes. I won't ask you to change except to stop criticizing me all the time, but I will always talk to roses, Arlene. Could you be married to a husband who talks to his roses?"

"I'm not sure I can," she said slowly. "I...I would hope you would be willing to stop doing that."

"I'm not stopping," he said firmly. "I will *always* talk to my plants, and I'm not going to sneak around to do it."

"I wouldn't want you sneaking around. I just want you to be normal."

"Arlene," he said with a sigh, "I *am* normal. I am Joseph Zook. That's normal for me, and I think you have your own problems if you would be honest."

She stared at him for a moment. "That makes no sense."

"There you go, Arlene. We only go in circles."

"But you did say that you would consider me for your *frau*?" Her face brightened.

"*Yah*, I did, Arlene. I'm not sure it will work, though, because if you expect me to change, I will disappoint you."

"There must be a way to cure you from talking to roses," she said, almost to herself.

Joseph sighed. "You're not hearing me."

She gulped. "I don't know what to say, Joseph."

He looked at her and said, "Well, we could try what Isaiah and Esther are doing. Maybe you could come over once a week to cook supper for Ben and me. That plan seems to be working for them. I could try to be more practical, and perhaps love would come, although—"

"You want me to cook for you? Once a week like Esther does for Isaiah? Oh, Joseph! Is that really all you want for us to begin our walk to the holy marriage vows? *Supper?* Why didn't you say so? I've done all this work at the greenhouse and tried so hard, and cooking is the easiest thing of them all. I've racked my brain trying to bring you around, and you simply want me to cook supper?"

He swallowed. "It's worth a try. Let's think about cooking supper once a week and maybe..."

"Maybe what, Joseph?"

"Just maybe...that's all."

Arlene fell silent and continued harvesting the cabbages. Joseph glanced at her. Would Arlene now spread word all over the community that they were officially dating each other, even if those dates were just meals she prepared for him? *Yah*, most likely, but he had asked for this and had no one to blame but himself.

In the end, perhaps this would be for the best. Esther was right in a way, and he didn't want another *frau* who would demand that he fall in love. His heart was locked away forever. Maybe Arlene was the right choice, the best choice, if she could keep her tongue in her head.

They would have to see about that.

THIRTEEN

Esther slipped between the wooden tables set up at the Saturday morning produce market on Fords Bush Road. Her arms clutched a carton of lettuce heads, their green goodness rising almost to eye level. She set them down with a lurch and caught her breath before returning to the wagon for another load.

Dawn had flooded the sky an hour ago, and the place would soon be swarming with people as the market opened. She had nothing to sell of her own, but she had agreed to help when Joseph asked her yesterday.

"I'm willing to pay," he had said with a smile.

"While I'm using your greenhouse for a garden? No way will you pay me. Besides, it's not as though I have a lot to do here at home."

"I'll be expecting you to carry your share of the work," Joseph teased.

Diana had stood beside her *mamm*, clapping at the news. "I'll help too!"

Today, Diana was shadowing Joseph's every move as he set up the bouquets of roses he was offering for sale. Esther had to admit they were gorgeous with their beautiful white and orange blossoms.

Was it a secret among Amish women that they, too, liked the beauty of flowers around them?

There was nothing wrong in liking roses, and there was nothing wrong with Diana's continued fascination with Joseph. Esther would have to tell herself that often. Her unsettled feeling came from the move and her rapid introduction to the innermost affairs of this small valley community. Lancaster County had been much larger, with multiple districts spread across many miles. One didn't become drawn in as quickly to people's lives unless they were family. Here, everyone seemed like family, which was exactly what she wanted—practical, down-to-earth family.

"Confound the roses," Esther muttered to herself.

"What did you just say?" Arlene chirped from a few feet away.

Esther ignored the question but waved her hand down the long table, which was laden with fresh lettuce heads. "How in the world does Joseph plan to sell this many?"

"Oh, that won't be a problem!" Arlene declared. She whipped out her tablet and scanned the page. "According to my figures of the sales from past Saturdays, these should not even begin to satisfy the demand for lettuce."

"Okay," Esther allowed. "That's impressive. You're doing a *goot* job tracking sales."

Arlene glowed. "*Yah*, I am. And I have to thank you for something. The Lord has finally opened Joseph's heart to me."

Esther jerked her head around. "How is that? I thought you didn't like what I had to say the last time we talked."

"Oh, it wasn't what you said to me, but to Joseph, and what you're doing with Isaiah. Joseph has taken your example. I'm going to come over to cook supper for him once a week." Arlene leaned closer to whisper, "Joseph doesn't know this, but that will soon be twice a week, and only the Lord knows what lies beyond that. We might even be saying the wedding vows by this fall."

"How did this come about? I had no idea Joseph had changed his mind about you."

"I'm not sure myself," Arlene mused. "Well...*yah*, I do know that your practical ways made an impression on Joseph. But I'm thinking that beyond your influence maybe my trying to change him is finally paying off. He's so hardheaded and unwilling to see his own foolishness. Why..." Arlene's voice lowered to a whisper again. "Maybe you never heard everything. See, Joseph talks to his roses all the time, and when I corrected him, he said lots of fancy *Englisha* words that I couldn't understand. But I didn't give up. I prayed and prayed, and Joseph invited me to cook supper for him one night a week."

Esther drew a long breath. "Wow. I still don't quite understand. Can you tell me more about what happened?"

Arlene demurred. "One shouldn't share the secret things that pass between a man and a woman. Do you tell me about the sweet conversations you have with Isaiah on Friday evenings over supper, or about how you keep him coming back?"

"But—"

"Oh, Joseph said the sweetest things to me. My heart could hardly contain itself. I'm half afraid I'll pass out while I'm serving him supper on Tuesday evening—that's when I'm going over to his house for the first time. Early, of course, and straight from my work at the greenhouse. Oh, Esther! I never dreamed this day would come."

"Won't you at least go back to Dorrine's place to clean up before you make supper? I mean, greenhouse work is kind of...I mean, look at us right now."

"You don't understand, Esther. Joseph doesn't want any of that fancy stuff. He just wants a woman who will cook supper for him. He's not worried about dirt-stained aprons. Underneath all his fancy talk and odd notions, the man still needs someone to cook supper and care for his *kinner*. Ben needs a *mamm*, just as all boys do, even if they have strange fathers."

"I see," Esther allowed, even though she didn't. "But how is this going to work? Joseph will still be strange to you, and he will still talk to his roses."

"*Yah*, I know." Arlene nodded, solemn-faced. "Joseph told me that himself. But he doesn't know the *wunderbah* powers a woman has to change her man for the better. I'll bide my time, but my foot is in the door now. Supper will soon be on the table."

Arlene's face glowed as she hurried away with her head held high.

Esther took a moment to collect herself before returning to the wagon for the last carton of lettuce. Setting it with the others, she walked over to where Joseph was still setting out rose arrangements.

"Looking for your daughter?" he asked.

"I saw her go into the greenhouse a moment ago. I'm assuming you sent her on an errand."

"*Yah*, she went to fetch me the spray bottle. The sun will be up soon, and we have to keep water on the roses until they're sold." Joseph took a step back and looked at the array of his arrangements. He smiled. "Silvia would be so pleased at how her rose turned out. I know this valley loves them. They sell out quite quickly and at decent prices." Joseph turned to face her. "Are you done with the lettuce?"

Esther didn't speak for a second. "Joseph, I need to ask you something...and it's not about roses. What made you change your mind about Arlene? She claims you are dating."

Joseph's smile spread to his whole face. "Arlene has been letting you in on our arrangement? Well, I don't mind. I'm just trying to follow your advice. Isn't that *goot*? By tomorrow the news will be all over the community. Arlene will see that her conquest receives the attention she thinks it deserves."

Esther didn't move. "Why are you doing this? It doesn't seem right...or even like you."

"Come on, Esther. Isn't this how you live? What's so difficult to understand? I have loved once, immensely and deeply. I don't need that again, but Arlene does need help, and perhaps I can learn to like her a little...after some time, of course. Women can change, you know. For the better, one hopes. Arlene understands I can't love her the way I once loved Silvia. To pretend that I could would not be fair to her or to me—and I'm not *goot* at pretending anyway. Arlene knows this and doesn't care. It's a practical arrangement—if only I can tame her sharp tongue. You're a practical woman, Esther. This should make perfect sense to you. No two flowers smell alike, remember? I'm not one to pretend that they do."

Esther stepped back. "And you think I pretend? Do you think that's what I'm doing with Isaiah? Pretending? That I'm trying to repeat what I had with Lonnie?"

"Esther, you give me too much credit. I'm a simple man who was given the love of a great woman. By that I will always be blessed and forever changed. But I know not to look for that kind of happiness again. I'm not telling you how to run your life."

"No, but aren't you trying to teach me by example? You expect me to see the foolishness of how I'm acting with Isaiah as you act out the same thing with Arlene."

Joseph laughed. "Do I strike you as a man who would put up with Arlene's criticisms just so I could make a point with you? I enjoy my own life too much for that. I'm beginning this relationship with Arlene because I want to. I took your words to heart,

Esther. You are right. Something can be made out of her and me that hasn't been before. I have faith, but I'm not stupid. I don't think or dream that my heart will ever be hers the way it once was with Silvia. But that's okay."

"It sounds as though you're just settling, and I find that sad. But it's your life."

"See, then why are we fussing about it?"

"Because I still think you're doing this to rub something in."

Joseph laughed again. "If the salt burns, it's only because there is a wound, Esther. Maybe you should be thankful I have the salt shaker in my hand."

"So you *are* doing this to teach me a lesson."

"I'm just living the way I want to, and if you can learn from it, fine. But I'm truly doing this for myself, not for you."

"Okay, but that doesn't make me feel any better."

"Perhaps you need a man who can grow a rose for you, Esther. That's what you've never had, and one should experience such a thing once in one's life."

"Are you proposing to be that man yourself?"

Joseph smiled. "I have been that man—for Silvia. I don't need to travel the road twice, even if such a thing were possible."

"But I don't want roses from Isaiah...or *anything* like that."

"Have it your way," Joseph said with a shrug of his shoulders. "People are starting to come in. We need to be ready for them."

Diana's voice piped up in the distance. "Joseph! I found it."

"And here's Diana with the water sprayer," he added. "I have to see to my roses, Esther."

She watched him walk away and forced herself to move down the aisle. She didn't need a rose in her life, or a man to grow her one. But as for Joseph, surely he could find another woman he loved the way he had once loved Silvia, just as she had found a man who fit the life she had once lived with Lonnie. Roses were for Joseph, but they were not for her. Anyone could see that plainly enough. But what if Joseph was right? What if she could have with Isaiah what she hadn't had with Lonnie? Was there something to what Joseph had said? But how would Isaiah be different from Lonnie? How was she different all these years later? She was still the same woman, and Isaiah was so like Lonnie. They were two flowers that looked the same—but did they also smell alike? Did she want flowers and butterflies in her stomach—a love to take her breath away?

FOURTEEN

The following Friday afternoon, Esther opened the oven door and removed the cake from the rack with her mitt-covered hand. She set the round cake on the stove top and bent down for a closer look. Her arms still ached from the severe beating she had given the egg whites earlier in the day to produce a decent angel food cake. She hoped the effort had not been wasted. Even then, Isaiah might not appreciate the cake, enraptured as he was with pecan pie for dessert. Not that she was complaining. She liked a man who was so easily satisfied with the basics. How else could she pass muster? She had no fancy frills or daydreams to offer the relationship. She was Esther Stoltzfus, a simple woman who lived a simple life.

Joseph's words from the produce market last Saturday had disturbed her all week, but she was not going to take them to heart. She was building a solid relationship with Isaiah. Why even think about disturbing things with fancy thoughts of love and roses?

Esther squinted at the browned top of the angel food cake. "I hope you taste better than you look," she muttered.

"I want a piece of that cake," Diana piped up from below.

"Where did you come from?" Esther patted her daughter on the head. "You sneaked right up on me."

Diana grinned. "Can I have a piece, please, especially if it's no *goot*?"

"You hear too much." Esther smiled down at the little girl. "I'm afraid you'll have to wait for supper."

"Is Joseph coming?"

"No, Isaiah is coming."

"I want to see Joseph. I haven't seen him all week."

"We're going to help with the Saturday market again tomorrow. You can see Joseph then. Tonight Isaiah is coming."

Diana pouted. "Isaiah doesn't tell me anything interesting. I want to know about new things."

"Maybe you can ask Isaiah about his farming," Esther suggested. "He has many acres of grassland, black cattle, and a nice house."

"He does?"

"*Yah*. I should take you over there sometime."

Diana didn't appear impressed. "I want Joseph to come for supper tonight."

"Well, he's not coming, but you can have a piece of angel food cake after we've eaten the main course if—" Esther stopped short when she heard the sound of buggy wheels coming up the driveway. "There's Isaiah now. Right on time, as usual. Go give him a hug and a big Stoltzfus welcome."

"You don't ever give Isaiah a hug."

Esther drew a sharp breath. "Diana, that wouldn't be decent."

"Why not? I give him hugs."

Esther bent on one knee to wrap her daughter in both arms. "It's difficult to explain, sweetheart, but it wouldn't be right. Now shall we go welcome Isaiah together?"

Diana's head bobbed up and down. Esther took Diana's hand to lead the way out the front door. Isaiah had already tied Echo to the hitching post and waved toward them. They came close to greet him.

He looked at both of them and smiled. "*Goot* evening. Is supper ready?"

"*Goot* evening yourself," Esther told him. "Diana can't wait for angel food cake, so we'd better eat soon."

Isaiah bent on one knee and opened his arms. "How are you tonight, Diana?"

"Okay." She cheerfully returned his hug.

"So I hear you like angel food cake?" Isaiah asked. "Meat and gravy—now *that's* what a person can grow strong on. Don't you want to grow up big and strong so you can help your *mamm* in the garden?"

Diana looked at him with a puzzled expression.

"I think you need a son," Esther told him.

He bent down for another hug. "I guess I don't know much about little girls."

Diana's face lit up. "Tomorrow we're going to help with the Saturday market, and I'm taking along a piece of my angel food cake for Joseph."

"Really?" Isaiah glanced over at Esther.

"Oh?" She looked at her daughter. "That's news to me."

"Joseph *loves* angel food cake," Diana insisted.

"And you know this how?" Esther pressed her lips together. Why did Diana have to bring up Joseph again?

"He just does."

"Did Joseph tell you this?" Isaiah asked. "Maybe while he was telling you that no two flowers smell the same?"

Diana's perplexed expression was back.

"I'm sorry," Isaiah said again. He picked up Diana for the walk toward the house. She wiggled out of his arms at the front porch and ran inside ahead of them.

Isaiah turned to Esther with a smile. "So how have you been doing? It's *goot* to see you again."

"And you." She returned his smile, holding open the front door. "Supper's getting cold. We can't have that."

"Nope," he agreed. "We certainly can't."

She led the way to the kitchen and motioned for Isaiah to sit down. Diana was already perched on her chair with an eye on the cake.

"Shall we pray?" Isaiah asked, bowing his head without waiting for an answer. "We give You thanks tonight for this delicious food before us, dear Lord. Bless Esther for the hard work she put into the preparations. Bless both Diana and Esther, and their precious home. Thank You for bringing them to the community safely and in Your time. Bless our evening together. May You always be the center of all our actions and thoughts. Amen."

"Amen," Diana echoed.

Isaiah gave her a warm smile.

Diana giggled, and Isaiah reached across the table to serve her first. Esther watched with a catch in her throat. What more could she want than this? *Yah*, this was home. Her life was being given back to her. She had been selfish to think she should ask for more. Joseph was wrong about Isaiah and her, as he was wrong about his relationship with Arlene.

Diana dived into her food when Isaiah handed her a plate. He watched the child eat for a second before he filled his own plate with meat loaf, mashed potatoes, and gravy. Esther glanced away. Why couldn't Isaiah dish out her food the way he had served Diana?

But where had that thought come from? What silliness. She wasn't a child in need of attention.

"Here's the bread." She passed him the plate of thickly cut slices.

He smiled and buttered his piece as she filled her own plate.

"So tell me about your day," Isaiah said to Diana.

Diana thought for a moment. "I played with my dolls in the backyard, but it's not as fun as playing down at Joseph's place with his boxes. We didn't go down there all week."

"But you're going tomorrow," Isaiah prompted.

"*Yah*." Diana's interest increased. "There will be lots of people there, and loud talking as they sell things, and Joseph's roses. They're so beautiful."

"They are beautiful," Isaiah agreed. "Will you be buying any?"

Diana giggled. "I don't have to. Joseph gave me one last Saturday, but it didn't last very long. I dropped it."

"That's too bad," Isaiah commiserated. "I'm sure Joseph can give you another one tomorrow."

Diana peered across the table at him. "Do you have roses?"

Isaiah laughed. "I'm not a rose man, myself. Just a common fellow, you could say. But I'm glad you like roses."

"I do."

"Are you a rose admirer like your daughter?" Isaiah asked Esther.

"Oh, I guess. They're beautiful and they do smell nice. Did you bring some for me?"

Isaiah's fork nearly fell from his fingers.

She forced a laugh. "Isaiah, I'm just teasing."

He laughed with her. "You startled me for a moment. I thought some fancy ways had suddenly taken hold of you."

Esther concentrated on her food, hoping there would be no more talk of roses. Where had that all come from? What was wrong with her?

Isaiah paused with his fork halfway to this mouth. "But...now that we're on the subject, what was the story you were going to tell me about Joseph's rose?"

"Maybe we should finish supper first."

"You have me worried, Esther. You're always pushing this off. What's the big secret?"

She tried to smile. "You're helping me wash dishes afterward, aren't you? We can talk then." She sent a quick nod toward Diana.

"I see. Then this is serious."

"No, not really," she hastened to say, but he was clearly not convinced.

"I think we do need to talk," he added, taking another bite of food. A heavy silence fell in the kitchen.

"Can I have some angel food cake now?" Diana asked, her face uplifted.

Esther cut the first piece of cake as Isaiah dished himself out another helping of mashed potatoes.

Diana took a bite, her face rapturous.

"Is it *goot*?" Isaiah asked.

Diana nodded, grinning from ear to ear as she took another forkful.

Obviously her daughter was impressed with her extra effort baking the cake. But would Isaiah notice?

"Why aren't you eating, *Mamm*?" Diana piped up. "This is so yummy."

Esther forced herself to cut a piece, put it on her plate, and bring the fork to her mouth. The spongy goodness practically melted in her mouth.

"It is *goot*," she agreed softly, and Diana seemed satisfied. She finished her piece, but Isaiah hadn't yet helped himself to one.

"Let's pray," he said, bowing his head.

After the amen, Diana asked Isaiah, "Aren't you going to try a piece of angel food cake?"

"Maybe later," Isaiah said. "I'm full to the top right now."

Diana giggled and scurried off.

"Okay," Isaiah said, turning to Esther. "Start talking."

"It's nothing really," she protested. "It's just that Joseph has a hybrid rose he created himself, and he had Silvia's *daett* enter it in some rose-growing competition in California. You have to submit your seeds two years in advance, he said, and they grow them on their own land and judge the live specimens. The judging is this year. The award is a big deal for Joseph, who named his new rose after his deceased *frau*. That's it."

"And you know all this how?"

"Joseph told me. Beyond that, I know a little something about roses, but not as much as he does."

"And what happens if Joseph wins this award for his rose?"

"There could be some fuss, I suppose."

"Like what kind of fuss?"

"Oh, you know, maybe a newspaper would want to report a story like his. Especially with it being Amish related."

"And what has this to do with us?"

"Nothing."

"I agree," he said. "This sounds like Joseph's problem if he causes a ruckus in the community."

"So now you know as much as I do," Esther said, forcing a quick smile.

"Why didn't you tell me this before?"

"I didn't think it was important. Can't you just forget about Joseph and his roses? Won't you have a piece of angel food cake? I spent extra time whipping the egg whites, and they turned out real well. Try a piece and see if I'm not right." She cut a piece of the cake and put it on his plate.

"This is not like you, Esther, wanting attention for what you do. You're avoiding something. Tell me—are you in love with Joseph?"

She shook her head. "Of course not. It's you I want to fall in love..." Almost the words had slipped out. What must Isaiah think? What they had was love.

He took a large bite of cake and chewed slowly.

"Is it okay?" She dared a glance at him.

"*Yah*, it's delicious. You did a *goot* job, Esther. Maybe you can bake one for the barn raising at my place next Friday. Not that I'll have much chance of getting a piece with everyone else in line."

She lowered her head. "I'll see that you get some, Isaiah. And I'm sorry about what I said. I'm ashamed that I should want more than what you're giving me. You give me plenty of attention and care."

His smile was thin. "Joseph can put strange ideas into one's mind and heart, but we are a down-to-earth people, Esther. I'm sure you understand that."

"I do. Thank you for coming tonight. Your presence is always a great joy to me."

"And your suppers are splendid," he replied. "I couldn't ask for better food."

"You are very kind, Isaiah. You give me much more than I deserve."

"You'll soon have me falling in love," he teased, and they laughed together.

FIFTEEN

Early the following Tuesday morning Esther dug her fingers deep into the dark soil of Joseph's greenhouse, pulling up weeds in bunches. The row of seedlings in front of her faded in and out of focus. Everything had gone well at the produce market on Saturday, but yesterday the Sunday service had undone her again. She envisioned Isaiah's handsome face as he preached his sermon. His voice had been sure and steady, but his gaze rarely drifted in her direction. What had Isaiah thought of her strange statement on Friday evening—that she wanted to fall in love with him? Isaiah had joked and they had laughed at the end of the evening, but things were not the same anymore. They both knew something was wrong.

Those words should never have been thought, let alone spoken. How could she think that she wasn't in love with Isaiah—and then tell him so? What an insult she had handed him. What immaturity on her part.

Her heart was pounding but for the wrong reasons. Had she not loved Lonnie with all of her heart, as Lonnie had loved her? The same love must have existed between Isaiah and Mandy. How embarrassing for her to blurt out what she did. It was a wonder Isaiah hadn't walked out of the house.

Joseph was to blame for this. Isaiah hadn't said anything to her about staying away from Joseph, but perhaps he wanted her to use common sense and keep her distance from the man. Perhaps she shouldn't even be here in his greenhouse. And yet, how awkward would that be? Avoiding Joseph might be seen as an admission, confirmation that her heart had strayed. Such an admission should disqualify her as a minister's *frau* right on the spot, so staying away from Joseph was not the right choice. Neither could she abandon her garden. What a waste that would be.

Esther's face flamed at the memory of her words, and she yanked at the weeds in front of her all the harder, pulling up several of the young carrot plants along with the weeds. Esther took a deep breath and stilled her thoughts. This was no way to act.

Joseph's soft shuffle behind her turned Esther's head. She forced a smile and stood.

"Keep pulling," he said, motioning with his hand. "I don't want to disturb you."

"You certainly have a green thumb. You have things growing quite well here."

"*Yah*, including the weeds," he said with a grin. "If I could just figure out a way to stop them from helping themselves to the nutrients."

"That's the Lord's doing, I'm thinking. Much like life—we take the *goot* with the bad."

He nodded. "It does seem so. If you don't mind my asking, what weeds are growing in your life, Esther? Also, where's Diana?"

She turned away. "I dropped her off at Dorrine's, and we'd best not speak of the other, Joseph."

"I'm sorry to hear that. I hope something hasn't come between you and Isaiah. I wondered on Saturday if something was troubling you."

She studied the ground. "No, we're okay..."

He winced. "So there *is* something wrong? I hope I'm not to blame."

Esther sighed. "Joseph, you did nothing wrong."

"It seems I did." He shifted off his lame foot. "Does Isaiah object to you having a garden here?"

"No!" she exclaimed. "It's what you said at the produce market the Saturday before last. And your stories about love, Joseph... they've gone to my head and stirred my imagination. As a result, I said something very stupid to Isaiah on Friday night."

"Oh, I doubt that, but I'm sorry that anything I said caused problems. I was just grateful for someone to speak to after Arlene's obtuseness."

Esther forced a laugh. "Like I said, it's not your fault."

"I have led a blessed life, Esther. A rare one in some ways, though most people who know me probably wouldn't understand that. The truth is, not many men receive the *wunderbah* kind of love that Silvia gave me."

"There you go again. When you say things like that, I feel like a cold fish. A woman who will marry a man without really loving him."

"I'm sure you love Isaiah—"

"Then why did I tell him that I want to fall in love with him? I made it sound as if I don't love him already!"

Joseph studied the ground at his feet. "Your carrots are growing fine along with everything else."

"Joseph," she scolded. "Don't do that to me."

"Do what?"

"Change the subject. That's what men do when they don't want to talk about something uncomfortable."

He grinned. "Did Isaiah switch subjects on you?"

"*Yah*, he did. He complimented me on my cake."

Joseph laughed. "When an Amish man compliments a woman on her cooking, you have nothing to worry about."

Quick tears sprang to her eyes. "Do you really think so?"

"I know so. I think deep down in his heart, Isaiah wants something different with you than what he had with Mandy. I'm sure their love was *wunderbah*, as was your love for Lonnie, but surely Isaiah knows that no two women are the same."

"Like two flowers that smell differently?"

His grin grew. "We don't have to speak that plainly, I suppose, but *yah*—that's what I mean."

"But what if you're wrong about him?"

"If I am, you can blame me. Isaiah should understand that."

"No. He'll just wonder why I listen to you."

"I don't know what to say about that, Esther. I guess I've gotten you into enough trouble already." He glanced down the greenhouse aisle and whispered, "Here comes Arlene."

"Are you really having her cook supper for you tonight?" Esther whispered back.

He nodded.

"What are you two whispering about?" Arlene asked as she approached.

Esther gave her a bright smile. "I was just asking Joseph if you're cooking supper for him tonight."

Arlene glowed. "*Yah*, I am. Joseph needs to put on some weight, and Ben's practically falling out of his pants. I think I need to come over twice a week, maybe on Friday nights too, though this Friday is Isaiah's barn raising, I suppose supper will be served there for the workers who can stay past their chore time."

Joseph cleared his throat loudly.

Arlene ignored him. "But the following week should work

perfectly. I'll have these two fattened up and looking fit in a month or so. Shoofly pie is on the dessert menu tonight. When is the last time you had shoofly pie, Joseph?"

Joseph grunted. "Not in a while."

"Did Silvia ever bake shoofly pie for you?" Arlene asked.

"No, I don't think so." Joseph cleared his throat again.

"See!" Arlene proclaimed. "That's exactly what you need. *Yah*, I'll fatten you up quickly!"

"When do you plan to do all this cooking? I need help in the greenhouse, especially on Fridays."

"You never have to worry about that," Arlene retorted. "I will stay up late and awaken early if it's necessary to make you happy and improve your health. You just wait and see. Maybe this is why you talk to flowers so much. You're undernourished."

Esther hid her smile while Joseph struggled to keep a straight face. "I appreciate your efforts, Arlene. I'm sure supper will be exactly what I need, but I will continue talking to my roses. It helps them grow better and thus sell better."

She sighed. "I guess everyone is entitled to a few strange ways. But please don't talk to them when others from the community are around." Arlene glanced at Esther. "You won't be telling, will you?"

"My lips are sealed," Esther promised, busying herself with the weeds in front of her.

"Thank you, Esther. I appreciate that." Arlene turned to Joseph. "I just want a normal life, like Esther and Isaiah's. They're such a shining example for us, Joseph. Can't you see that?"

"We're not doing everything quite like them," he protested. "Having you cook supper for me the way Esther does for Isaiah is enough for now."

Arlene sighed again. "I guess a woman can't have everything she wants, so I'll be thankful for what I do have. Now I'd best get busy if I plan to serve supper on time tonight."

Joseph gave her a warm smile. "I think that would be a *goot* idea."

Arlene blushed and scurried off.

"I'm sorry I won't see Diana today," he said as soon as Arlene was out of earshot. "I had hoped to see her this morning."

Esther stood. "I can go get her and bring her here."

"No, no. It might send a confusing signal to Diana if you've told her to stay away from me."

"I didn't do that, Joseph," she protested.

"I'd understand if you did."

Esther gave him a warm smile. "Why don't I check on her at Dorrine's, and if things are going the way I think they are, Diana will be thrilled to come over. If not, we'll leave well enough alone."

"I hope I haven't made trouble for you, Esther." He shifted from one foot to the other. "That's the last thing I wish."

"What about me making trouble for you with that supper deal?" she teased.

He laughed. "Well, when you look at it that way, I suppose we're even."

She turned serious. "Are you sure about your arrangement with Arlene, Joseph? Is this what you really want?"

"I'm as sure as I am about most things these days, which isn't very sure. But I do want this relationship with her to work out. I'm thinking the woman might be *goot* for me, and I know it's different from where you're headed with Isaiah, but that's okay."

"So you know that I am changing? What if we're both messing up?"

"That's the danger, and the *thrill*, of love." He grinned.

"I think I would have preferred things to stay as they were," she muttered. "Life with Lonnie and Diana was so right. So very right."

Tears sprang to Joseph's eyes. "You'll get no argument from me there. Life was perfect with Silvia and Ben...but the Lord had other plans for us."

"Oh, Joseph. I'm so sorry."

"You loved too."

"*Yah*, I did." She turned to hurry outside and hide her tears. *Why the emotion now?* She had cried plenty at Lonnie's funeral, but not with such sting.

Esther paused to turn her face into the breeze that moved up from the valley floor. The tinge of redness in her eyes would be gone by the time she walked across the road. Dorrine didn't need to know about her conversation with Joseph or about the strange emotions stirring inside of her.

Esther glanced each way before she crossed Fords Bush Road. Dorrine peeked out the front door as she approached and called out, "Diana's in here. I was about ready to come and get you. She won't stop asking if she can go over and build playhouses with Joseph's boxes."

Esther forced a smile. "So much for my idea, I guess."

"Joseph didn't complain about Diana bothering him, did he? Because if he did, I'm chewing him out *goot*."

"You know he didn't. This was all my idea, which obviously isn't working."

Dorrine smiled. "There's no harm in trying, and I do know it's easier to pull weeds without keeping an eye on a young child."

As if on cue, Diana came running into the room and gave her *mamm* a quick hug.

"I want to see Joseph, *Mamm*," Diana begged. "I want to build a playhouse right now at his place!"

"Just wait a moment," Esther told her as Diana hopped around on one foot. "I have to tell Dorrine something."

As Diana skipped her way down the sidewalk, Esther turned to Dorrine. "Arlene's so excited about her supper tonight."

Dorrine's face lit up. "*Yah*, she is. You've been a *goot* influence for those two. I don't know how we made it before you moved to the valley."

"I'm sure you got along quite well," Esther assured Dorrine, and they laughed.

"Let's go, *Mamm*," Diana called from the sidewalk.

"I'll be seeing you then." Esther walked over to take Diana's hand. As they crossed the road again, Esther looked back to see Dorrine waving to them from the front porch with a big smile on her face.

SIXTEEN

Esther pulled back on Biscuit's reins before she turned into Isaiah's driveway on Paris Road. She pulled the buggy to a stop beside the barn. It was the Friday morning of Isaiah's barn raising, but she hadn't wanted to arrive too early. After that embarrassing statement to him last Friday evening, she still hesitated to meet him again. Joseph's words had comforted her, but what if he was wrong? The thought had kept her awake with worry for more than an hour last night. Now the moment of truth had arrived. She would speak with Isaiah today one way or another. She had to.

Esther hopped down from the buggy and then helped Diana. The distant beat of horses' hooves hung over the valley as more buggies arrived, so she had timed her arrival well. Bishop Willis and his *frau*, Beth, were already here, and Isaiah's place would soon be bustling with activity.

As Esther undid the tugs on Biscuit's harness, she asked Diana, "Why don't you go find Beth and let her know we're here?"

Diana nodded and ran toward the house. Esther waited until Beth opened the front door to greet Diana with a hug. The community had been so kind to them since their move. Beth made a point of speaking with Diana at all the Sunday services. What if Beth knew that she wasn't satisfied with Isaiah and their relationship? How embarrassing that would be.

Joseph's roses and his comforting words seemed far away on a morning like this. Maybe she shouldn't blame herself entirely. Part of the pain in her heart came from her sorrow over Lonnie's loss. But why had that reappeared? She had mourned Lonnie a long time ago and thought she had moved on. Obviouly she had been mistaken. There were tears of sorrow yet to cry.

Esther ducked behind Biscuit to wipe her face. She didn't want to lose Isaiah. What a tragedy that would be, one for which she would never forgive herself. Isaiah was coming out of the barn to greet her at this very moment.

Esther freed Biscuit from the buggy and called out to Isaiah, "*Goot* morning."

He smiled in return. "It's *goot* to see you, Esther. You're nice and early."

"I wanted to come early enough to say hello before all the work began."

"That was wise of you. I suppose you know I won't be coming to your place for supper tonight. I'll have plenty to do here."

"*Yah*, that's what I thought. But I can stay and help with supper if you like."

"I would love that. And there will always be Friday evening next week." He put his hand on Biscuit's bridle. "I told Beth you and she should be in charge of the cooks today. I didn't have a chance to ask you if that's okay, but I figured you wouldn't object."

"Of course that's okay! It's a great honor."

He grinned. "I know you can cook, so the honor will be mine." He turned and led Biscuit to the barn.

She wanted to run after him and kiss him on the cheek, but

that wouldn't be decent. She hadn't even hugged the man yet, and she knew they didn't need kisses to cement their relationship...but Esther stopped short. In her heart, she did want to kiss Isaiah quite badly. Had her feelings come from all the fancy thoughts she had entertained these past weeks about roses and Silvia's great love for Joseph?

Esther pinched herself. What exactly did she want? She had known what she wanted when she arrived in the community, and she still knew...but something had changed. The question the other evening had been real: What would she feel if she fell in love with Isaiah? Would Isaiah be the same? Would she be the same? Joseph was right. She was different from Mandy, just as Isaiah was different from Lonnie. She had been blind to that truth until she heard about Silvia and Joseph's roses. What would happen if a man brought a rose to life because of his great love for her?

Esther hurried toward the house as more buggies came up the driveway. She was sure several of them had seen her standing frozen in the driveway, staring after Isaiah's disappearing back. They probably figured she was love stricken, which was understandable. Most young women would find the handsome minister quite attractive.

Inside, she found Beth bending over the kitchen sink with Diana perched beside her.

"And he had miles and miles of roses again on Saturday," Diana was saying. "They were so beautiful, and he sells them and makes lots of money, and I got to build dollhouses at his place this week while *Mamm* worked on her garden, but first I had to stay at Dorrine's place, which wasn't nearly as fun as Joseph's greenhouse. That's the best place of all with..." Diana paused to catch her breath.

"*Goot* morning," Beth greeted Esther. "You're bright and early."

"You can say the same for yourself."

"Diana was just filling me in on the latest."

"Mostly about Joseph, I believe," Esther said, smiling at her daughter.

"Well, I'm glad you're here. There will be so much to do today. I'm sure you've been on hand during the week to help Isaiah prepare for the barn raising today."

"Actually, we haven't," Esther admitted. "And now that you mention it, I feel a bit embarrassed. Isaiah never said a word about helping to prepare, but that should have occurred to me. How could I have been so thoughtless?"

Beth smiled. "Don't berate yourself. Isaiah should have said something. We'll blame this on him."

"No, it's not his fault."

"Your loyal heart does you *goot*," Beth replied, comforting Esther with a pat on the shoulder.

Esther changed the subject. "Isaiah said you and I are in charge of the cooking."

"*Yah*—" Beth was interrupted when a flood of women came into the kitchen carrying cold dishes and food for the meals to come. Greetings were exchanged, and within minutes the kitchen was bustling with activity. Esther joined in with minimal fuss, and the time passed quickly. Two hours later—but in what seemed like only minutes—one of the women called from the kitchen window, "The first wall is going up already!"

"This serves as break time," Beth hollered, and everyone went out to the front porch to watch.

Several of the men waved their hats toward the house, producing a loud bellow from the foreman in charge. "Keep your attention focused, boys! You can wave to your sweethearts at lunchtime."

The young men hooted and waved their hats even more as the wall crept skyward.

"What if that thing should fall back down?" one of the unmarried girls asked.

"The men know what they're doing," Beth told her. "Now let's get back to work. We have to make sure the meal is ready in time."

Esther's conscience stirred. She had entertained romantic thoughts these past weeks like a silly teenager. This was exactly why she had always been determined to stay above this kind of foolishness. She had married one of the best men in the community, Lonnie Stoltzfus, who had been ordained to the ministry. It was an honor few of the men were given, and she had planned to repeat the feat...only she hadn't counted on getting to know Joseph Zook.

Joseph would be out there somewhere. The man would do what he could on a day like this, though he was limited in his abilities. This was no cause for shame, and she didn't blame Joseph for her emotional mess. She was no better than Diana in a way, or the young unmarried women who had waited breathlessly as the wall was raised—afraid that love would be snatched from their hands by a freak accident.

Esther returned to the kitchen with several of the women, and was busy preparing sandwiches when she heard Arlene's voice rise clearly above the group. "I tested this potato recipe on Joseph and Ben on Tuesday evening. It's my own version of a casserole and mashed potato combination. Joseph was so impressed that he was almost speechless, and poor Ben had a second helping. He's so neglected. I can't believe that Joseph has left his home without a *mamm* for so long. On the other hand, I'm thankful." Arlene glowed as she whipped the potatoes in her bowl to a white frenzy.

"I didn't know you and Joseph were dating," someone ventured.

"We're doing it the practical way," Arlene proclaimed with a flourish of her spoon. "Just like Esther and Minister Isaiah. I've tried for a long time to get through to Joseph and show him how much his life could be improved with a *frau* in the house, but I couldn't get anywhere. It seemed as if every time we talked we just went in circles. Then a miracle happened the other week, as it does when the Lord is in things. Joseph found the answer in Esther's example, and now I'm coming twice a week to cook for him, which shows him how much of a blessing I can be in his life."

Several of the young married women exchanged amused glances, and Esther wished the floor would open up and swallow her. She hadn't bargained for this. The way Arlene described her Friday night suppers with Isaiah held no romantic charm at all. But what did she expect? She hadn't aimed for romance, only practicality—so why did the shame burn so deep?

Did she expect Isaiah to arrive at the house with roses in hand? Esther slowly measured out the ingredients for a cake. Something had clearly happened to her since they had arrived in the valley.

But what? Did she really want to fall head over heels in love?

SEVENTEEN

Isaiah pushed his hat back on his forehead as the last exterior wall of the barn was nailed into place. Men were swarming, and the noise of the hammering was deafening. The trusses had been laid out this morning by Deacon Daniel, who had once worked in a truss factory back in Lancaster County. They were all nailed together and ready to lift into place. When people with various talents came together in commitment and love toward their community, an immense amount of work could be accomplished in a very short period of time. This was not unlike the barn raisings of Isaiah's youth, which he had so loved. There were fewer people, but the will to work remained—along with the pleasure of a day spent in one another's company.

"Liking what you're seeing?" the deacon shouted in Isaiah's ear.

"Yep, no complaints. And everyone's being careful, I see."

Daniel nodded. "I gave them a lecture before we started. Job safety is always a priority."

"*Yah*, it is."

"Can we step away from this noise for a moment?" Daniel asked. "You need a break anyway."

Isaiah nodded and followed Daniel around the corner of the

old building. "What? Did I transgress the *Ordnung* this morning already?"

Daniel grinned and ignored the joke. "I just wanted to tell you I wasn't able to find out anything more about Joseph and his roses. I checked with Deacon Lester from Joseph's home district in Southern Lancaster County, and the man wrote back with nothing but praise for both Joseph and Silvia. It appears that Silvia was the model of decorum and decency for the short time she lived after their wedding. So there you go, for what it's worth. I don't know that Joseph is doing anything wrong by selling roses, though he does sell a lot. There's nothing in our *Ordnung* about roses, so maybe you should raise a few yourself while you romance Esther."

Isaiah laughed. "I don't think a lot of romancing is necessary. I've never been the romantic type and neither has she."

"Ah, come on," Daniel teased. "Everybody has a little romance in them. You ought to make a special announcement today in appreciation of Esther for the contribution she's already made to the community. I heard that Arlene and Joseph are following Esther's example of having you over every week for supper. Looks like Esther has started a new trend for our community when it comes to second courtships. Or was that your idea?"

Isaiah lowered his head. "I'm afraid I can't take the credit for that."

Daniel slapped Isaiah on the shoulder. "There you go. Well, it looks like the women have lunch about ready. You're the man of the house here. Take the chance to say something a little special on Esther's behalf."

Isaiah forced a laugh, and Daniel left with a broad grin on his face. Indeed, the yard in front of his house was a hive of activity. The women had set up tables and covered the tops with white tablecloths and steaming dishes of food. Chairs were scattered about, ready for use once the men were called to lunch. Did he have the nerve to give Esther praise in public? What if he choked up? He was used to giving sermons, but this was something else. What if he got halfway through and Esther frowned, or, worse, fled into the house from embarrassment?

Isaiah grabbed a loose board that lay on the ground. There were still a few moments before dinner would be called, so he didn't have to make his mind up right away. From somewhere the decision would come, and the words—if they must be spoken. For one thing, *yah*, Esther deserved them. And her plan for their Friday night dinners was exactly what he had needed. She had been wise in her suggestion. His admiration for her grew each week as they chatted around the dinner table, and their times together were so much more enjoyable than his previous dating experiences. He had taken Mandy home each Sunday evening for more than three years. Those times with Mandy had been lovely, but this was different and better in its own way.

Isaiah jumped when the dinner bell rang. The clang broke through the barn raising din like the blast of a train whistle. Silence fell at once, but it was replaced by the soft scuffle of the men's feet and the drone of their voices as they unlatched their tool belts. One by one the men laid them all over the ground and rested their hats on top. Lines of men formed at bowls of water that were set up near the well pump. Isaiah hung back, as befitting his role today. This was his place, and the others showed him a great favor with their help. He would gladly go last to demonstrate his gratitude.

Plenty of water was splashed at the water bowls, as the younger unmarried men washed up. But no one objected to the fun. This was a day of joy and happiness, a gathering of the community in expression of love and care for each other. Isaiah took his place at the end of the longest line. A few minutes later he was at the bowl, pouring fresh water and washing himself with soap. Then he began to dry his hands and face on a moist towel.

"Here's a dry one," Beth told him as she hurried up with a smile. "How do you like the progress of the barn so far?"

Isaiah took the towel from her hands. "Thank you. Things are going great. Everyone is doing very well, and there have been no accidents, for which I am very grateful. I'm also grateful for what you're doing in the kitchen today." Isaiah motioned toward the food-laden tables. "This is no doubt your and Esther's handiwork."

"The others did their share, but Esther is a wonder, Isaiah." Beth patted him on the arm. "You are getting a *goot frau*."

"I know," Isaiah said with a smile. Beth turned to scurry back to the tables.

When someone tapped him on the shoulder, Isaiah turned to see the bishop's smiling face. "Are you giving a speech before we give thanks for the meal? The man of the house usually does that to thank everyone for coming."

"Of course." Isaiah drew himself up higher. "Everyone must be thanked."

"You're a preacher, so you shouldn't have problems with public speaking," the bishop teased.

Isaiah bit back his retort. Bishop Willis didn't know about the special words he'd decided to say about Esther right here in public. He was determined now. Hopefully he wouldn't offend Esther or make a fool of himself.

"Hello, everyone!" Isaiah hollered, waving his arms about.

Silence fell slowly, and all heads turned in his direction. Isaiah took a deep breath and began. "Before our bishop gives thanks for this *wunderbah* meal the women have prepared for us, I want to thank everyone for coming. I'm humbled that each of you took the time out of your busy schedules to take mercy on a poor farmer like me who took it into his head to build a barn addition." Chuckles rippled through the crowd, and Isaiah hurried on. "I know I didn't lose a barn through a tragedy, so your compassion for me must have come from the high esteem where you hold me." More laughter came from the men. Isaiah grinned and waited until silence had fallen. "So thanks to each of you, and to the cooks especially. Beth is in charge today, along with Esther Stoltzfus, who only recently moved to our valley. She has already become quite the blessing to the community, as all of you know so well." He paused and then continued. "Esther is a special woman in my life, and I want to give her my personal thanks for choosing this community as her home, and for..."

Isaiah searched for words. He simply couldn't go on. Thankfully, no one seemed to care about his pause as one young man slapped another on the back and called out, "How about that. Our minister's in love again."

Esther threw her apron over her face, but the women around her beamed smiles in her direction.

"That's all I have to say!" Isaiah hollered out.

He was red faced himself, but at least Esther hadn't fled the scene. What she would say to him afterward, he didn't know. Would she be angry? That was the most likely thing to happen. What had overcome him? This was the worst way he had ever heard of to make a woman fall in love.

"Let us pray now," Bishop Willis said loudly, lifting his voice above the chatter.

Everyone fell silent and bowed their heads for the prayer of thanks. After the amen was pronounced, the lines formed at the tables as each man piled his plate high with food.

Isaiah looked around, but Esther was nowhere in sight. Had she fled into the house after all, or had she gone there because of her duties? Isaiah hung back and filled his plate only after all the other men had gone through. The younger unmarried women were in line behind him, giggling and whispering. He couldn't understand their words, but their plans were soon evident. After he had settled in at the table, the first two girls carried their filled plates toward the table where the unmarried men were sitting.

A chorus of "Welcome, girls!" went up.

Still giggling, the two settled in beside their boyfriends and engaged them in whispered conversations. More of the girls followed once the ice had been broken. Was he to blame for the romance in the air today? Dating couples didn't usually sit with each other on barn raising days.

The men across the table from Isaiah glanced in the direction of the couples. "Looks like you've started quite a thing today, Isaiah," one of them said.

"We should certainly keep an eye on the young folks," Isaiah tried to tease.

Chuckles passed between them. "I suppose that's true," one of them allowed.

"A little romance never hurt anyone," another added.

"Really, Jonas. And this from a married man?"

The laughter rippled down the table.

"What's all the whispering about?" someone shouted from the end.

"Jonas wants his *frau* sitting with him."

Jonas slapped the man on the arm, producing more laughter.

The truth was, he would have welcomed Esther's presence beside him at the moment, but that wasn't going to happen. He had embarrassed her sufficiently for one day, and they were older and more sensible than the young people. She would never walk over to his table in front of everyone.

Isaiah glanced toward the house. There was still no sign of Esther. She had to eat, didn't she? He would go and apologize if she didn't come out soon. He took another bite and waited with his eye on the front door. Thankfully, she appeared before his plate was empty. Isaiah kept her in his sight as she filled her plate, but not once did she glance toward him. Oh, well. He would find some way to make things right with her. He had to. Esther was sensible. She would not end their relationship over some ill-timed words of praise.

The meal concluded, but he'd had no chance to speak with her in private. He would have to wait. Moments later men were relatching their tool belts, and in an hour the trusses were set on the roof. Isaiah joined in the chatter and the laughter. He was a man and could work even when distracted by a woman. This demonstrated exactly why he had never dabbled in this foolishness. Emotions only got in the way of true peace and happiness. Yet Esther had deserved the praise. Once they were alone, that was what he would tell her.

The afternoon drifted on, and only a few pieces of trim were left to secure when chore time arrived and many had to leave. Esther had stayed, Isaiah noted as he slipped into the barn to begin his own chores. Outside, the young men who didn't have any chore responsibilities banged away on the new barn. They would be done by the time he finished, and Beth and Esther would serve them supper.

Isaiah turned as the barn door creaked open behind him and Esther slipped in.

"Are you leaving?" he asked with a catch in his voice.

She came closer to whisper, "No. I came in to thank you for what you did at lunchtime. I had to come out and speak with you the first chance I had. That was so *wunderbah*, to say those words in public."

"But...I saw you blushing. And then you covered your face with your apron."

"*Yah*, I know, but it was worth it, Isaiah. To have words said about one like that..."

"I didn't say much, and I—"

"Thank you, Isaiah," she whispered, reaching up to touch his face. "Thank you so much." She turned and hurried away.

"Are you staying for supper?" he called after her.

"Of course!" she exclaimed before disappearing out the barn door at a fast run.

EIGHTEEN

The following Tuesday evening, Joseph pushed open the front door to his home and stepped inside. From the bangs and crashes coming from the kitchen, Arlene was still in a bad mood. She had been disgruntled all afternoon, which was unusual. She usually glowed with happiness on the days she prepared dinner for them.

"Arlene?" he called from the kitchen doorway.

She whirled about. "Joseph! Don't sneak up on me like that!"

He tried to smile. "I have to keep you on your toes."

She glared at him. "You already do that plenty. My patience has been on edge all day thinking about fixing supper for you and Ben."

He pulled out a chair at the kitchen table and sat down. "Then why are you doing this, Arlene? If don't enjoy preparing supper for us, you don't have to do it. We shouldn't go on with this if you're so uncomfortable with the situation."

"It works for Esther, and it will work for me!" she snapped as she opened the oven door. A wave of hot air burst across the small kitchen.

"Arlene, please." Joseph begged. "I don't like this in the least. I thought it might work, but now I'm not so sure. You're not Esther, and I'm not Isaiah."

A tear trickled down her cheek.

"You don't want to spend your life cooking for a man you don't love."

"I do too," she retorted. "I mean, I *do* love you. You can tell by my putting up with this situation. It's bad enough that you don't have the food or ingredients I need to make a proper supper. I have to scrimp and stretch and cut corners, and tonight's supper will be my worst yet."

Joseph leaned forward. "Wait a minute. What are you saying?"

"There are no supplies with which to cook." She didn't look at him.

"Arlene, come on. You didn't say anything about grocery shopping, so I just bought my usual items. I had no idea you needed certain things. I'm sorry."

"You mean you *would* buy them?" She eyed him a little suspiciously. "My father would never do that. Women aren't supposed to grumble about what their husband brings home for groceries."

"Where did the man get that idea?"

"I don't know." Arlene shrugged. "My father taught us that a woman should have influence on her man and make him better. *Mamm* was expected to help *Daett* look *goot* in public, but in the kitchen she should be submissive and accept what he provided."

Joseph rubbed his upper lip. "I'm sorry to hear that your father taught you such things, but I think he was wrong. If you cook here, you should have the groceries you need. I'm not that big of an eater, and neither is Ben. We're happy with about anything we have, but never mind. So you want different groceries?"

Her face went pale, "You would call *Daett* wrong?"

Joseph hesitated. "Okay, maybe I shouldn't have said that. I don't want to criticize your parents, but in this house we do things the way I do them. So do you want different groceries?"

She nodded.

"Okay. Let's buy them."

"Will you still let me cook for you now that you know?"

He stood. "*Yah*, it's okay. I have plenty of money. You can buy all the groceries you want, and you don't have to ask me before you buy them. Just tell me when you need more money."

"Oh, Joseph. You really would do this?" Tears were running down her face.

"Arlene, you're breaking my heart. What awful things you were taught."

Her mouth moved, but no sound came out.

"Of course I'll do it. Now, shall I give you a hug to prove it? Just a quick one? I think you need it."

She hesitated. "I would like to cook a *goot* meal first, and then I can look forward to a hug."

He shook his head. "Arlene, in this house we give hugs when they're needed, not just when you've done *goot* work. That's a lesson you will have to learn—or unlearn, I guess. This is so wrong, Arlene, but here I go again. I don't want to speak against your parents."

"I don't understand," she said, her feet riveted to the floor.

"You don't have to understand." He opened his arms. "Come."

She seemed transfixed.

"Arlene, please come."

She obeyed, her step tentative, and then, as she drew near, he pulled her close. As his arms closed around her, her tears came again, along with great gulps of pain that racked her chest. He held her until her crying had subsided and then helped her to a kitchen chair.

A second later she bounced up. "The bread!"

She ran to the oven, and with kitchen mittens she pulled two loaves out and set them on a tray on the countertop.

"They sure smell fine," Joseph told her. "Did you have enough flour and other ingredients for the bread?"

"I was missing a little salt, but I think it will be okay. Will you still give me another hug before I leave if it doesn't taste exactly right?"

"If you want hugs that badly, I'll give you another one right now. And if you need anything in the kitchen, you can go buy it without any fuss."

"I'll try," she whispered, stepping closer.

He opened his arms and held her tight.

Her face glowed when he let go. "Oh, Joseph, you have brought such happiness to my life. I can barely believe it. Not in a thousand years did I think you would do this."

"A man who talks to flowers does strange things," he teased.

A worried look filled her face. "So you don't always do this? Give hugs just because someone needs one?"

"Only to my family," he said, "and to people who don't mind that I talk to my flowers."

Her eyes were large again. "You can talk to the flowers all you want. I won't say a thing as long as you give me hugs like that."

He sat down with a sigh. "I was just teasing. There's no connection between talking to flowers and giving hugs when a person needs them. You take me too literally, Arlene."

She looked at him a little skeptically. "Well, supper's almost ready. Why don't you call Ben?"

"Shall I set the table?" he offered.

She paused with her mouth open. "That's not decent, Joseph. Men might sit in the kitchen and talk with women as they wait for supper, but they don't work in here."

He sighed. "On that you're wrong, Arlene. I work in the kitchen all the time, and I'm still a man. Lame, *yah*, but a man." He opened the utensil drawer. "I have to set the table when I'm here by myself with Ben. Some men have had women wait on them all their lives, but I haven't."

"That's pretty obvious. Speaking of that, I need to point out how much this house needs cleaning. The living room is untidy and... well, I peeked in your and Ben's rooms, and both are a mess."

Joseph tried to keep a sober face as he set the table. "How do you propose to find the time to do all this cleaning? You already work in the greenhouse, and you cook on Tuesday evenings—"

"And Fridays," she interrupted.

"*Yah*, on Fridays."

"I can find the time," she said, her facing turning red. "And I promise I won't stay in your bedroom longer than necessary."

Ben chose the moment to stick his head in the kitchen doorway. "Is supper ready?"

Joseph smiled. "Almost."

"Oh, good. I'm hungry." Ben took his usual place at the table.

Arlene turned from the kitchen counter and asked, "Ben, do you get hugs from your dad when you need them?"

Ben snorted. "*Yah*, I guess so. I faintly remember my *mamm* giving them to me too."

"She did?" Arlene said, taking a loaf and slicing it. She brought the food to the supper table and looked down at Ben for a second.

"Oh no. You're not giving me one." Ben pulled back. "I'm too old for hugs."

Joseph stifled a laugh, and Arlene's mouth worked soundlessly again.

"Just ignore him," Joseph told her. "He is almost a teenager. It's not personal."

She went back to the counter to slice more bread. "I'm confused. I'm going in circles." Arlene's knife cut the air a few times for emphasis. "You hug me, you criticize me, and then you praise me. I'll be passing out soon."

"Please don't pass out until after supper," Joseph teased.

Arlene drew a few rapid breaths and fanned herself with one hand.

Joseph shook his head, and Ben grinned. "You two are the strangest people I have ever seen."

"That's why we should wed each other," Joseph suggested. "See, you've hit the nail on the head."

Arlene paused her fanning. "Should do what?"

"Don't worry," Joseph told her. "Let's just eat. I'm starving."

The glow returned to Arlene's face. She transferred the bread to a tray, and with a flourish, she set it on the table. A moment later she was in her chair.

"Let us pray," Joseph said. "Our father, which art in heaven, hallowed be thy name, thy kingdom..."

After the prayer, Joseph started heaping his plate with food. Arlene spoke up. "This casserole should have had a layer of cheese on top, but there was only a little in the house. It didn't go far."

"It looks *goot* to me!" Ben declared.

"I agree," Joseph seconded, helping himself to a large portion. "Everything looks perfect, Arlene, but feel free to shop for the groceries you need from now on." He turned to his son. "So tell me how you're coming with the weeds in the back greenhouse."

Ben shrugged. "I only had a chance to work on them after school, but I got over half of the eggplants hoed."

"That's *goot*."

Looking over at Arlene, Joseph asked, "So did your *daett* or brothers ever help with the dishes?"

Arlene gasped. "Don't tell me you plan to help me with the dishes!"

"I'll take that as a no."

"Of course not! There were plenty of us girls to do that."

"But surely he helped your *mamm* when the *kinner* were younger."

Arlene didn't appear convinced. "I doubt it. It's just not proper."

"You will have to learn our ways now, Arlene. When I wash dishes with you, it will be very proper."

Ben looked at his *daett* and then at Arlene. "If this is getting... um...gooey-gooey, I'm leaving."

A smile played on Arlene's face.

"See? We're making progress," Joseph told her.

Ben made a face. "I'm still leaving."

"Do you think this will work?" Joseph asked, winking at Ben.

He winked back. "Maybe?"

NINETEEN

"Be ready at five o'clock next Friday night, and we'll eat supper afterward," Isaiah had told Esther when he helped hitch Biscuit to her buggy the evening of the barn raising.

It was now Friday and nearly five o'clock, and Esther was racing around the house in her white apron. What was she supposed to wear for whatever she was getting ready for? She was in her everyday dress, so Isaiah would simply have to wait if he expected her to wear something nicer. And the food? Would supper have to wait on the stove while Isaiah did whatever he was planning? Why didn't men explain themselves?

Maybe Isaiah had prepared another speech praising her, like the one he had spoken at the barn raising? She gasped at the thought. Or maybe he was bringing her flowers...even roses? Esther laughed. No Amish minister would ever be caught with a bunch of flowers in his hand, let alone standing with them at a woman's front door. Whatever surprise Isaiah had in store, the mysterious instructions held plenty of promise.

The sound of Isaiah's buggy wheels pulling in her driveway broke into her thoughts.

Esther placed the lid on the bowl of mashed potatoes and

pushed them to the back of the oven. She peeked out the kitchen window, but there was no sign of him. She heard voices outside, though, so Diana must have raced to greet Isaiah. At least the little girl was caught up in the evening's unknown plans. For once Diana hadn't invited Joseph for supper when they had been around him during the week. Esther hadn't told Joseph about Isaiah's mysterious instructions tonight, but Diana had no such inhibitions.

"Isaiah has a surprise for us on Friday night," Diana had sung out.

"Another speech?"

Esther had turned all sorts of colors. Blushing was another downside of being praised in public by the man you planned to wed.

Joseph had seemed pleased, though. She was too, if she faced the truth. Her heart had warmed under Isaiah's public words, along with her bright red face. But had the embarrassment been worth it? That was the question, and she was to blame for whatever the answer was. Isaiah would never have gone to such lengths if she hadn't talked about wanting to fall in love with him.

Esther tiptoed to the front window and sneaked a look around the drapes. Isaiah had Diana up on his buggy seat and was in an animated conversation with her. He gave Diana the reins to Echo and turned to head toward the house. Esther ducked out of sight and stilled the sharp intake of her breath.

A few moments later, when Isaiah knocked on the front door, Esther jumped. What was wrong with her? She had turned into a nervous teenager. She pasted a smile on her face and opened the front door.

"*Goot* evening, Isaiah."

He grinned. "Ready to go, I see."

"If only I knew where I was going. I'm in my apron. Will that do? And what about supper on the stove?"

"We're just going for a little drive in my buggy," he said with a warm smile. "If you don't object, that is. Diana seems all for it."

"I'd love to." Esther wiped her hands on her apron. "But how long will this take?"

"As long as you wish," he said with a mischievous grin. "But we won't go far. Maybe a ride along the ridge on Highway 5 back toward Little Falls."

"Don't blame me if supper gets cold."

"Esther, we don't have to go if you don't want to."

"Will this be as nice as your speech at the barn raising?" she asked. His face reddened above his beard.

"I think so. I hope so."

"*Goot.* Then let me check on the food, and I'll be right out."

"I'll be waiting," he said, turning back toward his buggy.

Esther hurried into the kitchen and slid several of the bowls into the oven. The others she left on the stove top where the heat could reach them. She then raced out to the buggy and joined Isaiah on the seat with Diana between them.

Isaiah winked at her.

"Giddyap!" Diana shouted, still holding the reins.

Isaiah had his hands over Diana's, allowing her to help direct Echo as they went down the driveway and pulled to a stop at Highway 5.

"Now we want to look either way," Isaiah told Diana, "to see if there's any traffic coming. Can you do that?"

Diana peered around Isaiah's arms on each side and sang out, "There's nothing coming."

"Then let out the reins," Isaiah instructed, and Diana complied with a look of rapture on her face.

Echo trotted easily along the ridge, and Diana rocked from side

to side in rhythm to his hoofbeats. "Where are we going?" she eventually asked.

"Maybe we'll go until the road begins to slope down to the valley," Isaiah said. "We have to get back soon to your *mamm*'s delicious supper."

"I want to ride all the way into town," Diana said, pouting a little.

Isaiah laughed. "I'm afraid we can't tonight, but maybe I can
take you the next time I drive into Little Falls on errands."

"Oh, would you?" Diana beamed.

"I certainly can." He glanced at Esther. "If it's okay with your
mamm."

Esther nodded, while Diana peered up at him. "Do you grow
things like Joseph does?"

"No, I keep cattle, and they eat grass and grow big. That's not
quite the same thing as what Joseph does."

"Do you do anything else?" Diana asked.

Isaiah chuckled. "Well, there's the farm to keep up, hay to make,
and plowing for the acres I have in crops. And then there's a chicken
coop out back of the barn—and we could get some rabbits for you,
if you liked that."

"Rabbits don't let you catch them," Diana said. "Joseph said
they're wild by nature, and that the Lord made them so. He said we
should just watch them and not try to pick them up. Joseph keeps
his rabbits inside a fence. No rabbit can get through a wire fence.
Did you know that?"

"I suppose I did," Isaiah allowed. "That's why you keep tame rabbits in wire cages. Did Joseph tell you about tame rabbits?"

Diana shook her head.

"Tame rabbits aren't just brown like the wild rabbits Joseph has.
Tame ones come in all kinds of colors. You can get white ones or

black ones, or black-and-white ones, or brown-and-white, or gray-and-black, or—"

"Are any of them orange like Joseph's roses?" Diana interrupted.

Isaiah laughed again. "I'm afraid not. Unless there are rabbits I haven't seen, which is possible."

Diana regarded him for a moment.

"Do you know what those mountains are over there across the valley?" Isaiah motioned with his hand.

Diana shook her head.

"They are called the Adirondack Mountains, though they aren't really big mountains. Out west the mountains are so high you have to tilt your head to see the tops." Isaiah demonstrated with his beard lifted high off his chest.

"Have you seen them?" Diana asked.

"Yep. With my own eyes. I worked out in Oregon one summer with a wheat harvest, back when I was young, spry, and adventurous."

"I didn't know that," Esther said with interest.

"That's because you don't know everything about me."

A smile flickered on Esther's face. "That sounds interesting. I've never been out west. How is it?"

"*Wunderbah.* I'll have to take you sometime."

"Can I go too?" Diana piped up.

"Certainly." Isaiah patted Diana on the head.

They continued on for several more minutes before Isaiah spoke up. "Well, I suppose we should turn back. Your *mamm*'s supper is getting cold, I'm sure."

"I want to go on," Diana protested.

Isaiah frowned. "Sorry. We can't tonight, but we should do this more often. Don't you think?"

Diana's head bobbed up and down.

After a quick glance over his shoulder, Isaiah took the reins into his own hands and expertly spun Echo around on the road.

"That was fun," Diana chirped. "Do it again."

"Then we'd be going the wrong way!" he said, pretending to be shocked.

"Well, you could turn around again."

"You are too smart for you own *goot*," Isaiah chided, and the two laughed together.

Esther glanced away to hide her tears. This was Lonnie's child, and Isaiah handled Diana tonight as if she were his own—with the same deftness and confidence that a real *daett* would display. She hadn't known how badly she wanted this to happen.

Isaiah smiled down at Diana and asked, "Did you know that Indians once lived on this land? Big, tall Indians who could run like the wind and hunt with bows and arrows?"

"What are Indians?" Diana asked.

Isaiah hesitated for a second. "They were the people who lived here long before the settlers from Europe came over in their ships. They lived off the land and moved about with the seasons. They didn't build homes and businesses the same way we do."

"Did they have tame rabbits?" Diana asked.

Isaiah laughed. "I think not. They shot the wild ones with their bows and arrows and made them into stew for supper."

"Why does *Mamm* never make rabbit stew?" Diana glanced over at Esther.

"Maybe she should," Isaiah suggested. "I could shoot one with my gun, and we could have rabbit stew like the Indians did."

Diana bounced up and down on the buggy seat. "Let's do that for supper next Friday night."

"Sounds like fun to me," Isaiah agreed. "But I'm afraid rabbits aren't in season just now."

"What is *in season*?" Diana asked.

"That's when you can legally hunt," Isaiah told her.

"I can buy one from Deacon Daniel's son. They raise them," Esther suggested.

"That would be great!" Isaiah proclaimed. "In the meantime, in preparation for the next open season on rabbits, we should get into form and practice with a bow and arrow like the real Indians did. Do you think you could hit one?"

Diana looked up at him. "Can I really shoot a rabbit with a bow and arrow?"

Isaiah wrinkled up his face. "Well, you could learn to do it."

"She would love a bow and some arrows." Esther jumped into the conversation again.

Diana joined the chorus. "I want to shoot a bow and arrow! And I want to shoot a rabbit!"

Isaiah gave Esther a quick glance. "Sounds like you have a tomboy."

"What's a tomboy?" Diana chirped.

"Now I have gotten myself into deep waters," Isaiah said with a sigh.

"You have been *wunderbah* tonight," Esther whispered in his ear. She gave his arm a quick squeeze and smiled down at Diana. "A tomboy is a girl who does things other than cooking in the kitchen and washing clothing, which is what most girls do. So a tomboy is a very nice thing to say about a girl."

Isaiah nodded his agreement. "So Diana, how about if I bring you a bow and some arrows next Friday night? We can practice in the backyard. I'll also bring over a rabbit on Thursday when I go to town to save your *mamm* a trip over to Daniel's place."

"That would be so *wunderbah* of you," Esther told him.

"Goody, goody." Diana bounced up and down on the seat. "I will get to shoot a bow and arrows in our backyard."

Isaiah's beard jerked up and down a few times, even though he attempted to hide his laughter. Arriving at Esther's house, he turned in the driveway and parked by the hitching post.

"Thank you," Esther whispered to him before she climbed down.

Isaiah said nothing, but Esther was sure his eyes were moist as he helped Diana down.

She gave him a sweet smile and waited until he had tied Echo to the hitching post before she took his hand. With Diana's in her other one, they headed toward the house.

Was this what falling in love felt like? She didn't know, but her heart pounded with joy tonight.

TWENTY

On Wednesday morning of the following week, Esther drove her buggy into Willis and Beth's driveway and parked beside the barn. She climbed down, then helped Diana down.

"Can I run and play?" Diana asked.

"Yep, off you go." Esther gave the girl a quick hug before Diana raced off toward the house.

Biscuit whinnied, his ears perking up when other horses trotted into the driveway and pulled up alongside him. She had timed her arrival at the sewing gathering in hopes of avoiding any undue teasing from the women—all of whom surely remembered the attention Isaiah had drawn to her at his barn raising some two weeks ago and with his Sunday sermon on the godly Proverbs 31 woman.

"Was Isaiah singing your praises again this morning?" One of women had asked during the meal on Sunday.

She had flushed, even though Isaiah hadn't looked at her the whole time he spoke that morning. He had fixed his gaze instead on the congregation. She had been married to a minister before, but she had never dated a minister—which was apparently something else entirely. Or was dating a minister while falling in love with him the problem? She hadn't expected any of this.

Esther hurried to the other side of the buggy and undid the tugs. Before she threw them over Biscuit's back, Dorrine's buggy drove past her. Dorrine's three sons were at the open door, ready to jump down when their *mamm* came to a stop.

"Howdy, Jason," Esther called to the oldest one.

Jason waved back with a smile on his face as he leaped to the ground.

Wouldn't it be wunderbah *if Jason chose Diana as his beloved someday?* The thought raced through Esther's mind as she whipped the tug over Biscuit's rump so hard the horse flinched.

"Sorry," Esther told him, patting his back. "I'm a bit distracted at the moment."

"What are you muttering to yourself?" Dorrine asked from a few feet away.

Esther gave her friend a wry look. "Just chewing myself out for being distracted."

"And what is distracting you?" Dorrine took a sly glance around. "I don't see Isaiah."

Esther tried to smile. "He isn't here," she said as she led Biscuit forward.

Dorrine giggled. "I haven't had the pleasure of seeing a minister in love in...well, I don't know for how long. Maybe never, but it's a *wunderbah* sight. Even John had to chuckle over Isaiah's sermon on Sunday. All about the virtues of a godly woman, while you were sitting right in the room. Every one of his words fit you exactly. And right after having sung your praises at the barn raising!" Dorrine stifled her giggles as another woman passed and waved to them.

Esther waved back and whispered out of the corner of her mouth, "You have that all wrong. Isaiah wasn't talking about me on Sunday."

"Oh *yah*, he was," Dorrine said, laughing. "What a delight it was to watch your face turn various shades of red. You were so pretty. No wonder the man has fallen in love with you. Confusion brings out your beauty like it does on few women I know. Now on me, embarrassment just shows off all the pimple scars from my youth."

"Stop it," Esther told her, which only made things worse.

"The woman of the Lord," Dorrine said in her best imitation of Isaiah, "is worth a price far above the rubies treasured by the world. Such a woman is made in the image of the Lord's grace and is prepared for some of the noblest tasks the Lord can give us. She is—"

Dorrine hid her face behind Biscuit as another woman walked past. "The man's eyes were practically glowing," she whispered.

"I am about ready to slap you," Esther whispered back.

Jason appeared in the barn doorway, and Esther composed herself. Dorrine scurried behind her buggy.

"Can I take Biscuit into the barn for you?" Jason offered.

"My, what a gentleman," Esther said, handing him the reins. "Thank you very much."

Jason pulled himself up a few inches higher as he led Biscuit away.

"Act your age," Esther chided when Dorrine reappeared. "You'll set a bad example for your sons, and here I was thinking about how Jason would be a proper suitor for Diana when they're older."

Dorrine's face glowed. Clearly the latter comment had undone the rebuke. "You were? Oh, Esther, shall we begin making the arrangements now or later in the week?"

Esther joined Dorrine in her laughter.

"It's so *goot* to be in love!" Dorrine exclaimed. "And to watch other people fall in love so deeply. You and Isaiah are sweet."

"I'm glad you're enjoying it," Esther shot back. "Shouldn't we go in now before someone thinks we have lost our minds?"

"There's plenty of work inside for hardworking, honorable,

Proverbs 31 women." Dorrine attempted another Isaiah imperson-
ation. "She looks at a field and makes a smart purchase. She keeps
her house well and her family fed with wholesome food. She is a
woman honored of the Lord, and such is our most beloved sister
Esther, who will soon be my *frau*."

"Isaiah did not say that!" Esther whirled about to face Dorrine.
"Now, please! Stop it!"

"You don't have to take my ear off! Isaiah might as well have said
it, and it's nothing you should be ashamed of. You arrived in the
community a widow and captured the heart of our esteemed minister, and I'm happy—as is everyone else. But here we go again, chattering when we should be working." Dorrine made as if to hurry
toward the house, but a moment later she dawdled again. "And
you haven't heard the latest news on Arlene and Joseph, have you?"
When Esther didn't answer, Dorrine leaned closer. "Arlene hasn't
told me a lot about what's going on. Every time she tries to explain,
the girl dissolves into tears, so I haven't pressed her for more information. She's—"

"What has Joseph done?" Esther interrupted. "Surely he wasn't
harsh with the girl? I can't imagine him being anything but gentle and kind."

"Oh, you would be right. Joseph has touched Arlene's heart in a
way I've never seen any man do before. But of course, Arlene was
always sure Joseph was the husband for her. I just never thought
things would turn out quite this...emotional." Dorrine smiled
wickedly. "Anyway, Arlene is really moved by Joseph allowing her
to come over and cook supper for him. They're doing it twice a
week now. Can you believe that? All because of your *goot* influence."
Dorrine clasped her hands and declared in Isaiah's voice, "She sews
her own clothing and those of her family. She—"

"I'm not listening to any more of this," Esther declared, hurrying up the sidewalk.

Dorrine caught up with her at the porch steps. "Okay, sorry, I won't start up again."

"Today, you mean," Esther quipped, sending both women into laughter again, right outside Beth's front door.

Beth greeted them with a smile. "I thought I heard the two of you laughing."

"You'll have to excuse us," Dorrine told her. "Esther is in love."

The protest died on Esther's lips. From the look on Beth's face, it was useless anyway.

"Has she seen Isaiah this morning?" Beth pretended to look down the road in both directions, which only drove Dorrine to giggles again.

"You'd better come in before more people see the two of you," Beth said with an even broader smile. "The capers you displayed on the way to the house this morning!"

"I'm so sorry." Esther put on her best apologetic face. "It's all my fault."

"I suppose most of us only get to fall in love once," Beth observed. "In your case twice."

All of the women smiled as Esther walked into the living room. She pulled out a chair and began to busy herself on the quilt they were making. This pattern was a Texas Star, and the quilt across the room was a random patchwork. From what she could see, both projects promised to turn into warm comforters that would bless some poor person this winter.

Esther forced herself to think about something other than Isaiah and his *wunderbah* words. The United Methodist Church in Fort Plain had agreed to find worthy recipients for the charity work these monthly gatherings produced. Blankets and baby clothing were always in demand. Beth had driven to town in her buggy when the Amish first moved here and made contact with the Methodist pastor. That the pastor was a woman had not been in anyone's calculations, but in the end it turned out to be a benefit. Pastor Alice had made this her pet charity project and gave the Amish women vital feedback on who received their gifts, which kept everyone's spirits up as they worked each month.

Sadie, pulled out a chair and sat beside Esther. "How are you doing today?"

"Quite *goot*, and yourself?" Esther asked.

"We're blessed as usual. Looks like you and Isaiah are coming along quite fine."

"I suppose so."

"Now, don't be bashful," Sadie chided. "Being in love is nothing one should be ashamed of, even the second time around. The Lord gave you a great sorrow, and now He comforts your heart."

"Sometimes I think I'm behaving like a teenager," Esther said, glancing at Sadie.

Sadie smiled. "It's clear Isaiah is quite taken with you. You've even crept into his sermons."

"Don't go there," Esther muttered, lowering her head to study the stitch lines and work her fingers nimbly.

Sadie's laugh was soft. "I don't mean that as a criticism, Esther. I'm pleased, and so is Daniel. Isaiah has been too long without a *frau* to comfort his home and heart, but it seemed like he couldn't find one on which to settle his affections. Now you show up out of the blue, directed by the Lord's hand, no doubt. Someday you'll have to tell me that story."

Esther made a face. "There's really nothing to tell."

"Oh, there's a story there, I'm sure," Sadie insisted. "I must hear it after the wedding vows are safely said and the dust has settled."

"Really, there isn't!" Esther countered.

"Love is very unpredictable, dear," Sadie said. "Just as life does not go the way we plan. You of all people should know that."

"I do."

Sadie's smile grew. "Let me say that I agree fully with Isaiah's assessment of you, and so does Daniel. He has been very glad to see Isaiah come out of himself again, and he has encouraged Isaiah whenever possible."

"Did Daniel tell him to preach that sermon?" Esther paused with her needle in the air.

Sadie hid her face for a second. "No, but he did encourage Isaiah to make that little speech at the barn raising. It was so much fun to see you turn all sorts of colors. You two are so dear, and it's such an honor to be part of a lovely couple's path to the wedding vows."

"Well, at least I wasn't fully to blame," Esther muttered.

"What did you say?" Sadie leaned closer.

Esther gave her a big smile. "Maybe I should keep some secrets in my life."

Sadie smiled. "It'll get better before long. You'll have the wedding vows said with Isaiah by this fall and be settled into married life by then. Best wishes, that's all I can say. Sorry to enjoy your discomfort, but it's nothing to be ashamed of."

"I suppose not," Esther allowed. She fixed her gaze on the quilt's stitches again. She still wasn't sure about all of this!

TWENTY-ONE

On Friday night Esther was stirring a pot of rabbit stew with a skeptical look on her face. An occasional change in the menu was fine, but she wasn't about to risk Isaiah's regular meal, so all around her lay the usual supper she always prepared for him—pot roast, mashed potatoes and gravy, coleslaw, and green beans. Pecan pies were set to cool on the counter, pulled fresh from the oven around noon. She and Diana had eaten light sandwiches at lunchtime as the little girl chanted, "Isaiah is coming. Isaiah is coming."

Esther held back her rebuke. This was such a change from Diana's earlier relationship with Isaiah that she could stand a little excess. In fact, maybe she had indulged in a little of that herself. Her emotions had been all over the place since the women's sewing circle on Wednesday. Yet the joy she felt from being publicly praised by Isaiah was followed quickly by stabs of guilt. She hoped she would be able to face him tonight without blossoming red like one of Joseph's roses. She had been tending her garden yesterday when Isaiah dropped off the rabbit, and she had come home to find a little note on the kitchen table, scribbled in a man's scrawl.

Sorry I missed you. Rabbit's in the refrigerator. Happy stew and best wishes. Love you.

Maybe Isaiah hadn't wanted to face her after the gush of his words lately, and he had timed his visit accordingly. But how would he have known she would be down at the greenhouse? He couldn't have. This was all coincidental, and she should stop speculating.

Esther twirled the spoon in the rabbit stew, sending a spray of liquid over the stove top. She gasped as smoke rose from the hot surface. What was wrong with her?

Esther let go of the spoon to reach for the wet cloth that was draped over the kitchen sink. Where had her calmness and steadiness gone? Those traits had always been some of her strongest virtues. Now she was reduced to daydreams in her kitchen and giggling fits with Dorrine on Beth's front lawn.

"Isaiah's here," Diana called. Esther startled. The spoon flew across the stove and landed on the floor.

Esther set her lips and cleaned up the mess. Enough was enough. She had to gain control over the situation. She moved the stew further back on the stove top to simmer and wiped her hands on her apron before going to the front door. There was no sign of Isaiah or of Diana, but a trail of straw led around the corner of the house. She traced the trail back to Isaiah's buggy, which was parked in her driveway.

So Isaiah had kept his word to shoot a bow and arrows with Diana. Not that she had doubted him, but the bale of straw was the surprise. Isaiah had brought one with him. Her brothers used to set those up in the yard for target practice, so Isaiah was sparing no effort in his attempt to please Diana.

Esther drew a deep breath and slipped around the corner of the house. Isaiah was standing by Diana's side with the straw bale a short distance away from them. A large bow and arrow lay on the ground, and Diana was holding a bow more her size. Isaiah was down on his knees with his hands overlaying Diana's and the bow was drawn back all the way, ready to shoot.

"I want you to take aim," Isaiah instructed. "Keep your eyes open and then let go."

The arrow flew across the short space to miss the straw bale by several feet. The arrow landed on the edge of the lawn with the point hidden in field grass. Diana whooped and raced off to retrieve the arrow.

Esther waved her hand in greeting and managed to smile. At least her face didn't light up like an *Englisha* Christmas tree. She hoped no one had told him about the happenings at the sewing gathering on Wednesday.

"Hello," Isaiah called to her. "I didn't hear you come up."

Esther moved closer as Diana returned with the arrow. "I can get you another bale of straw from the barn," she offered.

"That would be great." Isaiah grinned from ear to ear. "But wait. I can get it."

She stopped him with a shake of her head. "I'm sure Diana is going to complain if you leave even for a moment. She's been looking forward to this all day. All week, in fact."

"Let's shoot!" Diana declared, as if to emphasize the point.

"This time, we'll try to shoot straighter," he said.

"I can do that."

Esther left for the barn as the two bent over the bow again. She found the bale of straw near the horse stalls and lugged it outside. Diana was at the edge of the fields retrieving another arrow when

Esther came around the corner of the house. Isaiah noticed and hurried over to help.

"Here," he said, his strong hands gripping the bale. He heaved upward, the straw light against his strength.

Esther followed him as he placed the extra straw bale on top of the one he had brought. "Now there will be no missing," he declared. "And we can move closer."

Esther waited as Diana hit the straw this time but missed on the second try. She raced off and brought the arrows back with her face aglow. "Now it's your turn," Diana told him, peering up into Isaiah's bearded face.

"Okay." He smiled at Esther before he backed up with the larger bow in his hands, pulled the bowstring back, and let the arrow fly, singing its way to the center of the straw bales.

Dianna danced a jig as Isaiah went to retrieve his arrow. Esther slipped back into the house to check on the stew. She stirred it and then sampled a bite. The taste wasn't bad, almost like chicken stew with a wilder flavor. She had seasoned it to perfection, and Isaiah would be impressed. Of course, he would likely find anything acceptable tonight with the rose-colored glasses he was wearing. That was a downside of falling in love. One didn't see too well anymore.

How strange things were turning out. Arlene and Joseph had kept their heads together all afternoon in another part of the greenhouse while Esther worked on her garden. Other than an occasional hi and a nod, that was all she had gotten out of the two. But she was sure Joseph wasn't falling in love with Arlene. He didn't have the gleam in his eye that Isaiah had, nor did Joseph sing Arlene's praises in public. From the conversations she had overheard, Arlene's tongue still had its sharpness, but Joseph was patient with her.

Something confusing was going on in Joseph's life...and in hers. It was as if they had exchanged places. Maybe that was all part of falling in love. She needed to have a long talk with Isaiah after supper to see if some of her feelings could be dialed back. Not that she wanted Diana and Isaiah's relationship to retreat, but she did long for the simple and calm days of knowing how to behave herself around a man.

Esther set the table and brought the food from the stove. She opened the kitchen window to call into the backyard, "Supper is ready!"

Isaiah turn to wave as Diana jumped up and down. Several arrows were stuck in the straw bale, so the two must have fired only seconds before. Esther paused to savor the moment. She would not turn back from this. She had been selfish to say she wanted to fall in love with Isaiah, but wanting Diana to have a close relationship with the man she planned to marry was not selfish. Joseph had fascinated the child, but now Isaiah was winning Diana's heart. How the man had managed, she had no idea. Who would have thought that buggy rides, rabbit stew, and bows and arrows would outweigh Joseph's tales and playhouses built with boxes? But they had.

And Isaiah was in love with her. Even now, her heart pounded over that thought. She had clearly gone off the deep end. Never had her heart pounded this fast over a man—or rather, over the thought of a man who loved her. Lonnie had loved her in his own way, but he never would have said the things that Isaiah had, and most certainly not in public.

Did she really want to go back? Did she want to lose the joy that sprang up inside of her of its own accord? Could she turn the tide of this river even if she tried? At least she could make the attempt. They could have a long talk after supper to find a way for Isaiah and Diana's relationship to grow while he and she settled into a more normal one.

At least, a relationship in which her heart didn't have a mind of its own.

The front door slammed, and Diana raced in to take her seat at the table.

"Did you have a *goot* time?"

"*Yah!*" Diana exclaimed. "I could almost hit a rabbit now. I can take my bow and arrow down to Joseph's greenhouse, and Joseph won't have to put up as many wire fences when I shoot the rabbits."

Esther laughed. "You'll have to talk to Joseph about that. We'd have to eat the rabbits you shoot, so maybe you'd best taste this stew first to see if you like it."

Diana leaned over the bowl of stew to take a deep smell. "I could eat all of it myself!"

"Where is Isaiah?" Esther asked.

Diana shrugged. "He told me to run into the house and let you know that he would come inside in a moment."

"He must have gone to put away the straw bale," Esther guessed. She peeked out of the kitchen window and saw that both bales of straw were gone.

"I had so much fun tonight," Diana declared. "Can we do this every Friday night?"

"I don't know about that. We should be thankful that Isaiah visits us even when he doesn't do *wunderbah* things."

The front door opened, and the sound of heavy footsteps came across the floor. Esther glanced up to see Isaiah's bearded face peering around the doorway, but the rest of him was out of sight.

"Howdy."

"Supper's ready," Esther told him. "Is...something wrong?"

In answer, the rest of him moved into view. Isaiah's hands were clasped behind his back. He stepped closer and brought his hand around to reveal a bouquet of flowers, wild ones, with flashes of white, blue, purple, and yellow. His eyes twinkled with the surprise. "I brought you a few flowers for the table tonight."

"Isaiah, you can't do that!" The words burst out.

He seemed to gather his courage. "Too late. I just did."

In the meantime Diana bounced up and down in her chair and chanted, "Flowers, flowers, Isaiah brought flowers!"

"These aren't store bought or anything like that," he said. "They were growing along my hayfield fence behind the barn. So if the Lord can have them on display, I thought it might be okay if I borrowed them for one evening."

"Isaiah." Esther tried to breathe. "I don't know what to say."

Diana pointed to one of the flowers and said, "That one's yellow on the inside. Oh, they are so pretty." She jumped down from her chair to race across the kitchen floor.

"That's called a cow-wheat flower," Isaiah offered. "That's about all I know." He bent low to take a sniff of the bouquet along with Diana.

"I need to get a vase." Esther got up and hurried into the living room.

What had gotten into Isaiah that he would bring her flowers?

She grabbed a Mason jar from a small desk Diana used and emptied the pencils and erasers it held. The Amish didn't keep vases, so she would have to improvise. The pencils skidded all over the desktop, but she left them to return to the kitchen, where Isaiah and Diana were still hovering over the flowers.

Esther filled the Mason jar with water and set it on the table. "Let me take them," she offered.

Their fingers touched in the transfer, but Esther kept her eyes on the flower stems. Only after the blossoms were safely in place did she dare look up at him. He seemed uncertain of himself, and perhaps a little guilty.

"It's okay," she told him with a smile. "And thank you. That was very thoughtful."

He appeared relieved and took his seat. Isaiah had brought her flowers.

TWENTY-TWO

After supper, Esther moved the bouquet to the end table between the rocking chair and the couch. She reached over to brush the green leaves tucked in among the beautiful flowers.

"You shouldn't have, Isaiah," she scolded "You really shouldn't have. What if Daniel finds out you carried a bunch of flowers into my house for my enjoyment? That's the fancy way of the *Englisha*."

"You don't like them?" He knew good and well by now that she did, and more than that, she'd been quite overcome.

Diana hopped down from Isaiah's lap—where she had been sitting contentedly since supper ended—and ran over to the bouquet. She looked back at Isaiah. "Which one did you say was the cow...what was it?"

"A cow-wheat," Isaiah said, coming over to kneel in front of the flowers. "As you can see, that's the one with all the green leaves and only a little stem on top that's white and bright yellow on the inside."

"What are the others?" Diana asked. "They're so pretty."

Isaiah smiled. "I'm afraid I can't help you on that. We'll just have to enjoy them along with your *mamm*. I think she likes them. Doesn't she?" Isaiah winked over his shoulder at Esther.

She leaned out of her chair to slap him playfully on the shoulder. Where had that instinct come from? They were not wed yet. She looked away and forced herself to breathe evenly.

Diana spoke up. "Maybe we can go ask Joseph what the other flowers are called. He would know."

Isaiah's Adam's apple bobbed a few times.

Esther leaped to his defense. "No, Diana, we're not going down to see Joseph. You can enjoy the flowers without knowing all about them. See, I am."

Esther leaned over to take a long sniff. She came much too close to Isaiah's face, but he made no effort to draw away. She jerked upright and exclaimed, "The dishes!"

They still sat on the kitchen table. Never before had she left the supper dishes to sit and chat in the living room.

"I want to know what the flowers are," Diana pouted. "And Joseph knows."

"Stop it, Diana. Be thankful for what you have."

Isaiah had a big grin on his face. "Perhaps we can find an answer without making the trip to see Joseph. Do you have an encyclopedia in the house?"

Esther thought for a moment. "We haven't unpacked everything since the move, but even if they can be found, they're quite old."

"It would be worth a try! Do you know where the unpacked boxes are?" Isaiah asked Diana.

"*Yah*, I do." Diana bounced to her feet and took his hand. "Come. I will show you."

"You'd best take a lamp with you," Esther told them. "It's starting to get dark."

"That we can do," Isaiah sang out, picking up the kerosene lamp on the desk. "A match?" he asked.

"Let's look in the drawer," Esther managed as she moved forward to the desk. With matches in hand, she lit the flame as Isaiah held the lamp. He waited as she lifted the globe and lit the wick with trembling fingers. He gave her a smile when the flame caught, and then Diana led Isaiah up the stairs with her hand in his.

Esther returned to the couch and collapsed. Feather sticks! This is what came from falling in love. Whatever had prompted her to say such words, and now...oh, it was too late. That's all there was to it. Maybe if she had gone to wash the dishes some good sense would have returned to her. Now the image of Isaiah with Diana's hand trustingly in his danced in her head. The man seemed possessed overnight with the ability to wrench her emotions out of shape. The bouquet of wildflowers on its own would have undone her completely, but coupled with everything else this evening...oh!

Esther fanned herself and then hurried into the kitchen. Maybe doing something ordinary would help.

She gathered the dishes and moved them to the sink. She paused when she heard footsteps coming down the stairs again, and then Isaiah and Diana reappeared.

"Found it!" Isaiah declared. "*A* is for apple—or rather, Adirondacks, and its flowers are listed here."

Esther left the dirty plates in the sink and followed them into the living room, where Isaiah patted the empty space beside him on the couch. She sat as Isaiah opened the dusty book. The faded white pages still displayed the text well enough to read. He held the encyclopedia close enough for Diana, who peered at the book from over his knee. Isaiah's finger traced through the pictures of the flowers, as his glances went back and forth between the bouquet and the page.

"Here we go," he announced. "A dwarf ginseng, which is the all-white one with the long strings on the side and the pale yellow center."

Diana's eyes verified the match, and she bounced up and down to proclaim, "That's what it is!"

"Ta-da! One down." Isaiah winked at Esther. "Here's number two. A blue flag iris. That's the purple one with the four long tails brushed with yellow and white. I had to go down to my swampy area in the back pasture to pick that one." Isaiah made a face at the little girl by his side. "I got my feet wet."

"But it's so pretty!" She bounced up and down a few more times before she pointed. "There's one more."

"There it is, all right. A bog laurel." He glanced toward Esther. "What do you think?"

"I appreciate your doing this. Thank you."

He grinned and focused on the pictures again. "The bog laurel also came from the wet spot in my pasture," he told Diana. "The cows had stomped a few of them, but this one was left."

"I'm happy it was." Diana beamed up at him. "You got to bring the flower to us in a bouquet. Will you be bringing flowers every Friday evening?"

Isaiah gave Diana a quick hug. "Well, we can shoot some more arrows, perhaps, but there probably won't be more flowers..."

Esther came to his rescue. "Flowers are very special, Diana. He won't bring them every week."

"But I want them."

"You've had enough of what you want for one evening," Esther said. "You can play for a bit by yourself now, and then it's off to bed with you."

Diana smiled up at Isaiah before she ran off toward her bedroom. "Thank you for telling me what the flowers are," she said over her shoulder.

"You're welcome!" he called after her, but she didn't slow down.

"You have been very sweet to her tonight," Esther whispered. "That wasn't all necessary, but—"

He laid his hand on hers. "It was worth it, Esther. Diana is a very dear child to me. She grows closer to my heart every time I come over here, as does my heart toward her *mamm*."

"Isaiah, you'll have me a blubbering mess before long, what with your praising me, bringing flowers and rabbits for stew...It's all overwhelming."

"Not at all. And now, shall I help you with the dishes?"

"No!" Esther gasped. "That's not right."

"Come." He took her hand. "I want to help, and I do have some practice at this. You know I have to wash my own dishes at home. An awful task indeed, which will be much more pleasant tonight with you beside me."

She followed him into the kitchen. "You just want to see me in tears."

"They would be very lovely tears," he teased.

She slapped him on the arm, and he laughed softly. Glancing at the dishes in the sink, he commented, "You've been working already."

"Just a little while you were upstairs with Diana."

"Always working."

"Do you object?"

"Of course not! I like a hardworking woman."

She began filling the sink with water as he continued. "Opening myself to Diana has been a little scary for me...but I think I've kept my head above water so far. Haven't I?"

"You have," she assured him. "And then some."

"And you?"

She looked away. "Me what?"

"Am I keeping my head above water with you? You don't really mind the flowers, do you? The compliments?"

"You know I don't." She began slipping the dishes into the hot water.

"You're becoming quite dear to me, Esther," he said from close behind her.

Esther took a deep breath. Surely he wouldn't kiss her now. Surely not.

He stepped closer and reached for her hand. "I want to marry you, Esther. Will you?"

"Marry you?" she choked.

"*Yah*, marry me. We knew each other in the past, we're quite similar in nature, and we've both lost a mate and need another one. And Diana needs a *daett*. I remember your saying you wanted to fall in love with me—which I assume you want to do before you become my promised one. So, if you want to wait, that's okay. But I'm ready to commit, Esther." His eyes were pleading.

She couldn't breathe. There had never been any question in her mind about her willingness to marry Isaiah. Did she dare say that to him now?

"Isaiah, I...I moved out here in hopes of marrying you."

"And you haven't changed your mind?"

"No." She lifted her gaze to his. "I will marry you, *yah*. I admit I've become a bit confused since I arrived here in the valley, but I can get over that. You are what I want in a husband, and I hope I'm what you want in a *frau*. There's no need to go through any more emotional turmoil. You don't have to bring me flowers, or praise me in public, or worry about that stupid thing I said about wanting to fall in love with you. That was awful of me, Isaiah. I loved Lonnie with my whole heart, and I'm willing to give my heart to you. You don't have to do anything more to show me that you care.

I already feel that I made a mess of things by saying that I needed to fall in love."

He whispered in her ear, his hands soft on her shoulders. "If it is a mess we are in, it is a beautiful mess, Esther." He chuckled. "I had the wildflowers folded in an old newspaper in the back of the buggy, and my shoes are still wet from the swamp waters. Who would have thought I'd ever do something like that, but...I liked it. You have awakened things in me that I didn't know were there. Will you join me for the rest of life's journey, right through this fall and to our wedding vows? And from there, to whatever the Lord has for us beyond those years?"

She reached for his face and pulled him toward her and gave him his answer with kisses.

She didn't let go until the clock on the kitchen wall had ticked for a long time.

TWENTY-THREE

Early the following Monday morning, Isaiah drove Echo up Fords Bush Road from the south. The longer route cost him a few extra miles, and even then Esther might still see him pulling in the driveway to Joseph's greenhouse—but the risk couldn't be removed entirely. If she asked him later why he had been to see Joseph, he would admit the truth. After her kisses on Friday evening, he would never be able to hide anything from her. It was difficult enough to think straight.

His sermon on Sunday had been little more than muddled phrases and disconnected thoughts. Deacon Daniel had glanced at him several times with a hint of a smile. At least Bishop Willis had acted as though the stumbling sermon was a well-delivered one. Isaiah hadn't been able to help himself. All he had thought of on Saturday and Sunday morning was Esther's beautiful face. To make things worse, she was seated right in his line of sight with Diana beside her.

Isaiah pulled his hat down over his eyes as he drove toward Joseph's greenhouse, but his horse and buggy were what would give his visit away, not his bearded face. He rubbed his cheeks with his free hand. If he arrived at Joseph's greenhouse all aflame like a romantic teenager, he had no one to blame but himself. He should think about his farm duties. Maybe that kind of distraction would help. But he would still have to face the purpose of his visit. He wasn't here to see Joseph about his acres or crops, but about an idea. Indeed, what a foolish errand he had embarked upon this morning. Yet he couldn't help himself.

"Whoa there," Isaiah called to Echo as they bounced into Joseph's driveway and clattered to a stop by the hitching post. No one was in sight, and Isaiah hopped out to secure Echo's bridle with the tie rope.

He hurried forward and ducked inside the greenhouse without knocking. Joseph appeared from between the plants with a look of surprise. "Isaiah. What brings you out my way this morning?"

Isaiah glanced backward over his shoulder, and then he looked down the greenhouse rows.

Joseph chuckled. "If you're worried that someone might see you here, I'm by myself. Arlene will be here soon, though. Esther doesn't come down until Tuesday, unless she surprises me, which is possible of late. Seems as though there are lots of surprises happening around here." Joseph's chuckle deepened. "But there's still time to talk if that's why you're here."

"*Yah*." Isaiah rushed the words out. "I want to ask you about the roses...about what Esther told me."

"Told you what?"

"I'm sorry if you didn't intend for Esther to tell anyone about the rose you grew for Silvia, and the whole story behind its special nature, and the award you're trying to win."

Joseph smiled. "She told you all that? I'm honored, and I'm sure Silvia feels the same from heaven." He mused on his words and then added, "Don't you think those who have gone before us know such things...if it means a lot to those who stayed behind?"

"I don't know, Joseph. But I suppose if Silvia needs to know and it's dear to her heart, she may know."

"Thank you. But what about my story brings you here this morning? Do you want a handful of roses?"

"I already took her some flowers on Friday night, so I'm not here for a bouquet—"

"You did *what?*" Joseph interrupted.

"*Yah*, I know." Isaiah sighed. "They were wildflowers, and I picked them from my fence row and from my lower swampland. Surely there's nothing wrong with that."

"We could ask Deacon Daniel, I suppose," Joseph teased, and they both chuckled.

Isaiah hurried on. "Truth is, Joseph, I would like to create, or grow, or make—however you say it—a rose for Esther like you did for Silvia. I'd like to give it to Esther on our wedding night." Isaiah glanced around again and rubbed his warm cheeks with both hands. "There. I've said it."

Joseph studied Isaiah for a moment. "Let me get this straight. You want to create a hybrid rose so you can give it to Esther by this fall? Is that when the wedding will be?"

"*Yah*, but don't tell anybody. We don't have the exact date yet, but the planning has begun as of late last week."

"Well, congratulations." Joseph offered his hand. "It's not too often that one gets to extend one's best wishes this early in the game. I'm honored indeed."

"*Yah*, you played a part in all this, so all the more reason for the rose...if it can be done."

Joseph pondered for a moment before replying. "I have several hybrid roses I pollinated last year and planted in December. None of them are quite up to Silvia's Rose. I mean, you never know how they will turn out, and each cross is a guess in the dark, but they are nice. Do you want to see them?"

"Sure!" Isaiah followed Joseph's shuffle to the adjoining green-house, where tables of blooming roses were set.

Joseph motioned with his hand. "Most of these are tried-and-true versions of roses, which the public wants. And here's Silvia's Rose, which sells at the Saturday market like warm homemade bread."

"I can see why." Isaiah paused to take a long sniff over the white-and-orange blossom. "It has quite the sweet smell."

"Silvia was a sweet woman," Joseph said softly. "She loved me when few did, and for that I will always be thankful. She earned her crown of righteousness with the kindness shown to me, if for nothing else."

"I've heard she had a difficult life on the other side of the fence," Isaiah ventured.

"She did, but she never told me too much about that. Silvia wanted to live in the present with the short time left to her."

"An admirable view," Isaiah murmured.

"From an admirable woman," Joseph added. "You never knew her, did you?"

"No. I'm sorry I didn't. You lived in the Southern districts of Lancaster County back then."

Joseph smiled. "But what did Samson say? 'Out of the eater came forth meat, and out of the strong came forth sweetness.'"

"That's quite a description of Southern Lancaster County!"

"We can laugh at ourselves, or at least I can," Joseph told him. "And we do have our strange ways. It looks as if some of them have rubbed off on Esther and you. I mean, here you are at my place looking for a rose."

"That's just some of the sweetness that comes out of the strong," Isaiah teased. "But don't tell anyone, okay? They might never listen to my preaching again."

"Agreed," Joseph said, grinning from ear to ear. "But back to business. These are the three best splices I made last year. There's the deeper red one from a Red Rose Ultra and a Dark Night. That one is pretty. And this yellow version is from a Sunshine Rose and a Pink..." he paused to bend low to check the small card below the plant. "A Pink Desert Glow. But the one I like best is of course the white version here, a cross of my very own Silvia's Rose and a Yellow Pristine. Isn't that a beauty?"

Isaiah bent low to look. "It is lovely—both the smell and the color. All flowers do have a distinct scent, just as you told Diana—even though I usually can't tell. This morning I believe I almost can."

Joseph laughed. "Diana has been tattling on me, I see."

"*Yah*, she has."

"How are you two getting along?"

"Better, I think. I've been trying."

"That's *goot*." Joseph nodded. "I thought so from Diana's chatter. You will make a very decent *daett* for her, Isaiah."

"Thank you." He took another quick sniff. "These are all very lovely, Joseph. I can't thank you enough for the offer to help, but how would we do this? Do I—"

"Roses won't be blooming that well in November," Joseph interrupted. "But there are ways around that if we're dedicated and keep the bloom cycles in control."

"But I would still have a rose you created in the first place. I'd have to tell Esther that."

Joseph paused. "So you want to create a rose on your own? That's a lot of work, and it wouldn't be done in time. You would need to either wait until after the wedding to present your rose or postpone the wedding. I doubt if postponing is an option, though Esther would probably understand if you told her that a rose was coming."

"Maybe," Isaiah muttered. "Esther might like that—and the rose would be mine, right? You would teach me how?"

"You'd go to all that trouble? You'd need to spend a lot of time here in the greenhouse, and Esther lives just up the road."

Isaiah grinned. "How can I forget? She'll probably catch me this morning."

Joseph laughed.

"So what should I do?" Isaiah asked. "I want to make something special for Esther's wedding present."

The smile grew on Joseph's face. "There are other things that can be done with roses, all of which could be ready by your wedding date. I could give the roses to you at cost, and we'd be on our way. That is, if you're willing to follow a few instructions."

"Like what?" Isaiah eyed Joseph. "You've gotten me in deep enough water already."

Joseph stepped closer and whispered his idea to Isaiah.

Isaiah gasped. "*That*? What would I want with that?"

"You said it was for Esther."

"But our people—"

"And then there's..." Joseph bent closer again and whispered a second idea.

Isaiah jerked his head upright. "You're going to get me into all kinds of trouble! I have never heard of such things."

"Either would make a very romantic wedding gift, and they're not that hard to do. I can get you the instructions the next time

I'm in Fort Plain. I'll stop in at the library. And I doubt if Esther will get you in trouble by telling anyone about her wedding gift." Joseph gave Isaiah a wicked grin. "That's what I'm thinking. And she'll thank you a lot."

"This is indecent!" Isaiah declared. "What is the world coming to?"

"Southern Lancaster County," Joseph teased. "Out of the strong comes forth the sweet."

"Be quiet a minute and let me think." Isaiah stroked his beard and concentrated.

"You can take some roses home with you right now and begin their proper care until I get you the instructions you need," Joseph suggested.

After a little more thought, Isaiah agreed. "All right. Let's do it! Which roses do I take?"

Five minutes later they had sneaked a dozen rose pots into the back of Isaiah's buggy. After furtive glances up and down the road, Isaiah raced out of the lane to head home at a steady trot.

TWENTY-FOUR

Joseph watched with a smile on his face as Isaiah's buggy disappeared down Fords Bush Road. Silvia would be thrilled if she were alive. Isaiah's venture down romantic paths might open more of his people to the ways of the heart that lay beyond duty, faith, and commitment to the community. But most would be uncomfortable if they knew the full extent of his devotion to Silvia. The real test would come this year if Silvia's Rose won an award in California.

Joseph glanced toward the heavens. "Maybe You're sending me an ally in Minister Isaiah and Esther Stoltzfus. If that's the case, thank You. I appreciate it."

Joseph shifted his gaze across the road as Dorrine's front door burst open. Arlene came across the yard at a fast walk. Apparently she had noticed Isaiah's early morning visit and was curious—*too* curious.

"What's going on with Isaiah?" she asked as soon as she came within earshot.

Joseph tried a little charm to distract her. "And a *goot* morning to you. You're out bright and early."

Without answering, Arlene asked, "So why was he here? And why did you load those roses into the back of his buggy? When he left, I saw you talking to the sky. I hope you were asking for the Lord's forgiveness. What have you talked Isaiah into with your roses?"

"That's really none of your business," Joseph chided gently. "Maybe you should take a deep breath. Isaiah is a minister, and I am a man who owns a greenhouse. I can load a dozen roses into the minister's buggy without your becoming so curious."

Arlene struggled to calm herself. "I suppose you will be my husband soon, so perhaps I should listen to you. But Amish ministers don't go off with roses in their buggies. You must be in some kind of trouble, which affects me now that—"

"When did you become my promised one?" Joseph asked. "I don't remember—"

"Oh, I am," Arlene assured him. "We should really be talking about our wedding date instead of roses in the back of Isaiah's buggy. Don't you see how distracting all this is from what's really important in life? That's why your ways trouble me, Joseph. They did from when the Lord first placed the desire in my heart to wed you."

Joseph didn't back down. "Arlene, please tell me about the exact moment when, as you claim, you became my promised one."

"I've been making supper for you, and you gave me those sweet hugs awhile back, which was so dear of you, and I knew then what it meant—that you were asking me to wed you, and of course I agreed." Her eyes filled with tears. "You don't know what that meant to me, Joseph. You will never know, even if we live together for fifty years before the Lord calls one of us home."

"I'm sure it will be that long," he muttered. "The Lord wouldn't want to break our marital bliss."

"Oh, Joseph! That is so *wunderbah* of you to say! And you see now why I am so worried about the strange things you do..." She choked up a little. "You...you are so sweet on one hand and sometimes so strange on the other. Maybe that's just the way it has to be, and I have to live with it. Isn't that what a *frau* has to accept in her husband, that everything won't be perfect?"

"I suppose so," he allowed. "I hope you won't suffer unduly due to my...imperfections."

She attempted a smile. "I'm not sure what you mean, but your heart sounds kind, so I hope so too. Have you thought of a wedding date?"

"No, I haven't thought of a date. I'm sure you'll have to search for me in the greenhouse on the morning of my wedding."

"Oh, but I can live with that." Arlene threw her arms around his neck. "At least you'll be in the greenhouse and not in the *bann*."

Joseph extracted himself from her embrace. "It's the middle of the morning, Arlene, and in front of my greenhouse. What if someone sees us?"

"They will know that we're to wed," she chirped. "I want the whole world to know!"

"And what did you mean about me being in the *bann*?"

She sobered. "I will pray that doesn't happen, Joseph. I will pray real hard, and get on my knees every evening before I fall asleep and beg the Lord not to let your strange ways get you excommunicated before we can say our wedding vows. How awful would that be?"

"Simply dreadful."

"*Yah*, you in the *bann*. I don't know if I could go on living."

"Arlene, really!" He gripped her arms in both of his hands. "Come inside." Letting go, he motioned with his hand. "People will think we're having an argument out here."

"But we are. You won't set our wedding date."

He ushered her in and closed the greenhouse door. "Let's get this straight first. A hug is not an engagement. Surely you know that."

She hung her head for a moment. "But...it *could* be."

"But it *isn't*," he said firmly. "You need to tell me when things like that go through your head." He lifted her chin with his finger. "Listen to me. I'm serious. Things have to be done normally, or at least we should try."

She stared, and then he shrugged and laughed. "On second thought, I think we had better abandon that angle of the conversation."

"I just want a wedding date, Joseph." Tears began to trickle down her face. "I can set it if you can't."

"Okay, when will it be?"

Her face lit up. "Oh, Joseph. I can't believe this! We can wed this year. I was afraid you would make us wait until the next wedding season, and my heart would simply die in the meantime."

"Okay, so when?" He took her hands in his and waited.

"I don't know. I'd have to see a calendar, but maybe the last of October. Or would that be too soon?"

"You are marrying a strange man. Why not a strange date?"

"I still need a calendar."

He led her around the corner and motioned with his beard. "There you go."

She almost tore the pages off to arrive at October. Her finger stabbed the numbers. "This one! The last Thursday of October. We can have the wedding at Dorrine's place and begin to plan the meal menu right away."

"Will your parents pay for the wedding?"

She whirled about. "That's normal, right?"

"*Yah!*" He shrugged. "Though I've never met—"

"I'll have to tell them," she suddenly whispered.

"Will they approve of me?"

Her gaze traveled up and down his form and settled on his leg. "I guess they have no choice."

"Maybe I should meet them before we make this official."

She shook her head. "Dorrine approves of you, and *Mamm* and *Daett* will too." She gave a little nod of her head as if to drive home the point.

"You're not convincing me. We should settle this before we go too far."

"But they can't keep me from marrying you!" Her lips were set.

"Parents can do lots of things. You should write them and ask for permission. Believe me, you don't want to find out a month from now that they won't agree to our marriage."

"Dorrine will put in a *goot* word for you, and I will tell them it's already planned."

"Be sure to tell them that I am from Southern Lancaster County and that I have this…" he flung his leg outward.

Her eyes grew large. "But I won't tell them about the roses."

He laughed. "By all means, Arlene, do not tell them about the roses. Heaven forbid they know I grow roses because I once loved a woman with my whole heart."

"You also grow other things. I will tell them that. That's all they need to know." She gave him a huge smile. "And now I'll go and write the letter. Dorrine will help me, and it will be okay. *Mamm* and *Daett* won't forbid me from marrying you."

"That's very comforting."

"*Yah*, it is," she agreed.

"Well, you had better go now. Take all the time you want. Make sure it's done right."

"I will," she said before dashing off.

Joseph turned to approach the bench of roses on the far wall, their white-and-orange blossoms bright in the early morning sun. He had not given Isaiah any of these, and Isaiah had not asked for them. They had seemed to understand each other on that point.

He bent his head as the tears trickled into his beard, and he spoke to the roses as though they were Silvia. "I thought I missed you before, but I never knew how much I missed you until now. But someday we will see each other again. You, who taught me what love was, help me to love her just as you loved someone who could give you little in return."

Joseph shuffled away and then turned to look back at the long row of roses. "Arlene can be sweet in her own way, and she does adore me. Maybe I carry the smell of your sweet presence, Silvia?"

Tears came again, and he wiped them away. "Enough of this, and I'm talking to myself. Stop it, Joseph. Be normal."

He grunted and headed toward the other end of the greenhouse to work on his tomato plants.

TWENTY-FIVE

The following week Esther knocked on Dorrine's front door with Diana's hand in hers and waited. She heard quick steps coming across the hardwood floor, and then Dorrine threw open the door and greeted them with a cheerful, "*Goot* morning. What a pleasant surprise."

"*Goot* morning to you. I had a few spare moments and thought we'd walk down to say hello. Maybe we can even come in and help with something."

Dorrine sighed. "With three young boys and a busy husband, I'd never turn down an offer of help. And Arlene..." Dorrine lowered her voice. "Well, I'd best not say. But do come in, and make yourself comfortable."

"Arlene?" Esther asked as she stepped inside.

"*Mamm*, can I go out and play?" Diana said.

"The boys are in the barn doing late morning chores," Dorrine offered. "You want to watch them?"

Diana appeared skeptical.

"If you can shoot a bow and arrow, you can learn the boys' chores," Esther told her with a smile.

Diana's face lit up. "Do they have bows and arrows?"

"I doubt that, but I'm sure they have other interesting things."

Dorrine appeared puzzled. "Bows and arrows? The hunting season is still awhile off."

"It's Isaiah's thing with Diana," Esther said. "Don't ask me why, but I'm not complaining. Those two can use all the bonding they can get."

"Isaiah brought wildflowers, and we looked up all the names in the encyclopedia," Diana chirped.

"Hush," Esther chided. "You weren't supposed to say that."

"What's wrong with wildflowers?" Diana peered up at her *mamm*.

"Nothing, dear. Forget I said that. Run along. Jason will entertain you in the barn, I'm sure."

"Jason certainly will." Dorrine held the door open. After the little girl had raced out the door and across the front yard, Dorrine turned back to Esther. "Isaiah's bringing you *flowers?*"

Esther covered her face with both hands.

Dorrine giggled. "Now you have me curious."

"Diana wasn't supposed to say anything, and he only brought them once."

"Tell me the whole story."

"Okay." Esther took a deep breath. "Now that the beans are spilled, I may as well confess. Isaiah brought me a bouquet of wildflowers when he came for supper."

"A bouquet? Minister Isaiah?"

"*Yah*, I know, but—"

"Oh, I wish John would bring me flowers once in a while. You'll get no complaints from me. Maybe now that our minister is courting with flower bouquets, it will start a trend in the community."

"Dorrine, please don't say anything to anyone. For my sake, if nothing else."

"Okay, if you say so," she promised, her face still glowing. "But what exciting news this is, and with Arlene's troubles, I'd—" Dorrine stopped. "I really shouldn't be saying things to you about Arlene."

"I spilled my secret. What's happening with Arlene?"

Dorrine shook her head. "I'd tell you if it was about me, but Arlene..." Dorrine paused at the kitchen sink to peer out the window. "Here she comes."

Esther busied herself by bringing the dirty dishes on the table to the counter as they waited. The front door slammed, and she turned to greet Arlene with a smile.

"*Goot* morning," Arlene muttered, but her face was grim.

"Did you tell Joseph?" Dorrine asked from the kitchen sink.

Arlene burst into tears and collapsed on a kitchen chair. "Joseph knows something is wrong, but I couldn't tell him the news. It's just too awful! What is to become of me? I cannot believe this *wunderbah* open door is slammed shut in my face!"

"What's going on?" Esther asked, glancing between the two of them.

"Oh, plenty's going on," Arlene wailed. "After all this time, when I have waited and worked and prayed, and with our wedding date set, and with Joseph agreeing, now..." Arlene's wail rose even higher.

Dorrine stepped closer to take Arlene in her arms.

"What has happened?" Esther tried again.

Arlene lifted her head to wave in the direction of the living room. "You might as well hear from the beginning. Get the two letters on the desk."

As Esther waited, Dorrine hurried off and returned with several handwritten pages that she laid on the kitchen table.

"This is so awful," Arlene moaned, staring at the pages. "I was *so* close, and after such a miracle... The Lord had turned Joseph's heart!"

"Let Esther read them first," Dorrine suggested. "You have to control yourself, Arlene. It's not decent to make such a fuss about things."

Arlene sobbed. "This is not about *things*. This is about my wedding to Joseph after all this time. You know I'm well past marriageable age. No one wants me, Dorrine. No one! Only Joseph had ever given me an offer of marriage, and that after so much work. There will never be another man who would consider me." Arlene lifted her face to the ceiling in silent supplication before she covered her face in her apron.

"Just read the first letter," Dorrine told Esther. "The one Arlene wrote her parents. That's better than us trying to explain everything. Read them aloud."

"'Dear *Mamm* and *Daett*,'" Esther began. "'Greetings of Christian love in Jesus's name. I hope this finds all of you well and in *goot* spirits. Spring is almost over here in the valley at the base of the Adirondacks. Summer will be here soon. The seasons are a little slower to change than they are in Lancaster County, but I have nothing to complain about. Indeed, the Lord has blessed me greatly of late and has granted me a dream I have long prayed and worked toward. Joseph Zook, the man who owns a greenhouse across the road from John and Dorrine's place, has asked me to wed him this fall.

"'Oh *Mamm*, can you believe it? Here I am an old maid, but Joseph is a widower, so perhaps that's part of the reason he considered me. Still, he's a worthy catch. Please write and tell me you have no objections. I don't know why you would have any, and I wouldn't even have bothered you if Joseph hadn't insisted. He seems set on obtaining your permission before we proceed any further. Joseph offered to write you himself. He said this in a way that makes me think he's expecting you to object, but I don't think there's any such worry. Joseph can be a little strange. Let me assure you that he is an upstanding member of the district, and that his greenhouse, as well as the rest of his life, is all in the *Ordnung*. I have asked Dorrine and John whether this was true, just in case I missed anything, and they have assured me that they and the ministry think highly of Joseph.

"'Minister Isaiah has even developed a close personal friendship with Joseph, but I don't want to go into that. Joseph loves me, and I want to wed him, so please ease my mind with your quick reply. Then we can begin our wedding plans. Your loving daughter, Arlene.'"

Esther laid the page on the table. Arlene had lifted her head to listen, but now she wrapped her face in her apron again. A wail rose once more.

"Please control yourself," Dorrine ordered.

"I can't listen to anymore," Arlene said, leaping to her feet to bolt from the kitchen. Her sobs were still audible in the living room, filled with painful gasps for breath.

"The poor girl," Dorrine muttered. "Read the other letter quickly."

Esther grasped the paper.

"'Dear Arlene, greetings of love in Jesus's name. We received your letter last week, and we have taken our time to think about the matter and to ask around about Joseph Zook. What we have discovered is not *goot*. The man was once married to an *Englisha* woman who joined from the outside. True, this Silvia never made any trouble for the district while she lived, and she passed away a short time after her wedding to Joseph, leaving him a son. But we have heard that there are many who fear this woman may have corrupted Joseph more than what was known at the time. She was an educated woman and even had what the *Englisha* people call a PhD. If this had been known at the time, we were told, Silvia might not have been accepted into the community.

"'We fear for you greatly, Arlene. What is this Joseph like? You speak of his friendship with one of your ministers, but that can be a trick. What do you know about Silvia's influence upon him? Was Joseph changed by his marriage to her? And you said something about Joseph being strange. How is he strange, Arlene? These are all questions that must be answered before we can give our word to your wedding. I know you have wanted to wed for a long time, which is why we allowed you to make the move to the valley in the hopes that you would find a suitable young man. But this is not what we had in mind. Your reputation and happiness are at stake here. What if Joseph should make trouble in the community? What if he should decide that you aren't *goot* enough for him after the wedding? Silvia was a beautiful woman, we were told. How do you come up to that standard, Arlene? We are sorry, but under the circumstances, we can't give permission for you to wed at this time. In fact, it might be best if you gave up your dreams of marrying the man altogether. We have often warned you about your dreams. This is what we meant. Our confidence in you is severely shaken. We had thought you would know enough to choose a decent man as your prospective husband. With much love and concern, *Mamm.*'"

Esther laid the page down as Dorrine muttered, "If that doesn't beat all. How do we get around that?"

In answer, Arlene wailed loudly from the living room.

"*That's* certainly no way," Dorrine said. "Maybe you can talk sense into her."

"I'm not going to give up Joseph!" Arlene shouted from the other room.

"I'm not going to give up Joseph!" Arlene shouted from the other room.

"So what should she do?" Dorrine asked Esther.

"First, she should break the news to Joseph," Esther suggested. "Maybe things will get easier from there. Sometimes the first step is the worst."

"She could always choose not to obey her parents," Dorrine suggested. "We could have the wedding here."

Esther grimaced. "That might not work out well. Feelings between this community and Lancaster County could fall apart fast."

Dorrine sighed. "Suggestions, then. That's what we need, and nothing is coming to me."

Esther tried again. "Maybe Arlene should give up the idea of marrying Joseph."

Arlene appeared in the doorway of the kitchen, her face splotchy but dry. "I want your help, Esther, first in telling Joseph about this, and then in writing to my parents. You are about to wed Isaiah, and they will listen to you." Arlene's face brightened. "Better yet, Isaiah can write a letter to my parents. He's *goot* friends with Joseph."

"We should go talk with Joseph first." Esther stood. "That I do agree on, and from there Joseph can handle this. You should have told him right away."

Arlene hung her head. "I will go tell him right now." She scooped up the letters and scurried out the front door.

Esther followed Dorrine to the front window to watch Arlene run across Fords Bush Road. She looked at Dorrine. "It took a lot of courage to face this alone. Maybe Joseph wasn't wrong in his evaluation of Arlene. I hope they make it."

Dorrine smiled at her before turning back to the window, watching as Arlene entered the greenhouse. "So do I."

TWENTY-SIX

Late on Thursday morning, Esther entered the greenhouse looking for Joseph. She had come to tend her garden, but she also wanted to find out how he had received the news from Arlene. Diana bounced ahead of her, calling out for him. Esther paused to listen, and soon Diana's happy chatter guided her to Joseph. He was working on his asparagus plants, kneeling in the dirt, pulling weeds with both hands.

"You'll have to bring your bow and arrows down to the greenhouse and show me sometime," he was saying.

"But I would shoot holes in the walls," Diana declared. "The arrows are really sharp. I think I'll just play with your cartons and make a playhouse again."

"You go right ahead." He gave Diana a kind smile, and she scampered off. Looking at Esther, he said with a twinkle in his eye, "Making a hunter out of the girl, are we?"

"I don't know about that," Esther replied, "but she hasn't tired of the game yet. Maybe once she gets better at it, the fun will fade away. I'm thinking Isaiah will have thought up something else for her to do by then."

"Sounds like he's turned into quite the charmer." Joseph's smile lit up his face.

Esther nodded. "You could say that, but life is full of surprises."

"Ah, but surprises are *goot* for the soul and the heart," he said with a grin. "I'm glad to hear it."

Esther regarded him for a moment. "And what about you? You're sure cheerful despite the news from Arlene's parents the other day."

Joseph sobered. "She told me you gave her *goot* advice and a dose of courage. The poor woman. I was sorry to see her run into such rough waters."

"No regrets for yourself?"

Joseph sighed. "I suppose I could go down without a fight, but the right thing is for me to go see Arlene's parents in Lancaster County. In fact, I'm leaving tomorrow morning via Greyhound and should get there in time for the weekend. I was going to ask if you would mind keeping Ben for me."

"Of course not," Esther said. "But when were you going to ask?"

"I figured you'd be down soon, checking on me," Joseph said, his grin returning. "I admit I was bit shocked that I'm being put through such a test, but it's not unexpected. Silvia spoiled me the last time. A lame man normally would have gone through such trials on the first round."

"Surely it's not that," Esther said. "If it was your lameness, then there would be concerns about money, which are easily disproved by your business's prosperity. Arlene told them about the success of your greenhouse."

"Unless they didn't believe her."

"Then you go with your checkbook in hand and show them. But it's still a shame you have to go through this."

"So you think it's because of Silvia?"

Esther nodded. "Sadly, *yah*."

"Then that hurts even worse."

"You know our people are sensitive about all things *Englisha*, and they assume Silvia doesn't match Arlene from any angle. But the real question is, why are you stepping down the ladder? A man who had a love like yours doesn't have to settle for second best. Maybe they are afraid you have an ulterior motive."

"That Arlene doesn't measure up?"

"Or perhaps they themselves." She hesitated a moment. "You may have a difficult time convincing them."

"Do you think I should abandon Arlene? After she has gotten her hopes up so high?"

"No, but neither should you do this because you feel sorry for her."

He laughed. "I don't feel sorry for Arlene. She's sweet in her own way. But after my first wife, love is different for me. There can never be another Silvia."

"But won't you love the woman you want to marry?"

He gave her a sharp glance. "Not in the same way. Would you expect to love Isaiah the same way you loved Lonnie?"

She looked away. "I...I don't really know."

"You hoped to duplicate Lonnie, but one doesn't try for true love twice. At least I won't."

"Having loved once, I think it would be hard to settle for less, though," she protested.

"Perhaps," he allowed. "I didn't say it was easy, but that kind of love is not going to happen between me and Arlene. I'm lame, yet I was allowed the love of an *Englisha* woman. You see how that's causing problems for Arlene? How about a woman of your standing in the community?"

"Joseph, are you saying you want *me* to fall in love with you?"

He laughed. "We respect each other, Esther, and I value that highly. But love...you know that couldn't happen, though I never even thought to try. I mean, not with you, but with someone on your level."

"I was teasing. But tell me about Isaiah and your roses. Arlene mentioned something in passing last week, and then she dropped the subject as if I wasn't supposed to know. Surely he's not going to embarrass himself in public with a bouquet of roses for me at a barn raising or something."

Joseph stood upright and straightened his back. "There's nothing going on like that, Esther—at least that I know of."

"But you do know of something?"

Joseph chuckled. "Isaiah has a right to his privacy. You'll have to ask him, but I suggest you don't. Just allow the man to surprise you with whatever he has planned."

"And you don't know what that is?"

Joseph laughed out loud. "I'm not saying, Esther. There's no use digging."

She smiled and turned to leave, but then she stopped. Outside the greenhouse the blast of an *Englisha* automobile's horn broke the morning stillness, followed by a screech of tires.

"That doesn't sound *goot*," Joseph muttered. He swung his lame foot down the aisle and walked as rapidly as he could toward the greenhouse door.

Esther stood frozen for a moment, the sharp throb of her heart in her throat. "Diana!" she called down the length of the greenhouse. There was no answer. Joseph hadn't paused to wait but barreled out the door.

She forced herself to follow and nearly tripped over the sill as she dodged the swinging door. An *Englisha* automobile sat sideways on Fords Bush Road. Two women were on their knees on the pavement beside a small form lying between them.

"Diana!" Esther shrieked and tried to run, but nothing seemed to move. Her legs felt like lead, her body sapped of its strength. She fought for consciousness, for movement, for air.

Joseph appeared in front of her and grabbed her with both hands. "Stay here, Esther," he whispered. "Sit on the grass while we take care of things."

Esther threw him off and found the strength to lunge forward to where the unmistakable form of her daughter lay still.

"We are so sorry about this," one of the women said. "We already called 911."

Esther ignored them and slid to her knees, not noticing the pain of her skinned flesh on the pavement. She reached out with both hands and bent low to listen. The child breathed. She held back her sobs. From somewhere in the distant past she knew that an injured person should not be moved, but every nerve in her body screamed otherwise. She wanted to pick Diana up from the pavement, to cradle the little body in her arms, to give life back to the limp form, to heal what her carelessness had cost. This was her fault. She had been talking with Joseph in the greenhouse while Diana ran wild. What had possessed the girl to cross the road by herself?

This was her fault. Everything was her fault.

She lifted her face to the heavens to pray, but the words were stuck in her mouth. Joseph appeared beside her and also knelt. "She's breathing, Esther," he said, "she's breathing." He took her hand in his.

She nodded. There was no more she could do.

"Dear Father in heaven," Joseph prayed. "Look down from the heavens and have mercy on this child. Forgive us where we have failed her, and shed Your grace upon this young life. If it be Your will, grant her healing from her injuries. In Jesus's name, amen."

Esther clung to his hand and said nothing as forms appeared

around them. Dorrine came first and took Joseph's place beside her. John came next, followed by Arlene and the three boys.

Joseph took Arlene in his arms and held her. Dorrine's hands rested on Esther's shoulders as she reached out to touch her daughter's small form.

They waited, the silence heavy.

"I'm so sorry. This was all my fault," Esther whispered.

"I'm sure it was not," Dorrine whispered back. "We saw Diana run out of the greenhouse from the kitchen window. The girl was across the greenhouse yard in a flash, and the car came out of nowhere."

"Then I'm even more to blame," Esther said. "I was talking to Joseph and not paying attention. I—"

She was cut off by the wail of a siren as a police car appeared. The officer leaped out of his car, and Joseph approached him to explain. The officer came closer and bent down for a quick check on Diana. "The ambulance will be here in a moment, ma'am," he said.

He returned to his vehicle to produce flares, which he had set up along the road by the time the ambulance pulled in from Highway 5. Esther tried to stay close, but she had to move back as the attendants cared for Diana. She held her tears until the little girl was carefully placed on a gurney that was then loaded into the ambulance. An attendant helped Esther into the back of the vehicle to sit at Diana's side.

Joseph came up to the ambulance door. "I'll let Isaiah know at once."

"Thank you, Joseph. And thanks for the prayer."

He tried to smile. "Someone should go with you," he suggested. He turned to Arlene, who didn't hesitate before climbing in.

Esther glanced at the attendants, but no one objected.

"We'll be taking her to Little Falls," the attendant said.

Esther nodded. "Can you tell how bad her injuries are?"

He smiled reassuringly. "Not life threatening. The women back there told us they were able to slow down considerably before the impact."

"They won't be blamed for anything, will they?"

"That's up to the officer."

"I just want my little girl back safe and sound," Esther told him. "Oh, please, Lord. Please."

"We are all praying with you," the attendant assured her as the ambulance wailed along the ridge of the valley. "And we are giving your girl the best care we can."

"I'm sure you are." Esther tried to smile, but the effort was useless. Isaiah had brought them this way for a buggy ride only recently, and now through Esther's negligence Diana lay injured. She buried her head in her hands and wept.

Arlene put her arm around Esther. "It will be okay."

"Thanks for coming along," Esther said. The shame hung heavy—her neglect, her lack of discipline, her daydreaming about the surprise Isaiah might have for her—all while Diana had been in grave danger.

Worse, she wanted Isaiah's arms around her right now. She wanted him to hold her close even if she deserved none of that.

"It'll be okay," Arlene repeated as the ambulance rocked down the incline toward the small town of Little Falls.

Esther wiped her eyes and tried to compose herself. She needed to focus and be prepared for whatever medical decision lay ahead of her. Isaiah would be with her soon. She was sure of that.

TWENTY-SEVEN

Esther sat in the waiting room of St. Elizabeth's in Utica, where Diana had been transferred immediately after their arrival at the Little Falls Hospital. Arlene sat beside Esther, white-faced and apparently as traumatized as she was.

"She'll be okay," was all the information anyone would give her. But why had Diana been transferred if she would be okay? She knew enough about medical ways to know that only serious cases were sent to a better facility. What was really wrong with Diana? The girl had been breathing when she disappeared through the emergency room doors at St. Elizabeth's, but she had not made a sound on the way. What a change from only hours ago, when Diana had been filled with such vibrancy, happiness, and joy.

Esther tried not to go down the road of doubt and worry. The Lord had allowed this injury, but He had not taken Diana from her. Surely the Lord wouldn't—not after Lonnie's death. Not after the pain she had already endured.

But still, the Lord did what He thought best. What if Diana was needed in glory with the angels?

"It'll be okay." Arlene repeated the only words she seemed capable of uttering at the moment. "It'll be okay."

"Thank you," Esther whispered. "You comfort my heart with a little hope, at least."

"It'll be okay," Arlene repeated, squeezing Esther's hand.

"How are *you* doing?" Esther asked. Arlene appeared pale. "Maybe you should get something to eat in the cafeteria. It must be well past lunchtime by now."

Arlene shook her head. "I couldn't eat a thing. This was my fault, you know." A tear trickled down Arlene's face for the first time.

"Arlene!" Esther exclaimed. "I was the one who wasn't paying attention to what Diana was doing and let her get away from me."

"But she was running to meet me," Arlene choked. "If I hadn't called to her, she wouldn't have run across the road."

"That doesn't change anything," Esther told her. "Diana knows to look both ways before running across the street. I should have had a better eye on her. Usually I would have heard her leaving the greenhouse, but I was..." Esther looked away. "We just have to pray that she will get well. You can do that, can't you?"

Arlene nodded, still looking miserable.

Esther reached over to give Arlene a hug. "Nothing can be accomplished by assigning blame. Now we just have to make the best of things. And we must pray out of pure hearts, so let us give our blame to the Lord and ask for His forgiveness."

"I...I don't know if I can do that," Arlene whispered.

"But we must. It's the only way," Esther insisted. She took Arlene's hand and bowed her head. "Dear Lord, help us. Forgive us our many failings, and have mercy on Diana's broken little body right now. Don't hold my sweet little girl accountable for my faults... *our* faults. And help us both in the future walk closer to Your will. Amen."

"Amen," Arlene echoed. "I do feel better already. Shall I go get something to eat for both of us?"

"I can't eat." Esther forced a smile. "But you go."

Arlene retreated down the long hallway, and the minutes ticked past. Esther wished Isaiah would come, but it would take some time for him to find a driver and trace her route. Maybe Isaiah's *Englisha* neighbor would drive him for this emergency. No one in the community liked to impose on their neighbors, and they didn't ask for rides unless absolutely necessary. That was one of the blessings of life in the valley. Most of the stores and businesses were within driving distance for the community's horses and buggies. Maybe Isaiah would attempt the drive to Utica with Echo but...no, he couldn't. The distance was simply too much for a horse. But he must know to hurry. She needed him, as she had needed the Lord in prayer.

Esther stood to pace the floor. A young *Englisha* woman and her small son were seated at the other end of the waiting room.

The woman attempted a weak smile. "How are things going with you?"

"We don't know yet," Esther replied, walking toward her. "I'm waiting on word about my daughter, who was injured in a car accident."

"I'm so sorry to hear that," the woman said.

Esther offered her hand. "I'm Esther Stoltzfus. What brings you here?"

Tears formed in the woman's eyes. "My husband woke up with chest pains this morning, so we called 911. A light heart attack, they told us. He's supposed to be out once they've gone over things." The woman wiped her eyes and attempted a laugh. "Here's to healthy eating the rest of our lives, but at least we still have him with us." She wrapped her arm around the young boy and pulled him close. "I'm Phyllis, by the way, and this is Tommy."

"Hi, Tommy." Esther offered the little boy a smile and sat down beside them.

"My daddy will be well soon," he chirped.

"I'm very glad to hear that," Esther assured him.

"He won't be able to play ball with me for a while," Tommy continued. "Daddy's heart has to heal first."

"Shhh..." Phyllis chided him. "Don't talk so much."

"My daughter does her share of chattering when she's well," Esther said, her own tears stinging.

When would Diana again run free across the backyard? With Isaiah by her side, when would she be ready to shoot arrows at straw bales? Or bend low over the rosebushes to take in the scent of the flowers? The images agonized her. She was no stranger to loss, but this seemed different somehow. The hurt went deeper this time.

Phyllis reached over to hold Esther's hand. "We will pray that the doctors will soon have a good report for you."

"Please do," Esther whispered, unable to say more at the moment. She looked up to see Isaiah's tall form in the hospital hallway.

"Your husband?" Phyllis asked.

"No, my boyfriend," Esther managed.

Boyfriend was probably appropriate as she planned to fly into Isaiah's arms right here in this public place. She stood and managed to take a few steps before he caught her in his embrace. She buried her face in his chest and pulled him close. There was no shame in this. Isaiah would be her husband by this fall, and they had embraced before—though never under such awful circumstances.

"How are you doing, Esther?" His hand stroked her arm. "And Diana? I'm so sorry. I came as quickly as I could."

"I know you did," she said. "Come." She took his hand. "Just sit beside me. This was all my fault. I've already confessed to the Lord, but I must tell you too. I was distracted in the greenhouse, and I didn't hear Diana run outside."

"You mustn't blame yourself," Isaiah told her. "It could happen to any *mamm*."

"Oh, Isaiah!" Her tears came again. "That's so kind of you to say, but I was still to blame. I..." Esther stopped. She couldn't say the words and might never tell him about her conversation with Joseph. How foolish she had been.

"Have you any news from the doctor?"

Esther shook her head and leaned against his shoulder. "It's just so *goot* that you came. I was so...." Again she stopped. They were not wed, and she must not make a display of herself.

Isaiah nodded as if he understood. "Let me go talk with the nurse or perhaps the doctor. Someone should have news by now."

Esther smiled up at him. Maybe this was what she had also missed. A man who took charge and could order doctors and nurses around. She didn't have the courage even in *goot* times, let alone with Diana lying injured somewhere in a vast hospital.

Isaiah stood to walk back up the hallway. Esther watched his broad back until he vanished around the corner. Phyllis gave her a warm smile when Esther sat down again. "Do you have other children?" Phyllis asked.

Esther felt her cheeks grow warm. Clearly, the truth was always the better route. "No. I...I'm a widow," she managed. "Isaiah and I will be wed this fall if the Lord wills."

"Oh!" Phyllis's smile didn't dim. "He looks like a keeper."

"*Yah*, he is," Esther agreed, forcing herself to relax.

"Looks like your food is back," Phyllis said when Arlene reappeared.

"A sandwich," Arlene offered. "I know you said you didn't want anything, but I passed Isaiah in the hallway, and he thought you might be well enough now to eat."

"Thank you." Esther took a deep breath. "I guess I am now that he is here."

Arlene handed over the sandwich and seated herself beside Esther.

"This is Phyllis and her son, Tommy," Esther told Arlene, making introductions. "Phyllis's husband had a heart attack this morning but will be released soon."

"Hi," Arlene chirped. "*Goot* to meet you, although not under these circumstances." She attempted a laugh. "Sorry. I'm rather clumsy with words."

"That's okay," Phyllis assured her.

Esther took a bite of the sandwich but paused when Isaiah reappeared, accompanied by a doctor. The two men walked toward them, and Esther set down her sandwich to stand on trembling legs. Arlene stood with her, holding her hand.

"Mrs. Stoltzfus? I'm Dr. Kramer." He held out his hand. "I'm sorry about your daughter's accident, but you're a lucky mother. Everything will be okay."

"We are blessed, *yah*," Esther managed. "What is wrong with Diana?"

"A concussion for one, which is why we would like for her to stay overnight for observation. She also has a broken arm and some internal injuries—bruising to the spleen and the liver—but nothing that won't heal. We've done an MRI and know we don't have to operate. Your daughter is conscious, and you can be in her room if you wish."

"Of course! *Yah*! Where?" Esther stumbled over the words.

The doctor smiled. "A nurse can show you the way, and I wish you all the best."

"Thank you, Doctor. Thank you so much."

Dr. Kramer smiled before leaving them. Isaiah took her hand. "Come. I know where the room is."

"You do?" Esther choked on the words.

She wanted to see Diana, but she also wanted Isaiah to hold her and never let go. She wanted to drift off in his arms into a world where there was no trouble.

Esther gathered her wits and turned to Phyllis before she left. "Thank you for sharing our sorrow with us."

"And your joy," Phyllis said with a bright smile. "Your little girl will be up and running in no time."

"We hope so," Esther agreed. She responded to Isaiah's gentle pull on her hand, following him up the aisle and down a long hallway with doors on each side. Arlene quietly followed. Finally, Isaiah pushed open a door. Diana was inside, tucked under the covers of the bed with a nurse by her side. The girl looked up and burst into tears.

Esther let go of Isaiah's hand to rush across the room. She hovered over her daughter and stroked her hair across her forehead.

"Oh, *Mamm*, I'm so glad to see you," Diana whispered. "I thought you had gone far away."

"No, dear heart. I wouldn't do that," Esther whispered back. "And neither would Isaiah." She turned to allow him to come closer.

He reached out and held one of Diana's hands. "I'm sorry you got a little bang on your head," he said. "No shooting arrows for a while."

"What happened to me?" Diana asked.

"You ran in front of a car when you crossed Fords Bush Road," Esther said. A rebuke rose inside of her, but now was not the time.

"I don't remember it," Diana whispered. "I was just..."

"It's okay, sweetheart. Say hello to Arlene. She came along with me in the ambulance."

"I rode in an ambulance?" Diana's interest rose for the first time.

Esther held back her tears as Arlene came over to gently pat Diana's hand.

Moments later Isaiah whispered in Esther's ear. "I'll be leaving now, but I'll be back this evening for a visit."

"Thanks for coming," Esther told him.

"Would you like to come with me?" Isaiah asked Arlene.

She hesitated for a moment. "Maybe I should. I'll come back later this evening, Esther."

"That would be so kind of you."

The two waved from the doorway before they left.

Esther pulled up a chair and settled in by her daughter's bed.

TWENTY-EIGHT

Hearing the sounds of a buggy pulling in the driveway, Esther pushed back the drapes to peek out the living room window.

"Who is it?" Diana called from the makeshift bed Esther had constructed for her in the middle of the living room.

"Willis and Beth," Esther replied. "The Sunday service must be over, and they're coming to visit you."

Diana tried to sit up. "Is Isaiah coming too?"

"I hope so. But remember, he was just here yesterday when he brought you home from the hospital."

"I want to see him."

"I do too."

Esther stepped away from the drapes to open the front door. "*Goot* afternoon!" she called out. "How was the service this morning?"

"We missed you," Beth called back as Willis tied their horse to the hitching post. They slowly made their way up to the house.

"It's so *goot* of you to visit," Esther told them as she stepped to the bottom of the porch steps to greet the couple.

Once inside, they headed straight for Diana's bed. "Well, what happened to you?" Willis boomed. "Did you trip down the stairs like I almost did last week?"

Diana giggled. "A car got me. A big one that zoomed down the road while I wasn't looking."

"*Yah*, those *Englisha* cars sure can zoom fast," he said with a smile. "But you'll have to look extra sharp before you cross the road next time."

"*Mamm* has been telling me that," Diana replied. "I'll try to remember to do that."

"Well, now, tell me. Have you been out of bed yet?"

"I don't want to yet," Diana said with a scowl on her face. "It hurts too much. Maybe when Isaiah comes." Her face brightened. "*Mamm* said he would."

"Isaiah was getting his horse ready when we left," Beth told her. "In fact, here he is right now."

"Oh, goody," Diana sang out. She tried to sit up but gave a little cry and lay back.

"You just take it easy," Beth warned, pulling up a chair beside Diana's bed. Willis did likewise. Esther left them with a quick backward glance. The scene soothed her spirits and comforted her heart. What a blessing to have their bishop come to the house and pull up a chair beside the bed of her daughter to minister to her.

Esther slipped outside, where Isaiah was climbing down from his buggy. "How's the little one?" he asked with great tenderness.

"Eagerly waiting for you."

He opened his arms for a hug, but Esther shook her head. "Willis and Beth are inside."

"I know that. And they know we plan to wed."

"It's broad daylight, Isaiah," she protested. "And we're out on my front lawn. See, here come Dorrine and John with their buggy. They would have seen us."

"They would have understood, Esther, but it's okay." He touched her arm instead.

"I'm still feeling guilty about the accident." She looked up at him.

"You have to get over that," he told her as he tied Echo to the hitching post. "Accidents happen to children all the time, even to *goot* parents like you. There's nothing wrong with your mothering, Esther. I wish I could do something to help you believe that."

"You came." She smiled up at him. "That helps. And now you can help me make popcorn."

"That I cannot do," he said as they waited for the Kings' buggy to pull into the driveway. Arlene climbed out from the back first and helped the two youngest boys down.

Esther waved, but Arlene responded with only a slight nod of her head.

"How is everybody?" Dorrine called from the buggy door.

"Recovering," Esther said. "Diana's not too grouchy, so I'm thankful for that. Things could have been much worse."

"*Yah*," Dorrine allowed, making her way slowly down the buggy steps. "Did you know that the driver's insurance company will pay your bills even though it wasn't their fault?"

"I didn't," Esther reponded. "I've been too taken with Diana's injuries to think about hospital bills."

"The Lord be praised!" Isaiah proclaimed. "That's very kind of them, although the community would have stepped in to help."

"I'm sure they would have," John agreed from the hitching post. "But perhaps this is the way the Lord provides this time."

"I would have done my share." Esther spoke up. "This was mostly my fault."

"We're not going there again," Isaiah replied. "Come, I think someone said something about popcorn a moment ago. What more is needed on a Sunday afternoon to cheer a poor soul than *goot* company and popcorn?"

"You can say that again," John replied.

"All of you being here will certainly cheer Diana," Esther informed them.

Isaiah grinned. "Your company cheers me, Esther. In fact, I think popcorn would stick to my throat this afternoon if I didn't have you by my side."

Dorrine chuckled. "Do I hear Minister Isaiah singing your praises again? But where were these words in his sermon?"

"That's because Esther wasn't there to hear the sermon," Isaiah said, and they all laughed.

Esther lowered her head. She had not expected such teasing. She hoped things would soon return to normal after the awful shock of Diana's injury.

As they all made their way into the house, Arlene went into the kitchen to begin preparing the popcorn. Isaiah went over to Diana's bedside. "You poor little thing," he sang out. "All broken and fallen out of the tree with her limb in a white cast. What shall we do?"

Diana giggled and said nothing, but she beamed at her guest.

Esther left them to go help Arlene. A jar of kernels and a plate of butter sat on the counter. Behind them, the voices of John and Dorrine could be heard gently teasing Diana.

"How many batches shall I make?" Arlene asked.

Esther gave Arlene a hug before she answered. "I should be making popcorn for you. Diana's accident has consumed all of my attention these last few days. Is there anything I can do for you?"

Arlene shook her head. "I need to keep busy. That seems like the only thing that helps the pain."

Esther gave her another hug. "Maybe you can make two batches of popcorn. I'll go to the basement for oranges for orange juice."

"Let me get them," Arlene offered before racing off.

By the time Arlene returned, Esther had the popcorn and

popper over the heat. "Can you get a bowl, please?" she asked Arlene. "I forgot in my haste."

Arlene nodded and brought the bowl in silence.

"You should really talk about your sorrow," Esther suggested. "Maybe that would help."

"What *goot* will that do?"

"It might help you make sense of it."

Arlene sniffed, and then the words rolled out. "I'm so confused. There I had to sit today knowing that Joseph can no longer be my husband this fall—unless I can change *Mamm*'s and *Daett*'s minds, which I know won't happen. Joseph planned on making that trip to Lancaster County, but he hasn't gone because of Diana's accident. In the meantime, I haven't dared go over and make supper for him. Poor Joseph and Ben—they need what I can give them. To top it off, I just got a letter from *Mamm* yesterday saying they're coming to visit the community next week. That can mean only one thing. They probably want to take me home with them so I'm not tempted with Joseph so near at hand."

"Maybe you should speak with Willis and Beth about this problem," Esther suggested. She dumped the first popper of white kernels into the bowl.

"I don't know. That could just make things worse," Arlene said miserably as she pressed down on the juicer.

"Then we have to pray. You helped me pray at the hospital, and I'll do the same for you."

Relief filled Arlene's face. "Your friendship means so much to me, Esther. I can never say how much, nor can I thank you properly. You don't even hold it against me that I didn't stop Diana from running across the road."

"We're leaving that guilt behind," Esther warned. "Isaiah has been lecturing me on the same thing."

She twirled the handle of the popper as another round of kernels began popping. After she emptied the batch, Esther buttered and salted it. Together, she and Arlene entered the living room. Arlene carried the pitcher of orange juice and cups, and Esther brought the big popcorn bowl with smaller ones for individual servings.

The chairs around the bed scraped the floor as everyone turned around. Bishop Willis hooted, "What a sight for sore eyes indeed! Now our afternoon visit truly has reached the heights above the clouds."

Everyone laughed, and John teased, "You should wax eloquent like that in your sermons, Bishop."

"I try, I try. But there's no popcorn in church."

This was greeted with more laughter as Esther passed around the smaller bowls and Arlene poured the orange juice.

"Do you want some popcorn?" Esther asked Diana.

The girl shook her head. "I'm just glad everyone came to visit me."

"Ah, well said," Isaiah praised her. "That's my girl."

Esther filled her own bowl and joined in the light conversation. After an hour, Dorrine and John left with Arlene and the boys. Willis and Beth stood soon afterward.

"You get well quickly, now," the bishop told Diana. "I need to see your happy face in church again."

Diana smiled up at him, her face aglow. Esther escorted Willis and Beth to the front door, and Isaiah went out to the hitching post to see them off. He waited there until the bishop's buggy was out of sight.

She knew what he was up to. Esther went inside to whisper to Diana, "Isaiah's bringing in flowers." She laughed when the little girl shrieked with delight.

"I heard that," Isaiah said from the front door, his hands full of two rose pots.

Esther hurried over to take them from him. She set them beside Diana's bedside and whirled about to fly into Isaiah's arms. She never wanted to let go, as his strength enveloped her. From the look on his face, he felt the same.

TWENTY-NINE

Thursday morning dawned with dark skies on the horizon and another blast of rain and wind.

Isaiah ate his fried eggs and burnt toast and stared out the kitchen window. With this weather, there went his plans for a hard day's work in the hayfield. Maybe tomorrow the weather would clear. After three days of heavy thunderstorms, they were due a break, and he could get his second cutting of hay on the ground.

A streak of lightning lit the sky, its brilliance reaching deeply into the kitchen to splay flashes on the far wall. Isaiah smiled as the boom of thunder pealed. The truth was, he could use a few slow days after the awful accident Diana had been through last week. He had been past Esther's place yesterday to check on the two, and thankfully Diana continued to improve. Yet so much more could have gone wrong. How thankful they were for the Lord's mercy.

In the meantime life went on, and he could use this rainy day to catch up on things. There was, first of all, the little secret project he was working on. Yesterday he had stopped in at Joseph's greenhouse after he left Esther's and loaded up another dozen rose plants. They were in the makeshift greenhouse he had patched together behind the new section of barn the community had built for him.

If Willis knew he had pressed into service part of the structure for roses, the bishop might have things to say about the waste of the community's time on foolish ventures. But this use was only temporary until after the wedding. After that, the entire barn would be used for practical purposes.

Isaiah gulped down the last of the eggs and a final bite of toast. How *goot* it would be to have a *frau* back in the kitchen who could prepare a proper breakfast. He wanted to push for an earlier wedding date simply for that reason, but a rushed wedding for a minister wouldn't appear decent. And if his rose secret ever came out, he would have broken more than his share of the community's conventions.

Isaiah grabbed his hat and coat and dashed to the barn, but he paused when a buggy pulled into his lane. The wind blew and the rain slashed against the windshield, but he could make out Daniel's face along with another man he didn't know on the buggy seat.

They came to a stop by the barn, and Daniel leaned out of the buggy to call out, "*Goot* morning, Isaiah. The Lord has given us another rainy day, it seems."

"*Yah*, it seems so."

"This is one of our ministers, Isaiah Mast." Daniel turned his attention to the man in the buggy with him. "Isaiah, this is Peter, Arlene's *daett*, and in the backseat we have Edna, Arlene's *mamm*." The deacon smiled over his shoulder. "I'm giving them a tour of the community, even in this rainstorm, because they can only stay for the weekend and have to return to Lancaster by Monday morning."

"Greetings, and the Lord's blessings be on you." Isaiah smiled his brightest, his head tilted into the rain. "Would you like to come inside for a bit? Catch your breath?"

"Perhaps we will." Daniel turned his own head sideways and hopped out of the buggy to tie his horse to the hitching post.

Peter followed and helped his wife down from the back step. Isaiah waited until they were ready before he led the way back to the house. He held the front door open and settled them on the rockers in the living room. He took the couch himself, and Daniel found a chair.

"I hope you're finding us a decent community," Isaiah began. "We're not that old, but we have many stable people like Deacon Daniel and Bishop Willis, who get us into all kinds of trouble."

Everyone laughed at the joke.

"We could add you to that list, Isaiah," Daniel added.

"That is most kind of you to say," he said with a grin. "So what brings you to the community, Peter? Are you and Edna here for a visit with your daughter?"

Peter cleared his throat. "I'm sure you've heard about the marriage proposal that this Joseph Zook has made to our daughter. Your deacon didn't seem to know that they were even dating."

"And you think I know?" Isaiah leaned forward on the couch.

"As we understand it, the woman you're dating is Esther Stoltzfus." Peter didn't wait for an answer. "Esther and her family have a very good reputation in our community. They come from very decent people in Lancaster County. We are given to understand from Arlene's letters that Esther lives just north of the Kings' place where Arlene is staying, and that Joseph's greenhouse is just across the road. Esther and Arlene are friends, and you're a close friend with this Joseph. That's what Arlene has told us. Surely Joseph has told you of his wedding plans, or perhaps Esther has heard of this marriage offer through Arlene."

"Esther didn't tell me, and neither did Joseph," Isaiah said with a smile. "I wouldn't say that Joseph and I are close friends. He wouldn't necessarily tell me who he's dating, and women can be secretive about such things, as you know. Also, Esther's young daughter had a bad accident last week, which has occupied our minds considerably."

"*Yah*, we heard." Edna spoke up. "Our sympathies are with you, Isaiah, and with Esther and Diana."

"Thank you," Isaiah said with a nod.

"So you know nothing about this offer of marriage?"

"I do not."

"Have you any doubts about Joseph dating our daughter? Arlene said the ministry thinks highly of the man." Peter's gaze shifted between the two men. "Can you tell us what's going on, Deacon?"

"I'm afraid that I also haven't heard anything about a wedding between Joseph and Arlene," Daniel told him.

"This is simply beyond me. The man is dating *my daughter*, and no one in the ministry bothers to pay attention—all while thinking highly of the man, who apparently has already proposed!"

Daniel tried again, speaking calmly. "Maybe that's why we didn't pay attention. We don't usually hear of such things—that is, about marriage proposals. I suspect that Isaiah has extracted a promise from Esther to marry him this fall, but I don't make that my business."

Peter glared at him. "Deacon, I wish you would stop making excuses for what's happening here. I find it odd that you apparently don't pay proper attention to your members. Someone in the ministry should have known that Joseph was dating my daughter."

"Maybe you're right," Daniel allowed. "I'm sorry for our oversight."

"I should have paid more attention, I guess," Isaiah added. "But I was caught up in my own courting of Esther."

Peter huffed and sat quietly for a moment. "Since you both think so highly of the man, tell me more about this Joseph Zook, who mysteriously has approached my daughter with a marriage proposal."

Daniel glanced at Isaiah but said nothing.

"Well, have neither of you anything to say? The words ought to be flowing out of your mouths, or did Arlene make this all up about your good opinion of the man?"

"No, not really, but—" Daniel muttered.

"Speak up, Deacon," Peter snapped. "I get the feeling something is going on here that I'm not hearing. And this I can well imagine with the influence that Joseph's first *frau*, an *Englisha* woman, had on him. We have been told that she was highly educated in her world and taught Joseph everything he knows about gardening. In fact, before we left, our deacon told us there are rumors that Joseph knows secret things about roses, and has even created roses of his own." Peter paused to catch his breath. "Those are things which the Lord alone is granted the ability to do, but which the *Englisha* take upon themselves." He lowered his voice, "And there are even whispers about a rose contest that Joseph has entered with the roses he has made under his *Englisha frau's* direction. Do either of you know about this?"

Isaiah looked away, and Daniel stared at the living room floor.

"I see that you do!" Peter leaned forward. "So this opinion of yours for Joseph that Arlene speaks of is much misplaced. In a way I'm glad to hear this, as I can imagine that my daughter would take any gentle hand in dealing with Joseph as approval. Surely you as the ministry are taking a firm stand against this competition in California that Joseph has entered? You cannot have one of your members claiming they can create roses and then sending them out to the world for approval. What if Joseph wins this award and the community is brought to great disgrace? What a scandal that would be." Peter paused but hurried on when neither of them spoke. "Perhaps I'm wrong. Is Joseph under the observation of the ministry? In that case, some of this makes sense. You might have assumed Joseph would never date Arlene or approach her with a marriage proposal while under the community's disapproval."

Daniel shifted on his chair. "I suppose we should be honest with you. Isaiah himself came to me with many of these questions not that long ago. That was soon after Esther moved here and began to have contact with Joseph. But Isaiah should tell the story, as he seems to have settled any questions he used to have about Joseph. Perhaps that would help."

Peter turned toward Isaiah. "Okay. I'm listening."

Isaiah's mind swirled. He was not about to spill all that he knew about Joseph, nor about his own part in the matter. But what could he say?

"I'm waiting, Minister Isaiah," Peter prompted. "Your silence isn't making me feel any better about this. Has Joseph corrupted you, perhaps?"

"I do know about Joseph raising roses," Isaiah began. "From what he explained to me this is a perfectly natural thing one can do—this crossing of two types of roses to produce another one. *Yah*, Joseph learned this from his *frau*, Silvia. I have also heard the story of how Silvia came in from the outside and about Joseph's great love for her. Maybe this is what Joseph sees in your daughter, Peter. Perhaps he hopes to love again."

"Our daughter is not like an *Englisha* woman, Minister Isaiah!" Peter half rose out of his rocker. "I would say it is much more likely that Joseph is using these stories about his *Englisha frau* to lure Arlene, a true Amish woman, into marriage with him. You know that he tried often to find a *frau* among his own district in Lancaster County in his younger days and was unable." Peter gave Edna a

meaningful glance. "Our deacon also told us this when we wished
to know more about Joseph. So tell me, has Joseph been giving his
roses to Arlene?" Peter glared at both of them.

"I haven't heard Joseph or Esther mentioning any roses given to
Arlene," Isaiah offered. "But such things might not be said to me
anyway. If Arlene is in love with the man, they—"

"More excuses," Peter said curtly, cutting him off. "I'm sorry
about my shortness this morning, and I mean no disrespect to the
ministry, but this is my daughter's future, and I must get to the
bottom of the matter." He stood. "But I think it's best we be going
before I say too much. It's clear there's nothing more to be gained
here."

"We understand your frustration," Daniel assured him, as he
stood himself.

"Surely giving roses to someone you love isn't such a bad thing,"
Isaiah got in edgewise, but Peter didn't seem to hear him as he
helped Edna into her coat. Daniel kept up a steady chatter as he
ushered the two out the front door.

Isaiah hurried to pull on his own coat and follow them out into
the rain. By the time he got to the buggy, Daniel had untied his
horse, and there was little he could do but hold the bridle as everyone climbed in.

Isaiah waved as they drove out of the driveway, but with the
lash of wind all the buggy doors were closed. He didn't see any
hands waving back from the windows. With a sigh he entered his
barn and pulled the door shut tight behind him. He crossed over
the barnyard to his new shed in a quick dash and pushed aside the
flimsy greenhouse door to stare at his rose pots.

"For something so beautiful, you sure are causing a lot of trouble," he muttered to them.

THIRTY

Later that morning, with the rain still falling in spurts, Joseph drove his horse, Ali, toward Little Falls with Ben wrapped in a blanket on the seat beside him. They were on their way to the doctor's office. Joseph's phone call from the shanty beside the greenhouse had secured him an appointment at 11:30 after he had explained the gravity of his concern.

The boy had gotten himself soaked late Tuesday morning during the first of the severe thunderstorms that had rumbled through the area. For some reason, Ben continued to work in the downpour, moving several small implements into the barn for shelter. He was still soaking wet at noon when Joseph made his way inside the house at lunchtime. Joseph found him wrapped up in a quilt on the living room couch with his teeth chattering. A hot shower and a fresh change of clothing had followed, but apparently the damage had been done. Ben had done little but sneeze and cough all day on Wednesday, and now he was running a high fever.

To make matters worse, Arlene's parents, Peter and Edna, had been on his mind all morning. They had arrived yesterday. Arlene or Dorrine might have known what should be done about Ben, and perhaps he could have avoided the doctor's appointment—but he didn't dare approach the Kings' house without an invitation while Peter and Edna were staying there. His other option was Esther, who would surely know a remedy for high fevers, but Peter and Edna had been out on the front porch of the King house all morning peering toward his greenhouse. He had not dared run that gauntlet for the walk up the road to Esther's house.

In the end, he had given up and shuffled out to the phone shanty, and from there he had harnessed up the horse for the trip into town. As he worked, Daniel had shown up to load Peter and Edna into his buggy. He waved to the group, but other than a wave from the deacon, there had been no response. Perhaps it was just as well that he hadn't made that Greyhound trip into Lancaster County last week. Apparently, Peter and Edna had made their minds up about him and had traveled the distance to confirm their conclusions.

His decision last night not to walk over uninvited and make a plea for his cause had been correct. His effort would not have worked and would only have appeared suspicious. He managed a grin. He could have taken along a pot of roses to add fuel to the fire.

Joseph pulled back on the reins for the descent to the valley floor. At the bottom of the hill, he navigated through the maze of traffic lights off of Highway 5 and into the main part of town. He would have preferred making the trip into Fort Plain for a doctor's visit, but aside from an optometrist, the doctors in the area had their offices at the hospital in Little Falls.

The streets ran uphill toward the hospital, and Joseph slowed Ali to a walk. They arrived at Burwell Street to park the buggy, and Joseph tied Ali to a light pole. He left the blanket over Ben's shoulders as he helped him into the doctor's office. They made quite a sight. The nurse hurried out to check on them, but they waited another twenty minutes before Dr. Redding appeared. Joseph hadn't expected a female doctor, but what did it matter? *Englisha* women were as well trained as *Englisha* men.

"Good afternoon," Dr. Redding said in greeting. "Is this your son?"

"*Yah*, this is Ben." Joseph nodded. "He got caught in a downpour on Tuesday and continued working for a while. I didn't catch the situation until lunchtime."

"I see," she said. She continued her examination in silence, other than some short instructions for Ben to breathe deeply.

Eventually she turned to Joseph. "I think your son has a mild form of pneumonia—'walking pneumonia' in layman's terms. But I would like to take an X-ray to be certain."

"That's not necessary," Joseph told her. "I trust your judgment, and I suspected it myself."

"Tell me again exactly how your son acquired this condition." Dr. Redding focused on Joseph, who ran through the story again.

"Did you know your son is also quite run-down, Mr. Zook? Children normally survive summer rain showers without any problem. Is he eating properly?"

Joseph hung his head. "Perhaps not. The boy has no *mamm*, and we make do the best I can. We did have a..." He stopped. "My personal troubles are of no interest to you, I'm sure."

"If they concern the health of your son, they are," she said. "You will have to take some measures to improve your son's eating habits, Mr. Zook. Can you afford a housekeeper, perhaps, or a cook? How do the Amish handle such things?"

"I grow vegetables. There are plenty of those around."

She wrote something down on her tablet. "Vegetables are not enough, Mr. Zook. A growing boy needs protein."

"I will see that something is done."

She didn't appear convinced. "I will leave a prescription for anti-biotics at the front desk, but I need to see Ben again in a week—whether he is getting better or not. Do you understand, Mr. Zook? See that the boy gets some decent food and a steady diet of it. We may need another checkup the week after that, even if he shows signs of improvement."

"I will see that things are made right." Joseph winced as she left the room.

"What does that mean, *Daett*?"

"We have to get some better food in you, and regular-like."

"I'm eating all I need now. I'm not complaining."

Joseph sighed. "Maybe you should, son. You don't know what the care from a proper *mamm* is, and that's my fault."

"I was very thankful for the suppers Arlene made. Maybe she could be talked into coming back again."

"It's the rest of the meals that are a problem, but come on." Joseph put his arm around Ben and led him out into the hall. He paid the bill at the desk and collected the prescription. Back at the buggy, he helped Ben inside and drove over to the drugstore. Ben held the reins while Joseph went inside to make the purchase.

Ben had the blanket wrapped tightly around him when Joseph returned. The boy was coughing sharply at regular intervals.

"You're not doing too well, are you," Joseph stated. "And you need food."

"I'm fine, *Daett*," Ben assured him.

"No, you're not. I'm taking you down to the Subway on South Williams. And I'll stop at the grocery store and get some ready-made foods. What we have in the house from Arlene's shopping needs to be cooked."

Ben didn't object, and they drove to the Subway first. Joseph hopped down to tie Ali again and then helped Ben down. They left the blanket in the buggy.

"Get whatever you want," Joseph whispered in the boy's ear.

"What kind of bread?" the smiling woman behind the counter asked. Ben answered and then watched as the sandwich was piled ever higher. Joseph made sure that Ben got a bag of chips and a bottle of orange juice. He passed on the chips himself and chose apple juice instead. They carried their food to the buggy, and Ben chowed down on his sandwich with a grin on his face. Joseph drove them to the Price Chopper on East Main, and Ben stayed with Ali while Joseph went inside and stocked up on lunch meats, bread, canned soup, and other easy-to-prepare items. He didn't expect Arlene back anytime soon, if ever, so they would have to manage somehow with his limited cooking abilities. Joseph paid for his purchases and carried the half dozen bags to the buggy and piled them into the back.

Joseph climbed in and drove out of town. They said little on the drive home, but Joseph muttered, "How are we going to get more food down you, Ben?"

"I'm fine, *Daett*. Really."

Joseph glanced toward the Kings' place when he turned down Fords Bush Road. There was no sign of Arlene's parents on the front porch, but that didn't mean they hadn't returned with Daniel. He would have to take the chance.

Ben was sick, and Joseph needed help. He now knew he had to win Arlene back—which meant facing her parents. He should have paid them a visit sooner for Arlene's sake, but he hadn't. Perhaps this was the Lord's way to move on his heart. If they were home, he'd brave the conversation with them at once. If they were not, he could speak with Dorrine about Ben now and face Arlene's parents later.

"Whoa there," Joseph called to Ali. He pulled into the Kings' driveway. Ali objected with a shake of his head because they hadn't ever turned into the familiar driveway across the road. Joseph kept him in place with the reins taut until they came to a halt at the hitching post.

"Can you hold the reins for a bit?" Joseph asked. "Or would you rather I tie up and you run across the road?"

"I'll wait," Ben said, nestling under his blanket.

Joseph climbed down from the buggy and muttered, "Somehow I have to make this work, for both our sakes."

He shuffled up to the front door and knocked. Dorrine opened the door with a surprised look on her face. "What are you doing here, Joseph?"

"I need to speak with Arlene's parents and with you."

"You don't need to speak with me. I can't do anything for your situation with Arlene, and her parents are breathing fire right now. You'd best let someone else speak on your behalf."

"I'm sorry about this. About everything."

"There's truly no need to apologize to me. For what it's worth, John and I spoke up on your behalf, and Daniel is stopping in at both Willis's and Isaiah's places to chat. Maybe that will help."

Joseph forced a smile. "I'll hope for the best, then, but in the meantime I have an immediate problem. I just brought Ben back from the doctor's office. He has walking pneumonia, and—"

"Oh, no! And at a time like this!"

"*Yah*, when it rains it pours. Literally and figuratively."

Arlene appeared for a moment in the kitchen door behind them, and she gave a strangled cry before she raced upstairs.

Dorrine glanced toward her retreating figure and winced. "If it helps, Joseph, we're praying hard that this whole mess can be straightened out, but only the Lord knows how. Things are quite up in the air, as you can imagine. And Ben needs a *mamm* more than ever."

"*Yah*."

"This is such a shame! Things were going so well. Arlene had nothing but *goot* things to say about your treatment of her these past weeks, and your marriage proposal was so gracious. For so long we have waited and prayed that things could work out, and now... poof!" Dorrine threw her hands in the air. "Why this had to happen, I have no idea. But you're not the only one who mourns, Joseph. It seems so unnecessary, and with Ben..." Dorrine paused. "Shall we take him in for a few days? Would that help?"

"You're very kind." Joseph studied the porch floor for a second. "I don't think that would be wise with Arlene's parents here, but now that she no longer comes over to the greenhouse, I'm shorthanded to say the least. Could Jason perhaps help at least a few days of the week?"

"Maybe the problem with Arlene's parents will straighten out this weekend," Dorrine said, brightening considerably.

"The way they were looking across the road this morning..."

Dorrine's face fell. "I guess you are right, now that you put it that way. But...oh, this is awful."

"It is. What about Jason helping?"

"I don't know. I'll have to speak with John and Arlene too. This will break her heart. She will think she's being permanently replaced."

"I'm sorry about that." Joseph studied the porch floor again. "I'm ashamed to admit this, and it sure won't help my case with Arlene's parents, but the doctor said I'm not feeding Ben right. We have another appointment in a week, and the week after that. I have to get Ben's health in better shape. The boy won't complain, and I have no idea how things are done in the kitchen. Could you and Esther perhaps give me some pointers or some easy recipes?"

Dorrine let out a breath. "*Yah*, I will see that something is done. But we must keep this from Arlene's parents, and maybe from Arlene herself, lest she let it slip. They will give you black marks and say that this is your only reason for wishing to wed their daughter."

"Right now that wouldn't be far from the truth," Joseph said with an embarrassed look. "But I know that's not right, and I should have tried to make peace with Arlene's parents sooner."

"Don't even breathe such a thing, Joseph! You did nothing wrong, and you were going to make the trip to Lancaster County last week. Look, I'll come over myself tonight to check on Ben and bring a dish. Now you'd better go before Arlene's parents come back."

"I really do appreciate this, Dorrine." Joseph moved back a step. "But how can you come over with Arlene's parents in the house?"

"I'll think of a way," she promised, shooing him off the front porch.

THIRTY-ONE

On Friday afternoon Esther set her lips in a straight line as she hurried down Fords Bush Road with Diana ensconced in a small wagon behind her, wrapped up in quilts. Desperate times called for desperate measures. Clearly something must be done.

"Where are we going?" Diana asked again.

"Down to Dorrine's and then over to the greenhouse. The outing will do you *goot*."

Diana smiled weakly and settled in with her white cast resting on the quilts.

"Is it too bouncy? Are you in any pain?" Esther asked.

Diana shook her head. "I want to see Joseph's greenhouse."

"But you can't play or run around," Esther warned. "You have to be careful."

The little girl didn't answer. Her gaze had shifted to the roadside and the distant horizon, and a touch of color filled her cheeks. This short outing was the right choice, if for no other reason than to get Diana out of the house.

Dorrine had been up to Esther's that morning with the sad tale of Ben's illness and Joseph's predicament. Esther had been wrong to ever oppose Joseph's plans to marry Arlene. Clearly the man had been on the right track. She should have done more to help him. Hadn't she always taken pride in her practicality?

If only she had kept Isaiah apprised of the situation and been more sympathetic. She could about imagine how the sessions between Isaiah and Arlene's parents had turned out. Once Peter learned about Silvia's Rose and the competition, he would conclude that his fears had been justified. He would be certain that something underhanded had been going on, though Joseph had simply been influenced by his past love for Silvia. The whole situation was unusual but not wrong. That's what Peter and Edna needed to see.

She would march in this morning and spill her side of the story to them. Honesty was the only choice at this point, even if it added further fuel to the fire. She would even have to admit that she had kept information from Isaiah because she herself had entertained doubts about Joseph and Arlene.

On top of everything, the produce market was tomorrow, and Joseph no longer had Arlene's help. Ben was sick in the house and needed care. Dorrine had told Esther that Jason had gone over this morning to help, but he was a poor substitute for either Arlene or herself. Esther pulled the wagon into the Kings' driveway just as the door burst open.

Dorrine rushed out and exclaimed, "What are you doing here, Esther?"

"Just give me a chance. I know it's a risk, but I must speak with Arlene's parents."

"Are you sure? We're all on pins and needles around here already." Dorrine lowered her voice as Edna appeared in the doorway behind them.

"*Goot* morning, Edna," Esther sang out. "I'm Esther Stoltzfus. I hope you remember me from Lancaster County."

Edna came closer. "And *goot* morning to you, Esther. *Yah*, I was hoping to see you sometime before Sunday. We spoke with Minister Isaiah yesterday." Edna's appraising gaze traveled up and down Esther's length. "Your Isaiah seems like a decent man, which is what my memory of him was when he lived in Lancaster County. The same is true for you and your family, of course."

"*Yah*, Isaiah is the man of my dreams," Esther said shyly, her face flaming. What was wrong with her? She couldn't even speak sanely.

Edna studied Esther for a moment. "I guess we all have our dreams, but they must be in line with the Lord's will. That's what we've told Arlene. I suppose you know all about her troubles with Joseph. From her letters, you seem to be the one person who has her finger in all of this." Edna gaze traveled up and down Esther's length again.

"I...I try to help out where I can," Esther managed, her face still flushed.

"I see," Edna said. "You do plan to wed Isaiah soon, I hope."

"This fall's wedding season, *yah*," Esther croaked.

This was none of Edna's business, but she had to answer the questions.

Esther tried to collect herself. She must proceed, but a change of plans was in order. "Would you and Peter like to come to my place for supper tonight?"

Dorrine stared, open mouthed.

"Come for supper?" Edna peered at Esther. "To your place?"

"*Yah*, Isaiah will be there too. It's our normal date night, but you would be very welcome, and we could all become better acquainted."

"You say this is a date night? Whoever heard of such a thing?" Edna said. "But then you do have awfully strange ways around here."

In the silence that followed, Peter walked out on the porch to say, "*Goot* morning."

"Esther has asked us for supper tonight," Edna told him. "Isaiah will be there."

"I see." Peter hesitated for a moment. "I suppose it would be a chance to ask a few more questions after our conversation with him yesterday. Are the Kings coming too?"

"We wouldn't think of it," Dorrine interjected. "Esther's invitation was to you and Edna alone."

"Then why not?" Peter turned to Edna with a smile. "It seems as if we might get more of our questions answered. Around here our daughter only babbles about things that make no sense."

"Supper's at six," Esther told them. "And now I should be going. I was hoping to check in on my garden and maybe help Joseph a bit with the produce harvesting for tomorrow's market."

"With a child in that condition?" Edna's eyes were fixed on Diana. "Wasn't she in the hospital last week? This young generation, I do declare. They leap out of the sickbed before the drapes can be drawn. Now in our time, we—"

Peter patted his *frau*'s arm. "Esther's daughter appears to be enjoying the outing. It's best to get *kinner* out of the house, and I'm sure Esther has perfectly *goot* sense on the matter. She was married to Minister Stoltzfus, you know."

"I'll be going then," Esther said, turning to leave.

A minute later she and Diana had crossed the street and were at the greenhouse driveway when Joseph came to the door.

"*Goot* morning, Esther." His words were for her, but his eyes looked across the road toward the Kings' front porch. He seemed worried.

"Are they still there watching?" Esther asked.

"*Yah*." A slight grin slipped onto Joseph's face. "You're not scared of them, are you?"

"They sure are causing a lot of trouble. But let's not discuss it out here."

"No argument there." Joseph chuckled as he opened the door wide for Esther and her wagon.

"Maybe you shouldn't have done that, Joseph. They'll think—"

"Think what?" he asked, and then he finished his own question. "That you shouldn't be such *goot* friends with me? Esther, you can't let people like that dictate your life."

"Those are brave words, considering the mess you're in."

He tried to smile. "*Yah*, I know. I have many faults, but I won't stoop to groveling in hopes that Peter and Edna will approve of me. I will not disgrace Silvia's memory. I'm thinking that's what they want."

"Did you speak with them about the rose contest?"

"Not yet, but when I do, I won't deny it or back down. If I win an award, it will be Silvia who has won, and I will not take that honor from her, whatever the cost to me."

"I imagine Isaiah has already told them." Esther sighed. "No wonder Peter and Edna accepted my supper invitation so quickly. They probably wish the bishop was coming too so they can push for your excommunication."

Joseph chuckled again. "I doubt if things have come to that."

Esther assumed a skeptical look. "If it keeps Arlene from casting her affections on you, I wouldn't be surprised. They seem quite determined to protect the honor of their daughter."

"*Yah*, I suppose so." Joseph looked away. "I may sound brave, Esther, but I'm not so brave on the inside. I thought all of this was behind me—people questioning me and looking at me sideways. I grew up being judged, but I forgot about all of it while Silvia loved me. Should I perhaps jump the fence and find myself a *frau* out there in the *Englisha* world?"

"Most certainly not! Wipe such an awful thought from your mind, Joseph Zook."

"You support my marrying Arlene, don't you?"

"I suppose all of this has pushed me there faster than I thought. Arlene needs you with parents like that. I can see it now, and she does love you. Not the way Silvia did, I know, but I think we're foolish to try and re-create what once was. You talked me out of that mistake, remember? With all that stuff about flowers that never smell the same."

A smile spread over Joseph's face. "That seems like an awful long time ago. You came to the community so recently, yet it feels as if you've always been here."

"I know," Esther agreed. "But hadn't we better get to work? I came to help, not chat the morning away."

"You're kind to offer, Esther. I'm not sure what I'd have you do, though." Joseph smiled at Diana, who was still wrapped up in her blankets. "You look comfy enough, Diana."

"I am," she said, returning his grin.

Joseph turned back to Esther. "I appreciate your offer, Esther, but Jason is here. I have him sitting on a bucket right now washing tomatoes. We'll be okay."

"Are you sure?" She eyed him skeptically.

"I'm very sure, but thank you for your offer and your kind thoughts toward us."

"Well, just know I'm on your side, and so is Isaiah."

"I appreciate that," he said, shuffling to the door to see them off.

Esther rattled across the driveway and up the road again to the Kings' house to knock on the front door. There was no sign of Peter and Edna when Dorrine appeared and asked softly, "What happened?"

"Nothing," Esther whispered back. "But could you do me a favor and run over to Willis and Beth's place right away and ask them to supper at my place? Please?"

"*Yah*, of course."

"I'm so worried about tonight."

"Well, it will be good for you to have Isaiah and Willis there."

Esther nodded and hurried back out of the driveway. Her supper might help...or it might make things worse. At the moment she wasn't sure which.

THIRTY-TWO

That evening Esther passed the food around the table with a bright smile on her face. She had prepared dishes she normally served Isaiah—pot roast, mashed potatoes and gravy, sliced corn and green beans, and fresh pecan pie. She had taken the pies out of the oven moments before Isaiah pulled into the yard. It was the Lord's mercies that he had arrived first, and that he didn't make a fuss when she told him about the visitors she'd invited.

"Just help me get this mess straightened out with Joseph and Arlene," she'd pled. "You know it's partly my fault, and—"

Isaiah had pinched her cheek and grinned. "Nothing is your fault, dear."

Her heart had pounded from those sweet words, and now it pounded even harder from the tension around the table. Peter and Edna hadn't relaxed since they arrived. They each kept a wary eye on things right through the prayer of thanks, even after the hearty welcome Bishop Willis and Isaiah had given them. Nothing seemed to impress the two. Esther couldn't remember them acting like this in Lancaster County, but she hadn't known them that well and they'd lived in another district.

Isaiah helped himself to a generous helping of mashed potatoes before he passed the bowl to Peter. Perhaps she should have started the potatoes at the other end of the table, but that would have meant passing up the bishop—the guest of honor by Amish standards. Preferential treatment for Peter might have made things worse. The man was impossible, yet it was important that Joseph receive permission to marry Arlene. Any labor on her part was well worth the effort.

Esther gave Isaiah a quick smile when he glanced toward her, and he winked back. However, she sobered moments later when Peter's gaze pierced her. Maybe this was what came from abandoning the practical and sensible road to marriage. Joseph wouldn't be in a pickle either if he hadn't loved his *Englisha* wife so deeply.

Bishop Willis finally broke the silence. "It was quite nice of Esther to invite us all to supper tonight. And a real special treat too."

"So when was this invitation given to all of you?" Peter asked, his gaze still icy.

Willis turned to Beth with a smile. "When did you know, dear? I was told late this afternoon. Thankfully, I learned of it before leaving for a trip into Little Falls that would have made me late for supper. It's not every day that we get visitors from the old home districts. So, of course, I changed my plans at once."

Beth nodded and returned her husband's smile. "Esther sent Dorrine over to invite us after lunch. And we gladly accepted." She turned to Peter and Edna. "It's so *goot* to get to know both of you better. A meal is the best way, rather than the church service on Sunday. We should have come up with the idea ourselves, but with all the fuss going on after Diana's accident and now Ben's illness, things kind of slipped my mind."

"Seems as though Esther has her fingers in almost everything around here," Peter said. "And yet she's new to the community."

"Just moved in," Isaiah chirped. "And spoken for already."

Isaiah wasn't being helpful, but Esther kept her smile firmly in place as she passed the corn and green beans. Peter shot insults the way Isaiah shot arrows from his bow, but she had to take the darts sent her way in *goot* humor. Things would only get worse if she didn't.

Willis cleared his throat. "Of course, the real reason we didn't extend a supper invitation to you and Edna, Peter, is because we thought you might want to use your time here working on your daughter and Joseph's relationship. Hopefully, what we told you when Daniel brought you around to visit was helpful, but I'm assuming that Esther knows more recent information and thought a meeting with all of us would be helpful to you. Am I guessing correctly, Esther?" He turned to her with a warm smile.

"*Yah*," Esther whispered. She could have hugged the bishop, but that would have been very inappropriate. Peter and Edna would have been out the door and on their way back to Lancaster County at a run.

"Edna and I are finding nothing to reassure ourselves so far." Peter sent a glare around the table. "We had hoped to find a stable community where men like Joseph could at least find solid ground and perhaps be pointed in the right direction. Instead, we're finding a community that honors the man, even with his strange ways. I mean, Joseph is sending roses off to the *Englisha* world for judging, and worse than that, he apparently has great influence in this community. For example, Esther and Minister Isaiah seem to be friends with him. What are we to think of this? We cannot allow our daughter to marry such an odd man, and we are, in fact, considering asking Arlene to return home with us on Monday."

"Oh, that's too bad." Willis spoke up. "I'm very sorry to hear it."

"Can you give us any other interpretation of what we've found?" Peter asked. "To confuse matters further, Esther makes supper for us and invites everyone over to this strange courtship ritual she and Isaiah have embarked upon—dating on Friday nights by cooking supper and eating together as a family—all while holy marriage vows have not been said. This is quite indecent in our opinion. Has Joseph perhaps had a hand in this also?"

All eyes turned to Isaiah. "I...I don't think so. Esther invited me for supper soon after she came, but I never heard where she got the idea."

"So Esther asked you for a date like *Englisha* women do?" Peter half rose from his seat.

"That's not how it was," Isaiah objected.

Peter clearly didn't believe him. "I have never heard of anything like this! And from a minister? What has our world come to, that we are exposed to these awful *Englisha* influences?"

The bishop spoke up. "Peter, I'm sure you're not seeing things in quite the correct light. I know Isaiah, and I was here the first evening when Esther came. They knew each other from way back, and you could clearly see that Isaiah was quite taken with her. There was no question of Esther starting anything. I can assure you of that."

"Is this true?" Peter turned to Isaiah.

"I made my intentions very clear to her," Isaiah replied. "Don't blame her for beginning our relationship." He turned to reassure Esther with a smile.

"Why did she move to the valley in the first place?" Peter leaned forward to ask.

"I assume because she thought she liked our little community," Willis said, attempting a smile of his own.

"But as usual none of you know what Esther is up to," Peter snapped.

Silence greeted his observation.

"Why *did* you move out here, Esther?" Peter asked, addressing her directly.

Esther turned to face him, her cheeks aflame. "I suppose I wanted a new start, or rather..." She clamped her mouth shut. She was not about to share her innermost secrets with a man who would only shred them into an unrecognizable mass.

"Go on," Peter insisted.

Esther got up to bring the pecan pies to the table. "I think it's time for dessert, don't you?"

No one laughed.

"I would like my question answered," Peter continued. "I have a right to know. Did you move here knowing that Isaiah had an interest in you? Did you two write each other?"

"We did not," Isaiah said. "As far as I am concerned, Esther was guided by the Lord's hand. She is a righteous and just woman."

Peter ignored the praise. "So Esther came on her own."

No one answered.

"Esther's *goot* food is going to waste," Willis said, "while we're fussing worse than schoolchildren."

"I want honesty. That's all," Peter insisted. "And I'm getting nothing but the royal runaround. Before I leave tonight, you'll have me believing that Joseph has persuaded your courting minister to come around with roses and flowers in hand. At least I'll be spared the blow of learning that your leaders practice the ways of the world, when the old-fashioned love of our fathers has always produced a marriage and *kinner* in the will of the Lord." Peter fixed his gaze on each person in turn, stopping with Isaiah, whose face had also blazed red.

Willis chuckled. "I'm sure Isaiah is no flower minister. He's a faithful and caring man, but he can show that to Esther and Diana without flowers. I'm sure he..." The bishop paused and laughed at the thought.

Esther didn't move. She had no blood left in her veins. This was all her fault, and now Isaiah would soon be publicly shamed.

Peter's gaze was still fixed on Isaiah's face. "I'm thinking you might be wrong, Bishop. What do you have to say for yourself, Isaiah?"

"I brought some wildflowers from my land to Esther in a bouquet," Isaiah admitted. "And some roses after Diana's accident. I do not think that is wrong, and hopefully Bishop Willis won't either."

Peter bowed his head for a moment. "This is a sad evening indeed. It makes no difference to me if you can persuade your bishop to support you or not, Isaiah. I will not accept these *Englisha* practices or give my word to my daughter's marriage to a man who lives in such a community. If that causes trouble for anyone, I am sorry. Perhaps someday you will thank me, Bishop, for exposing this weakness in your district. You know that the *Englisha* sneak in like wolves in sheep's clothing. I have smelled a wolf ever since we received Arlene's letter. Now we find out that your own minister has been deeply influenced by this Joseph Zook. I don't envy you, Bishop. You have a lot of housecleaning in front of you. That's all I can say."

Silence settled in the kitchen, broken only by the tinkle of forks as everyone tried to eat. Tears stung Esther's eyes. No one made an attempt at cheerfulness, and her pecan pie was barely touched.

Peter and Edna stood the minute the bishop said the final prayer of thanks. "We really should be going," Peter said. "We have to start packing tonight, and we will be on the road first thing in the morning. Arlene will go with us. I thought you all should know, but I do want to say that we carry no hard feelings against any of you."

"Surely something can be done about this," Willis tried again. "I know that bouquets of flowers are not the ordinary thing in a time of courtship, but I can see nothing here that we should be ashamed of." He glanced hopefully toward Isaiah.

"I agree." Isaiah said, but the damage had clearly been done.

"We really have to be going." Peter looked at Esther. "Thank you for supper."

"You're welcome." She nearly choked on the words.

Peter gave her a final nod on the way out of the kitchen, his arm around Edna as if the wolves were already on their heels.

What was left now? Isaiah's reputation would suffer from the embarrassment he had undergone at her supper table. Here she had tried to help Joseph and ended up dragging herself and Isaiah down with him.

"I should be going too." Isaiah stood.

Esther followed him to the front door. "I'm so sorry about this," she said, wringing her hands. "I never would have invited everyone to supper on our special evening if I had known this would happen. You're a minister. I've shamed you, and you are not guilty."

"I did what he said I did. You're not to blame, Esther. We'll make it through this together, okay?" He reached for her hand.

She clasped his fingers in hers. "There was nothing wrong with what you did. I loved the wildflowers you brought me. That was the sweetest thing."

"I know." He tried to smile. "I guess we'll have to put this all back together somehow, but it will take a little while. I hope you understand."

She nodded and bit her lip. "You won't leave me, will you?"

"Of course not." He squeezed her hand. "You're not to blame. Just hang tight in the weeks ahead, okay?"

"I will," she whispered as he pulled his hat on and went out the door. She watched him go amid a flood of tears. Without meaning to, she had hurt the man she loved so deeply. Beth's arm slipped around her shoulder about the time Isaiah's buggy turned out of the driveway.

Her bishop's voice rumbled behind them. "I'm very sorry about this, Esther. I still say this is a bunch of fuss about nothing."

"I've messed up everything," Esther wailed. "And I couldn't even help Joseph and Arlene." She buried her face in her apron and sobbed.

THIRTY-THREE

The next week began with a blast of heat from the south that crept up the valley and threatened to stay. Esther opened all the windows in the house each night and pushed the drapes back, but she still tossed and turned until the early morning hours when a slight breeze blew down from the Adirondacks. Exhausted, she groped for the alarm on the nightstand by her bedside, shut off the switch, and stumbled toward the bedroom window for a peek at the faint dawn on the horizon. The promise of another hot day was in the air.

The ache in her heart continued, and she knew something should be done. Perhaps she should go back to Lancaster County for a visit and spend some time away from the community and the current sad situation. Isaiah had preached yesterday at the church service because he had to. Amish ministers didn't get to avoid their duties unless they fell into sin or heresy. Isaiah's embarrassment at Peter and Edna's hands had been neither, but the wound had cut deep into his sturdy nature, and she was to blame.

Isaiah had hung his head throughout the sermon, his voice rising to none of the heights or eloquence he normally attained. For this she was also to blame, and for the snickers the young men engaged in behind Isaiah's back. After the reason had become known for

Peter, Edna, and Arlene's sudden departure from the community, the men had dubbed Isaiah the "flower minister." Such things could not be kept a secret in close-knit community circles.

Isaiah had not been back since that awful night. She didn't blame him. They would face things and attempt to place their lives back on track—but how? Their engagement was still in place. Isaiah wouldn't leave her, especially now that their wedding date had been set for the last Thursday in October. But they hadn't gotten any further than a date with their plans, caught up as they had been in their newfound love for each other. She had led Isaiah down the fairy path of romance and ended up in the ditch, with Isaiah's reputation in tatters.

How much better things would be if she had never heard of roses, or of dreams, or of all those silly things, and had stayed the practical, down-to-earth woman who moved into the valley from Lancaster County this past April. She had fallen so low, and her plans—which had once been so sure—were now broken. She had held Isaiah in the palm of her hand that first night she arrived, only to foolishly squander what the Lord had so graciously given her.

On top of all that, Joseph was stuck with no help at his greenhouse except for Ben and young Jason. She went down when she was able, but Diana was still recovering from the accident and her cast wouldn't be removed for another two weeks. Joseph seemed appreciative of her efforts, but nothing she could do healed the wound that festered in both of their hearts. They were two injured people, drawn together at first by a common cause, now caught in a whirlwind of events that threatened to take them both.

Joseph did little at the services. He kept his head low and shuffled out of the house right after the meal to hitch Ali to the buggy and drive home with Ben. Dorrine took dishes of food to the Zook residence twice a week, but beyond that Joseph was alone with his rejection. Ben appeared to have put on a few pounds, so Joseph had obviously found the strength somewhere to fix that problem, even as his own frame grew gaunt.

She would weep and wail if it would do any good—but it wouldn't. Tears were a thing of the past when it came to fixing problems. She wanted to drive straight over to Isaiah's place this morning, throw her arms around him, and comfort him. But what comfort was she to him now? That truth stung the deepest. She had brought this upon him. Isaiah's first *frau* had never shamed him like this, and Esther had not even made it to the wedding vows before bringing disgrace upon his head.

But maybe there was time yet to redeem herself. She could change her ways.

Esther turned away from the bedroom window and dressed. Each pin felt like a pound weight, and she pricked herself twice—the second time badly enough that blood trickled down her finger. Perhaps she ought to bleed herself like the sick were bled in medieval times, to cleanse herself of her illness. But how morbid that would be, and self-serving. She would only sink deeper into this dismal hole of despair.

Esther pressed in the last pin and closed the bedroom door behind her. The dawn was bright in the sky without a cloud on the horizon, and the heat moved through the house with tentacle-like fingers. She entered the kitchen and stoked the fire. The flames quickly rose from the kindling, the smoke misdirecting for a moment into the room. She waved the offending fumes away and closed the stove's lid.

She soon had bacon in the pan and the eggs frying. Esther poured in the oatmeal when the water boiled, and dashed around the stove to blow out the flame when she spilled oat kernels on the hot surface.

"Clumsy me," she muttered to herself, brushing the smoking debris into the wastebasket with her apron and placing the lid on the oatmeal.

Now to get Diana up. She should have woken the girl earlier. Diana needed to begin her journey back to the bouncy child she had once been, but who was she to blame Diana when such a cloud hung over the house? The girl missed Isaiah terribly, and Diana had gone over to talk to him yesterday after the service. Esther hadn't dared ask about what the two had said—and Diana hadn't offered to tell her.

Esther entered the living room and stopped short. Joseph's shuffling figure could be seen coming across the lawn, his thin frame outlined against the dawn sky. She gasped and hurried to the front door.

"Has something happened?" she called to him.

He shook his head. "I would have gone to Dorrine if it had." He lifted his bearded face and attempted a smile.

"Oh, Joseph." Esther stepped out on the front porch. "What is to become of us? I feel so awful for how things turned out, and I'm to blame."

He perched sideways on the upper porch step and peered up at her. "Those are exactly the thoughts I'm thinking, Esther, and we can't both be right."

She stared at the dawning horizon. "It was all me, Joseph. Don't fool yourself. Only a woman could mess things up so completely."

His laugh was gentle. "It all starts with a man, Esther, and I was the center of that storm. Me, my roses, and my stories of Silvia and our great love."

"But they were true."

"Oh, *yah*, only too true. But that doesn't fix the present situation. I could promise to back off the rose contest in California to please

Peter and Edna, but I won't because of my memory of Silvia. And I doubt if that would help anyway."

"I would never want that to happen. And I agree. It would do no *goot* now, at least for us. Isaiah's trouble would still remain."

"I'm sorry for what happened there." He hung his head. "I must say that was a sad sight yesterday, to see a great preacher reduced to such shame by nothing at all."

"By roses," Esther mused. "And by a woman who lured him into all of it."

"Do you think you can go back, Esther?"

"I don't know. I'm close to trying, I think."

"I feel so badly about everything. I felt I had to come up and say so this morning. Not a lot of *goot* that will do, but it soothes my feelings at least."

"It's not your fault, Joseph," she told him, her voice resolute.

"You're just beating around the bush with that attitude, Esther. Maybe if you'd blamed me instead of sticking up for me—which is what I assume you did when Arlene's parents were here—things might have turned out differently."

"I didn't dare say much in front of those people," she said honestly. She paused a moment. "Why don't you come on in for breakfast? Feeding you is the least I can do for you. I'll run down and get Ben. I want him here too."

"Really?" Joseph sounded relieved at the invitation. "I'm ashamed of myself, Esther, but the kindness of a woman still touches my heart deeply."

"Sit comfortably on the couch in case Diana wakes, and I'll be right back."

He entered and took a long breath. "It seems breakfast is on the stove."

"*Yah*, and almost ready to serve."

"Do you mind if I set the table and help get things ready?"

"Of course not, but you don't have to."

He shrugged as she left the porch steps to run down Fords Bush Road toward the greenhouse.

If anyone from the King house happened to look out a window, they might wonder why she was hurrying along so early to the greenhouse—but what did their opinion matter at the moment? Serving Joseph and Ben breakfast was the important thing. Perhaps the simple gesture would help heal the pain in both of their hearts. Something must be done.

Esther ran across the greenhouse driveway and found Ben sitting on the living room couch. His hair was still mussed, and he had sleep in his eyes. "Hello, Ben. You're invited to breakfast this morning."

His eyes grew large. "Where is *Daett*?"

"He came up to my house to tell me something, and I invited him to stay. He's up there right now in my kitchen, so let's get back before he burns down the place."

Ben grinned and followed her out the door. They made their way at a slower pace back up the hill.

"How are things going for you?"

"Real *goot*. *Daett* has always done a great job of taking care of me."

"I'm sure he has," she said, tousling his hair. "You're getting to be a big boy, Ben." He objected with a shake of his head, and then he ran his fingers through his hair for a comb.

No one peered out of the Kings' windows as they passed. In her mind's eye, she could still see Peter's and Edna's faces as they scrutinized her that day from Dorrine's front porch. The memory sent a shiver up her back.

"What's for breakfast?" Ben asked.

"Bacon, eggs, oatmeal, and toast."

His face glowed. "That's a real breakfast."

"And I'll be making pancakes to finish things off, now that you have come."

"You will?"

"*Yah*, Ben, I will. When did you last have pancakes?"

"I don't know. It's been a long time."

"Then we'll have to make them this morning for sure," she said, holding the front door open for him.

Diana was seated on a kitchen chair with her arms propped on the table. The cast was banging on the top as she chatted with Joseph.

"Back they are!" Joseph proclaimed, taking the plate of eggs and bacon from the stove top where he had been keeping them warm.

"Yep," Esther chirped. "Now sit down and let's give thanks. Then you all can eat while I stir up some pancakes."

"You are making pancakes? I don't know if—"

"Just sit and say grace. I'm making pancakes."

THIRTY-FOUR

More than two weeks later on a Wednesday afternoon, Esther held Diana's hand as the Greyhound bus pulled into the small town of Gap in Lancaster County. Both *Daett* and *Mamm* would be at the bus station to greet her and drive her home to the old place on Hoover Road. It was where she had spent her childhood and then left all those years ago to marry Lonnie, and here she would return to lick her wounds.

Somehow she must figure out how to recapture Isaiah's confidence in her. They hadn't spoken more than a few words since the horrible evening when Peter and Edna had humiliated him. Isaiah had said nothing about resuming their Friday evening suppers, and she had decided not to tell him about her trip to Gap. Dorrine had driven her to the bus station in Little Falls, full of sympathy for her state and breathing hopes that a break might be exactly what was needed.

Dorrine had stayed to wave goodbye to them as the huge bus carried them southward. Esther had never liked bus travel, and this trip hadn't improved her opinion. Thankfully, Diana hadn't seemed to mind. The little girl's interest was taken up by the small towns they had passed through and the foreign sights her young eyes had never seen before.

"We're almost there," Esther said, squeezing Diana's hand.

Diana didn't say anything, her eyes heavy with sleep.

The bus driver shifted gears—the engine whined slower now—and bounced the vehicle into the small station marked by the image of a stretched-out greyhound.

"Gap!" the driver hollered. "No time out here. That's coming up in Lancaster, where we stop for thirty minutes."

Esther took her daughter's hand and lurched into the aisle of the bus, making her way forward. The cast had come off Diana's arm last week, which was the main reason Esther had waited this long to make the trip. The idea had come to her that morning when Joseph and Ben had joined them for breakfast. The delay had also provided time for a letter to travel to her parents, who had responded that a visit would be greatly welcomed.

Esther helped Diana down the bus steps and collected their single suitcase from the luggage compartment. Diana waved first when *Mamm* and *Daett* appeared around the corner of the station. There was a hitching post for the Amish a block away, which was where her parents must have parked.

"Have a *goot* trip?" *Daett* called as he and *Mamm* approached. His gray beard was slung over his shoulder, his hat was firmly on his head, and a smile stretched across his face.

"Oh, Esther!" *Mamm* exclaimed, almost falling into Esther's arms. "It's so *goot* to see you again. It seems like years since we dropped you off in your new home, even though it's only been some months. I told *Daett* we ought to pay you a visit, and here your letter comes the very next day. We must have been thinking the same thing." *Mamm* let go of Esther to embrace Diana. "How are you, little darling? My, you have grown. How is that arm of yours?" *Mamm* conducted a long inspection as Esther shook her *daett*'s hand.

"*Goot* to be home," she said, wishing she could fly into his arms. But she was a grown woman now, no longer a little girl. She was also in the middle of a major effort to become sensible and sane again. A flood of tears was exactly what she *didn't* need.

"Are you okay?" he asked, tickling her chin the way he used to when she was a girl.

"Oh, *Daett*...I'm doing the best I can," she said, tears beginning to form.

He pulled her close even as she muttered protests. "You're still my little girl," he whispered. "Even though you're all grown up and a *mamm* yourself, I think you still need a loving *daett*." He held her at arm's length. "You look well, Esther."

"I wish I was as well as I look," she choked. "Oh, *Daett*, you don't know how I've messed up everything."

The words came out in a wail, and several *Englisha* people who had come off the bus glanced in her direction.

Daett appeared concerned. "What's wrong, Esther? Is there some other reason for your sudden visit home—other than what you've told us?"

"*Yah*," she admitted. "But I'll tell you everything once we're in the buggy." Esther grasped her suitcase, but *Daett* took it from her. With Diana's hand in *Mamm*'s, they made their way up the street to where *Daett*'s horse, Westby, was tied.

Daett put the suitcase in the back of the buggy, and they all climbed in. A few moments later, they were clattering out of Gap toward Hoover Road. *Mamm* sat in the back with Diana, and Esther sat in front with *Daett*. The whole story spilled out in bits and pieces—about those first days after they left her in the beautiful valley below the Adirondacks, her subsequent contact with Isaiah, and the confirmation that the Lord was on her side. Then came Joseph and his story of Silvia, the *Englisha* woman who had loved him so greatly in spite of his lame foot and his strange ways. Finally, Esther confessed how she had embarrassed Isaiah and failed in her attempt to bring Joseph and Arlene together. *Daett* and *Mamm* listened until the end without comment.

"Isaiah is still humiliated beyond belief," Esther said. "I don't know how to make things right."

"Now, now," *Daett* said. "It can't be that bad."

"But it is!"

Mamm leaned up from the backseat to slip an arm around Esther's shoulder. "Just calm down, dear. There's nothing that a few days at home won't fix. We'll think of something."

"Like what? There is nothing to think of." Esther covered her face and groaned.

"What's wrong with *Mamm*?" Diana asked.

"See, you're scaring the child," *Mamm* chided.

Esther turned to face Diana. "I'm sorry, dear heart. It's just that... being home where I was once a little girl makes me feel like the little child I really am on the inside."

"That will make no sense to her," *Mamm* said, smiling at her granddaughter. "We'll go out to the barn and look at the new baby pigs when we get home. Do you remember that we have pigs?"

Diana appeared skeptical but still nodded. "I want to see them."

"They are all pink and wiggly and cute," *Mamm* cooed.

A smile grew on Diana's face, and Esther turned her attention back to *Daett*. "What do you think is to become of me?"

Daett grunted. "You're a big girl, Esther. You were the *frau* of a minister, and both of you were well liked in the community. There's no reason things won't be the same again in the valley."

Esther kept her voice low. "That's what my plans were! But don't you understand all that happened, *Daett*? You should have seen Isaiah on Sunday as he was preaching. I have broken him and shamed him."

"He'll be okay, Esther. Isaiah's a decent man from what I know of him, and he'll be fine. You did the right thing in coming here to rest and recover. Take whatever time you need. There's no sense in rushing back. In the meantime, the whole family will be at our place tonight for a big supper. *Mamm* has been doing nothing but rushing to the bulk food store and cooking up a storm the past few days. I can hardly set foot inside the house without being sent off for an errand somewhere."

"Oh, you poor thing," she said soothingly, and then they laughed together.

Esther exhaled as they turned down Hoover Road from Highway 30. "Thank you so much for letting me come home, *Daett*. You had to know I was running from something, yet you are only kind to me." Her tears threatened again, and Esther gave his arm a quick squeeze. "Thank you for being here for your little girl."

"You are very welcome." *Daett* smiled down at her, and his eyes twinkled as he brought the buggy to a stop by the barn. "That wedding date with Isaiah will be coming off just fine, I'm thinking, and I'll be getting to see that *wunderbah* valley of yours again."

"And *wunderbah* Isaiah," Esther said as she jumped down. "I think I've truly fallen in love with him now."

Mamm climbed down more slowly and headed for the barn with her granddaughter as Esther undid the tugs on her side.

"So you did fall in love with him?" *Daett* asked over Westby's back.

"*Yah*," Esther said, feeling her cheeks grow warm. "But now I feel a little guilty for not telling him I was coming home."

"Perhaps you should have. But if he loves you, he'll understand."

Esther made a face. "I feel as if we're doing this backward. What usually seems to happen is that people fall deeply in love the first time and then settle the second time around. But I don't think I settled in my first marriage. I was quite happy with Lonnie and he was with me—at least, he never said otherwise. But Isaiah...oh, my. We had best not go there. I'm trying to get my thinking straight."

"Maybe you shouldn't?"

"What? Not get my thinking straight?"

"*Yah*." *Daett* chuckled. "Trying to fall out of love may be a little difficult, and I suppose Isaiah is having the same problem."

"Then what am I to do, *Daett*?"

"That's what you're here to find out," he said with a smile before leading Westby into the barn.

How could *Daett* be so lighthearted and sure that everything would turn out okay? Isaiah had kept his distance since the disastrous evening, and she had left the valley without a word to him. How did couples survive such separations?

She wasn't unscathed, but she was still in love. Coming back here had driven that truth home. Her heart pounded at the thought of Isaiah and his wildflowers. When she had kissed him that evening for the first time and held him close, she knew she was in love. There was no question there.

She sighed and entered the house by the familiar front door. She smelled something delicious, and tears stung as she walked to the stove and lifted the lid on the scalloped potatoes. This was a staple from home, and she had always made Lonnie scalloped potatoes over the more traditional mashed potatoes Isaiah preferred. He'd never said anything, but somehow she'd known he loved mashed potatoes. She couldn't remember how. Had she overheard some conversation from his sisters in those long ago *rumspringa* days? Or perhaps his *mamm* had said something on the few visits she had made to the Mast home after her marriage to Lonnie? She didn't know how she knew. She'd just known.

How much easier things had been with Lonnie. Here in this living room, her relationship with her first husband had begun. They had enjoyed long talks on Sunday evenings after the hymn singing. Was this where she wished to return? Was this what she wanted with Isaiah when their relationship resumed?

"Confound it," Esther muttered. "I am really confused."

THIRTY-FIVE

Isaiah paced the floor of the small makeshift greenhouse behind his barn. The few rose plants he had left sat on the small table, their blossoms dull and lifeless. He should at least water them. The last time he had splashed a few drops on the roots was last week before his pitcher ran dry. That was the day Esther chose to visit her parents in Lancaster County without a word to him. Not that he blamed Esther for her sudden trip. He'd conducted himself shamefully since the night of his great embarrassment. His pride had been injured deeply, but that was no excuse.

The flower minister! Even Bishop Willis had chuckled over that one, along with the community's young men. Isaiah glared at the roses as if they were to blame. He was not used to laughter at his expense. His courtship with Mandy had included none of this upheaval and turmoil, and neither had his marriage. Isaiah clenched his teeth. In spite of his embarrassment, he had to get up in front of the congregation to preach at the services, all while sly grins played on the faces of the unmarried men.

At least the community members had been sober faced this past Sunday. Everyone knew that Esther had gone back to Lancaster County for a visit, and that the reasons ran deeper than connecting with her parents. In the end, the sympathies of the community lay with Esther and Isaiah in spite of their chuckles over his initial plight.

He had thought that all of this would blow over. He and Esther were both mature people, and they would settle this mess eventually. In the meantime, he needed action and a decision on what should be done about these roses.

But what? That was the whole problem. At heart Esther and he were both practical, down-to-earth, no-nonsense people who had been caught up in this foolish rose business. He ought to throw these rose pots out and bury the plants behind the barn where they would be out of sight and mind. Only they wouldn't be. The damage had been done. He would forever remember that he had honestly enjoyed the journey of romance he had embarked upon with Esther.

Now that road lay pothole filled and rock strewn in front of him. They had best turn back. But how? He'd wanted to visit Esther these past weeks, but his cheeks had burned with shame at the thought. He'd avoided the sorrow in her eyes on Sundays, except for the few times they had passed each other in a crowded room and whispered a few words. He had tried to smile, the effort feeble, though Esther had smiled back.

He was in love with her. There was no question about that. Heart pounding in love with her. Sweaty palms kind of love. Mandy had been a beautiful woman, and he had loved her, but not like this. With Mandy there had been no roses and no embarrassment.

Isaiah gritted his teeth. He really should have thrown out the half-finished bottle of rose oil the first evening he came home from Esther's place after his humiliation. His fingers had closed often around the neck of the bottle, but he had always stopped himself from tossing it aside.

Esther's face would rise in front of his mind in those moments. The sweet tenderness in her eyes, the softness in her face, the way she set the dishes on the kitchen table on Friday evenings. The woman had a grace and a wonder about her, a specialness that drew him. Did he want to lose that? Maybe he wouldn't have to. Maybe they could go back to what had been before. Was it possible?

Isaiah glared at the roses. They seemed to smile up at him even in their drooped state, as if they knew something he didn't. Things had to be made right between him and Esther. Isaiah fixed an even sterner glare at the plants. "I will not be losing my mind completely," he told them.

Oh, great. Now *he* was talking to roses. Isaiah grabbed a pitcher and addressed them again. "Okay, you win. At least for now. I'll water you. Are you happy?"

He hurried outside without waiting for an answer. He was losing his mind, but what was new about that? He had been losing his mind since the roses entered his life—since that first time Diana had taken him to see her roses along the split rail fence. That seemed far away and distant, as if it had happened to another man. But he knew better. He had learned to not only love Esther deeply, but also Esther's daughter.

Isaiah plunged the pitcher into the horse trough and returned to the greenhouse to dash water on the plants. "You could say thank you," he muttered, hurrying to the next pot. He stopped at the last one to study its petals. The water would soon bring life to the drooping plants, and the blossoms would regain their glow. He could use them to extract their scent and continue his project.

But did he want to? Wouldn't the easier path be to turn back and allow events to take care of themselves? Yet...he'd lived that way after Mandy passed, and look what had happened. Esther had moved to the community to marry him. There was no other way to say it, and he had been honored, if the truth were known. The whole community had seen the rightness of Esther's move and understood how the Lord had led her to him.

Esther would soon be back. She couldn't stay away forever, and Esther wouldn't move back to Lancaster County. She wouldn't break their engagement unless he did—which he had no intention of doing. Esther would marry him this fall and be the dutiful *frau* he had originally wanted. They would forget roses and bouquets and bows and arrows. How foolish that had all been. Even Diana would get over her exuberance once her arm was fully healed. Things would return to normal.

"*Yah*, they will," Isaiah said to his roses. "Stop arguing with me."

But he was arguing with himself. That was the problem. He didn't want to return to the way things had been. Mandy had been a *wunderbah frau*, but the Lord had taken her. He had a chance for live a new life with Esther—a life rough and scattered with the rocks of embarrassment that had tripped him up, but one of forgiveness. She probably would forgive him even if he didn't ask. All he had to do was show up at her house once she returned from Lancaster County and mutter a few words about how he was ready to carry on.

And could he come on Friday evenings for supper?

Diana would hop up on his lap and Esther would smile, but her eyes would be sad, and so would his. They would always know that life had offered them more, that they could have grown beyond the hurt, if only he had the courage to continue the journey. And Diana? The girl would never understand what had happened to him. If the accident hadn't occurred to occupy her mind, the hurt of misunderstanding over his continued absence might already have caused irreparable damage. That must be why Esther had made the trip to Lancaster County. This was Esther's last effort before the bridge collapsed completely between them.

Yah, Esther would still wed him, but the glimpses they had been given of each other's hearts would withdraw. Perhaps forever.

Isaiah stomped over to the barn window and looked out. He needed to work on his project today. That was the truth. He needed to tie on an apron and face the embarrassment head-on. He could practice alone in his kitchen, cooking oils to extract rose scents from petals. But if anyone saw him wearing an apron and bending over rose petals on his stove, he would never want to leave the house again. But they wouldn't see him if he locked the doors, pulled the drapes, and—

Isaiah stopped himself. This had to end. This *wunderbah* new life he had been given with Esther was worth a few chuckles from the community people. He could live down his new nickname, the "flower minister." That would all go away after the wedding once he said the vows with Esther and she was his *frau*. Let them laugh. Esther was a woman worth almost anything, and more than that, their love—which had blossomed like roses when watered—was worth much more.

He would drive to Joseph's greenhouse today and purchase a few more rose pots, and if anyone saw him, he would smile and wave and comfort himself by imagining the joy in Esther's face once he gave her the scented rose oil on their wedding night. He couldn't grow roses the way Joseph could, but he could extract the scent from rose blossoms. And if he was the only Amish minister in the whole world who set about to accomplish such a foolish thing, then so be it. He was the only Amish minister who would wed Esther. That was enough of an answer to satisfy him.

Isaiah jerked open the back barn door and whistled to Echo.

The horse came at a trot, and ten minutes later they were going up Highway 5 at a fast trot. He wouldn't even bother with the southern approach. Esther wasn't at home, and right now he didn't care who saw him.

"Whoa there," Isaiah called out as he pulled into Joseph's greenhouse driveway with a flourish.

Joseph appeared in the doorway with a puzzled look.

"*Yah*, I know," Isaiah said as he hopped down and tied Echo to the hitching post.

"And a *goot* morning to you," Joseph responded, his smile uncertain. "What brings you out?"

Isaiah wrinkled up his face. "What do you think the flower minister wants?"

Joseph chuckled. "I'm sorry about that, but it is a little funny, don't you think? Who would have thought only a few months ago that—"

"You can stop it," Isaiah ordered, and Joseph's chuckle deepened.

"So what are you going to do about *your* problems?" Isaiah shot back. "Both of our girlfriends are in Lancaster County, it seems."

Joseph sobered. "Maybe we should solve our problems together."

"I doubt if I can do much about Peter. But you could help me by selling me a few more pots of roses."

"That sounds like digging oneself in deeper to me."

"Maybe, but the tunnel might also lead to the sunlight on the other side of the hill."

Joseph laughed. "Now I believe all the rumors I heard. You are the poetic flower minister."

"Hush," Isaiah warned, but he soon joined in the laughter.

Minutes later six pots of roses were sitting in the back of Isaiah's buggy.

"Are you going to visit Esther in Lancaster County?" Joseph asked as they closed the buggy flap.

"I suppose I will. That would be the thing to do, I guess."

"I'm leaving tomorrow with a hired driver," Joseph told him. "Want a ride?"

Isaiah shook his head. "Thanks, but we'd best do this our own way. Don't you think?"

"You're probably right."

"Are you going to try to win Arlene's parents over?"

Joseph grinned. "*Yah*, I am."

"That sounds downright dangerous if you ask me."

"And this isn't?" Joseph motioned toward the back of the buggy with his beard. "Cooking roses in an Amish minister's kitchen?"

"We will say no more about that," Isaiah said as he jiggled Echo's reins. "I'm trusting you to keep your mouth shut."

"The same goes for you if you hear things about my trip," Joseph called after him.

Isaiah managed to smile and wave out of the buggy door. What had they gotten themselves into? But he couldn't imagine that Joseph would do anything worse than he had done by making homemade rose oil on his kitchen stove. Some might say this was silly and beneath his dignity...only it wasn't. This was how it really should be between a man and his intended *frau*.

Isaiah comforted himself with that thought.

THIRTY-SIX

The following day, Joseph directed his *Englisha* hired driver, young Ralph Wilson, with a toss of his beard. "Down that road is where I'm headed."

Ralph made the turn with a smile on his face. "You still haven't told me what this trip is all about, or what it has to do with what we're carrying in the back. You didn't come all this way to sell vegetables."

"I come bearing gifts."

Ralph shook his head and smiled.

Joseph had carefully wrapped the choicest offerings of his greenhouse in wooden crates yesterday for the journey south to Lancaster County, but he also had other gifts he was bringing that Ralph didn't know about.

"I'm hoping for a decent reception, at least," Joseph continued.

"Do you want me to wait until you know whether you're staying before I head into Gap for a motel tonight?"

Joseph cleared his throat. "I'll need a ride for later because I'm going down to my folks' place for the night in Southern Lancaster County, so let's say..." He thought for a moment. "I'll take the risk that I'll be invited for supper. Let's make it eight o'clock that you pick me back up."

"I'm yours to command." Ralph grinned. "Eight o'clock it will be."

"Thanks." Joseph managed a smile.

Now that he was here, his whole body was tense. His plan had seemed so foolproof back in the valley, but now...what if Peter ordered him off the place on the spot? He would have to depend on Ralph's presence to prevent any overt hostility, such as shouting. After that, Joseph hoped he would have a few hours to make his case. Even if he had to sit outside on the front porch and speak through the living room window, he was determined he would have his say.

The truck bounced onto Peter and Edna's driveway on Mentzer Road. The house's paint was peeling in places, and the barn was equally shabby. The front porch leaned on its pillars, with the posts crooked above them. He hadn't expected such obvious signs of poverty, but he had known from Arlene that Peter's financial situation wasn't *goot*. Why this was so, he didn't know, although Peter didn't strike him as a man given too much common sense—which was necessary in the management of a prosperous business. Why else had Peter and Edna reacted so irrationally in removing their daughter from the valley?

"Here we are," Ralph announced as he brought the pickup to a stop by the barn. "Shall I help you unload?"

"Perhaps that would be a *goot* idea."

Chills ran up and down Joseph's back. What if he was wrong in his calculation? He had chuckled over Isaiah's discomfort with his roses, but this had the potential of being a real disaster. He would never live this down if Peter sent him packing before he could even unload his vegetables.

"Let's set the boxes in the yard," Joseph decided, pushing open

his door. He shuffled toward the back of the truck and dropped
the tailgate. Then he lifted the first crate. He almost lost control of
it, but he managed to lower the box with some measure of dignity.
Ralph didn't seem to notice as he unloaded two more and Joseph
grabbed another one. They soon had them all on the ground, and
there was still no sign of anyone in the yard or on the front porch.

Ralph glanced around with a face full of questions.

"I'll see you at eight," Joseph told him.

Ralph shrugged and climbed in to drive off. Joseph caught his
breath and tried to order his thoughts, but maybe a prepared speech
was not for the best. Better to rely on his instincts, as there was no
way to know how Peter would react to his arrival.

The front door opened, and Arlene stepped out onto the sagging
porch, only to gasp and dash back inside.

"Well, that's a *goot* start," Joseph muttered to himself.

If Peter wasn't at home, maybe he could make his case with
Edna...but then again, that might not be wise. Peter would be
affronted by the obvious maneuvering around him, and he'd never
get the man to see the light of day.

Joseph turned and shuffled toward the barn. Peter had to be out
here and was likely ignoring him. Maybe he was waiting for him to
go away, or perhaps Peter was in shock that he had dared show up
after having his promised one removed so abruptly from the valley.

Joseph pushed open the barn door and hollered, "*Goot* evening.
Anybody home?"

The only answer was the thump of an animal in its stall and the
distant bray of a mule in the barnyard. Joseph shuffled on in and
peered out of the back barnyard door. There was still no sign of
Peter. A small building stood off from the barn that was even more
ramshackle than the rest. Joseph headed across the barnyard, but
he stopped when the small door jerked open.

Peter appeared with his hat pushed back on his head and a block of salt in both arms. He stopped short and stared.

"Hello, Peter," Joseph greeted him. "Can I help?"

Peter dropped the block of salt with a start.

"Let me carry that." Joseph came closer and bent down to pick up the block. "Where are we going?"

"To the pasture." Peter gestured, apparently dumbstruck. Seconds later he seemed to recover himself and grabbed the block of salt from Joseph's hands. "What in the world are you doing here? Thinking to charm me by helping with the chores?" Peter's laugh was harsh. "Even that should be beneath you, Joseph. I told you to stay away, but apparently you can't even follow simple instructions." Peter hurled the block across the pasture fence and turned to face Joseph. "But I can understand that in a way. Arlene is quite a catch, as I've been telling her since we came back to Lancaster from that valley of yours. She'll have no problem finding a husband in the community. So now you've showed up and confirmed this exact point. For this I thank you, but nothing else. Now go, Joseph, before Arlene sees you and you cause a scene."

"She already has seen me," Joseph said, regarding the man. "She ran back into the house."

A pleased look crossed Peter's face. "I see the girl has some sense, and there's your answer in case you don't believe me."

"I believe she was quite happy to see me," Joseph ventured. "She didn't talk to me, but she wants to. Look, Peter, we have to make peace somehow. I want to wed Arlene, and she wants to wed me. I want to love a woman again the best I can, and Arlene wants to be that *frau*, so let's talk."

"There is no use talking," Peter snapped. "Not with you or that flower minister of yours. What a joke your community has become!

And now is this one of your romantic gestures, coming all the way to Lancaster County to woo my daughter? Well, you've wasted your time. That's just all there is to it."

"I don't think I have wasted my time," Joseph said. "Come see what I brought along. It's in the front yard, and it's just the beginning."

Joseph didn't wait for a response. He shuffled across the barnyard and back into the barn. Peter's footsteps followed behind him and out through the barn door. "There." Joseph gestured toward the crates.

Peter laughed. "What is this? Vegetables from your greenhouse? Are you expecting me to help you finally make a profit?"

Joseph pressed his lips together for a second. "They are for you and Edna, Peter. A gift."

"For a bride!" Peter laughed even louder. "Do you expect to trade a few crates of vegetables for my daughter?"

"No." Joseph fixed his gaze on the man's face. "But I expect to show you that I'd be a son-in-law you would do well not to reject. I'm talking your language now, Peter, since apparently you can't understand anything else."

Peter huffed. "So you can afford to give away a few vegetables to impress me. Well, I'm not impressed. I can raise my own vegetables."

Joseph glanced at the weed-choked garden. "*Yah*, I can see that."

Peter shrugged. "Edna's a little behind this year, but she'll catch up soon."

"Then my offering is just in time."

"It won't change my mind about you." Peter glared at Joseph. "You're not a worthy son-in-law just because you can grow vegetables. Everyone can do some things, and this trade of yours was learned from your *Englisha frau*. Was it not?" Peter's glare grew fiercer. "I have half a mind to throw these crates and you back out on the road, Joseph. What are you thinking anyway? Bringing your *Englisha* stuff here?"

"Can we go inside and talk?"

"Into the house? Of course not. You plan to charm Arlene even further and make more problems for her."

"Maybe I should just take Arlene with me and marry her down at the courthouse," Joseph muttered.

"What blasphemy!" Peter exclaimed. "I knew you were up to no *goot.*"

Joseph grinned. "Control yourself, Peter. Let's go back to the barn and talk there. I want to show you something." Joseph reached inside his coat pocket and pulled out a sheaf of papers. "These are my financial statements."

"What *goot* does that do me?" Peter barked, but he followed Joseph into the barn.

"Just look at these," Joseph said once they were inside. "My accountant prepared them in layman's language, but I also have the actual bank statements if you wish to dig deeper."

Peter's lips moved as his gaze settled on the first page. "Income of the year..." Peter's eyes grew larger and soon bulged. "This is income from your greenhouse?"

"*Yah*. Those figures were for last year, and I'm doing even better this year. That's all on the next page, and who knows where this will go if Silvia's Rose wins an award? That flower is fixing to make me an awful lot of money, Peter. Your daughter could be part of that. And even more, *you* could be part of that. As a gesture of *goot* faith, my accountant has written out a check in your name, which is attached to the back there. You are welcome to cash the check whether you agree to my proposition or not, but I think you should seriously consider me as the best prospect that Arlene will ever have in a husband. At least the best one you will see offered to her. I am not a poor man. Perhaps you hadn't realized that. As your son-in-law, I will see that Arlene is well taken care of, and that in your old age you and Edna will not suffer from lack of funds."

"You would *buy* Arlene's favor?" The papers trembled in Peter's hand.

"No. I already have that," Joseph told him. "I'm sure you know this. What I want is your blessing and approval on our marriage. I'm sure this mistake in not asking about my income was simply an oversight on your part when you came to investigate my marriage proposal. I take full responsibility for this oversight and seek only to correct what I have overlooked in providing you with proof of my ability to support Arlene."

Peter stared at the pages. "These are truly huge sums of money. Are you sure they are yours?"

"The bank statements are right there," Joseph assured him.

Peter turned the pages, but nothing registered from the look on his face.

"You are welcome to have this checked out in any way you wish," Joseph said.

"I...I certainly will."

"And do cash the check," Joseph said. "The money is yours with no strings. There is more where that came from. In the meantime, I would like to see your daughter and eat supper with you. I'm hoping Edna won't mind...and I'm quite sure Arlene won't. If I can't stay to eat, I would at least like to talk to Arlene. We have much to catch up on. And the wedding will be in a month, Peter. I'm not waiting around any longer. This issue must be resolved speedily."

Peter appeared speechless, but eventually he repeated, "This is an awful lot of money."

"*Yah*, it is. So will you go tell Arlene you've changed your mind and that we can wed? I'll begin moving the crates inside the barn if that's where you want them."

Peter nodded, but he seemed dumbfounded as he headed across the yard toward the house.

"I hope he can talk when he gets inside," Joseph muttered.

Goose bumps broke out on Joseph's arms as Peter neared the house. He had won, but now that the contest was over, his nerve failed him. This was so unlike him—this boldness, this brashness, this flaunting of money. But he had to win Arlene back. He simply had to, and he suspected this was the only way.

Joseph picked up a crate and shuffled toward the barn. He picked a spot off to the side and lowered the crate to the ground. He made another trip, and on the third round he stopped when a cry came from the front porch. Joseph lowered the crate to the ground near the barn door as Arlene raced across the yard. He opened his arms, and she flew into them.

"Oh, Joseph," she said, sobbing. "I thought I had lost you. I thought I would die. But you came. You *came* for me and persuaded *Daett*..."

Joseph held her tight. "It's okay now. We'll be wed next month. Everything will be okay now."

"Next month?" Her mouth dropped open. "Next *month*?"

"*Yah*." He smiled. "We have lots of planning to do."

She said nothing, but her eyes filled with tears as she launched herself at him again.

THIRTY-SEVEN

Esther stepped out on the porch early on Saturday morning with a warm cup of cocoa in her hand. The swing squeaked under her as she seated herself. She should have draped a shawl over her shoulders, but the breeze stirring across the porch floor still had a touch of summer in its caress. That would soon change here in Lancaster County, and even sooner in the valley at the foothills of the Adirondacks. Wedding season was not even two months away, and she was still here at her parents' home.

Esther swung gently, her feet pushing against the porch floor. What was to happen to her and Isaiah? The wedding date was set, but no further plans had been made. Perhaps she should be angry with him for how he had acted these past weeks. Perhaps she shouldn't even love him...but about that, *Daett* was right. One did not easily fall out of love.

The front door opened, and *Mamm* peeked out. "Oh, here you are."

"*Yah.*" Esther smiled. "Catching the wonderful summer breeze."

"Mind if I join you?"

"Of course not. Shall I make a cup of hot chocolate for you?"

Mamm smiled. "No, I'll make it myself and be right back. Don't go anywhere!"

The swing squeaked softly under Esther as she waited for *Mamm* to return. This is where she had come during her teenage years to enjoy the summer evenings. Her sisters had often joined her, but none of them had been given to deep introspections—just light chatter about their day and plans for the morning. They had always been a practical family, and she still was practical. Surely her practical brain would soon find an answer to her problem.

Mamm returned with a cup clasped in her hands and seated herself beside Esther. "I suppose you're thinking about Isaiah," *Mamm* mused.

"*Yah*, and wondering what I'm supposed to do."

"There's only one thing to do, dear. You've had some time away now, and you should go back to the valley and tell Isaiah you're ready to be the kind of *frau* I know you're capable of being. Forget about this romance business. I didn't raise my daughters to go flying around the countryside in pursuit of flowers. Why, I imagine before long even Arlene's parents will forget about Isaiah's bouquets and so will everyone else. Joseph might even get to wed Arlene once the dust has settled."

"But—"

"No buts, Esther. What's done is done. Go back to the valley next week, speak with Isaiah, and shut your house down for the winter. Then come back here where we can help plan the wedding. There's only a little over a month left—unless you want to have the wedding at the end of November instead of October."

"No, as soon as possible," Esther told her. "And that is the sensible thing to do. I'm sure Isaiah will agree, and yet...I don't know, *Mamm*. Are you sure?"

"I'm sure, *yah*. But you need to be sure too. The first step is for you to go back and see Isaiah. Straighten things out."

"I suppose you're right," Esther allowed.

Mamm glanced toward the driveway, and then she stood to get a closer look. "Someone's coming in an *Englisha* automobile."

Esther stood as well and looked to the car now pulling to a stop. "It's Isaiah!"

Mamm gasped. "Esther, you must act decent. You must do the right thing."

Esther reached for her mother's hand.

"Welcome him into the house," *Mamm* said. "I'll be going inside now."

"Send Diana out when she wakes up," Esther called after *Mamm*, who gave her a sharp look before retreateing inside. Esther's heart beat faster as Isaiah's familiar form came out of the car and bent near the car door to pay the driver.

The car left, and Isaiah studied her on the front porch for a moment before he left his suitcase on the lawn and came toward her.

He paused at the bottom of the porch steps. "*Goot* morning, Esther. I see you're up and enjoying the summer air."

"*Yah*," she replied awkwardly.

"Shall we sit?"

"*Yah*."

The swing squeaked again as she sat beside him. She gave him a smile. "I wasn't expecting you."

"I wasn't expecting to come," he replied. "But things happen, I suppose. I'm here to…" His voice trailed off.

She waited in silence.

"You don't seem upset to see me," he said.

"Should I be?"

"I don't know. I suppose you have *goot* reason to be upset with the way I've been behaving myself."

She glanced away. "You know it was my fault, Isaiah. I'm sorry for what happened. I can't imagine how you must have felt, and yet you went on preaching each Sunday. I don't know what to say. I guess I came home to try to—"

"You don't need to explain yourself, Esther," he said earnestly, interrupting her. "I don't blame you. I..." He reached for her hand. "May I?"

"Isaiah, my hand is yours whenever you wish to hold it."

"Please forgive me. I acted childishly when my feelings were hurt, and it was rude of me to stop coming to your house for supper without any explanation. I can't imagine why you're even talking to me."

"You know why. It's the same reason you're here. We belong together. I've come to see that in the time I've been here."

He took a deep breath. "You know I love you, Esther, even more than I did before. But I still want to say it. You are a jewel, a woman among the—"

"Isaiah, please," Esther begged. "Someone will hear us."

"I don't care what people think!" he declared. "For you, I'd even carry bouquets into the house right in front of Peter and Edna."

Esther tried to suppress a giggle. "That won't be necessary."

His hand moved in hers. "Necessary or not, I should have brought roses."

"You should not have!"

"I should have."

Esther's giggle escaped her. "Are we going around this all morning? I should be offering you hot chocolate. *Mamm* will think I have lost all of my manners."

"You are a jewel," he said again. "The hot chocolate can wait. I love you, Esther."

"If you don't stop, I'll be kissing you right out here on my parents' front porch," Esther warned.

He grinned. "We can't have that, can we?"

"But I will once we're—" She stopped as her face flamed.

"To the future then. And to the unknown." He faked a shiver.

Esther squeezed his hand. "Is it that bad?"

"Oh, every bit. I'm scared to death."

"You are not, Isaiah. I know better. I'm nothing to be afraid of."

"Maybe not, but I have a feeling life with you will be very interesting."

"So the wedding is still on?"

"Of course. Would I have come all the way to Lancaster County if the wedding was off?"

"I want to be married in the valley."

"Not here, as is tradition?"

"No. This won't be our home."

"I have no objections if your parents don't."

"They will do what I say," she assured him.

"Let's begin the plans, then."

He was holding her hand when the front door burst open and Diana raced out. Isaiah let go of his intended to open his arms, and Diana flew into them. Esther pressed back her tears as her daughter clung to Isaiah as if she would never let go. Before long those arms would be around her, and she would never let go either.

THIRTY-EIGHT

On Sunday morning, Esther was sitting on a bench in Minister Emil's home where the service was held that day in Lancaster County. Diana sat beside her, her eyes fixed on Isaiah's face as he preached. Never had Esther seen him preach better or with more confidence.

"Abraham told his servant to leave the country where his tribe lived and to return to familiar lands from where they had come to find a *frau* for his young son, Isaac," Isaiah proclaimed. "The servant obeyed, and the journey began. A virtuous woman is a delight in the eyes of the Lord, and worthy is any effort we make to search her out. Things do not just happen by themselves. Goodness does not grow on trees. It takes prayer, desiring the Lord's will, and courage on our part to stand for what is right. If we wish the next generation to maintain the truth, we must ourselves seek it out."

Esther drew a deep breath. Isaiah had the main sermon as the visiting minister, and if Bishop Beiler from the local district knew about the story of the flower bouquets or Isaiah's nickname as the "flower minister," none of that showed on the bishop's face. The man sat on the minister's bench, nodding his approval of the sermon, with his full white beard flowing halfway down his chest.

She had always adored Bishop Beiler. Today she could have given the old bishop a kiss on the cheek. Being asked to give the sermon was exactly what Isaiah had needed—approval and acceptance from church leadership away from the chuckles and snickers at home. In time Isaiah would grow stronger. His trip to Lancaster County had achieved its goal...and the time they had spent together yesterday planning their wedding had been most productive.

There was nothing wrong with romance and flower bouquets. Isaiah might flinch when the subject was raised once they returned to the valley, but he would recover. He might even bring her flowers sometime in the future, maybe even for their wedding anniversary once in a while. Roses would be a reminder of how things had begun for them and always would be. They were in love, the type of love usually experienced by youngsters. It was *wunderbah*.

Now, all was well. *Mamm* had agreed without much fuss to a wedding in the valley. Isaiah had winked at her when the discussion went off without a hitch.

Esther pulled Diana closer. Isaiah had never really considered cutting off their engagement. Nor had she. Likely this was because of their mutual practicality and maturity, which proved that all things played their part somewhere, as the Lord no doubt intended.

Esther focused on Isaiah as he reached the height of his story. "Now Abraham's servant prayed again to the Lord and decided on a test. The woman who would offer to draw water not only for the servant but also for the servant's camels would be the woman the Lord had chosen for Isaac's *frau*." Isaiah paused to smile. "From this part of the story we often draw the lesson that love is only hard work and dedication to the task, but love is much more than duty and devotion to one another. Love is a *wunderbah* thing that the Lord has given a man and a woman who are promised to each other in the holy vows of marriage. We chuckle sometimes at our youth when they speak of falling in love, but they have a point." Isaiah paused to sweep the room with his gaze as if he expected a challenge.

Bishop Beiler smiled broadly, and Isaiah continued. "It would do us all well to keep a little romance alive between our spouses and ourselves. As you all know, I lost my *frau* Mandy some years ago, but the Lord has chosen to grace my life again with another hope... which explains why I'm here visiting Lancaster County instead of staying at home today in our settlement in the valley."

Chuckles rippled through the audience, and Isaiah hurried on. "May the Lord bless all of us who seek a righteous spouse, and for those of you who are married, my counsel is that love—like a rose— does not flourish by itself. You must nurture your love by praying and sharing your time and heart with each other. Love is a *wunderbah* thing when it is lived in the will of the Lord."

Esther felt her face flush when several of the women glanced her way, but she didn't mind. Isaiah had suffered much worse in the valley, and he would suffer again when they returned. But it was worth the embarrassment, and perhaps his words today would encourage one of the Lancaster men to hold his relationship with his *frau* in higher esteem. Who would have thought that Isaiah would say this and bless others with his words? Indeed, he was a minister worthy of her love and respect.

Isaiah concluded his remarks and took his seat as the testimonies were given. Bishop Beiler was last on the list and said with a big smile on his face, "It was *goot* to have Isaiah with us again this morning. I know he visited for reasons other than seeing us, but the Lord has chosen to bless many through the story of Isaac and Rebecca and their love. The Lord chooses to bless us still today when we see love blossoming in the hearts of our people. Many blessings on Isaiah and Esther as they continue to seek the Lord's will and join their lives as husband and wife."

Chuckles were heard again as the name of the closing song was given out. Esther kept her eyes on the page in the hymnal, and she lifted them only to sneak a look at Isaiah. He caught her glance and winked. She could have slapped him or kissed him—she wasn't sure which. But the more she saw of his handsome face and heard the sermons he preached, the happier she was that they had been granted the privilege of loving each other.

Esther squeezed back tears. Here she was crying over a man, and it wasn't even her wedding day. How things had changed. The song ended before she had composed herself, but no one seemed to notice her. The happy chatter began almost at once, as the women hurried into the kitchen to prepare the noon meal.

Bishop Beiler had planted an idea in her mind this morning with his kind ways. She would invite him to travel to the valley and marry them there. The bishop was older, but he still enjoyed trips to unfamiliar territories. Isaiah could ask him before he left, and from the look on Bishop Beiler's face during Isaiah's sermon, the man would be honored.

Isaiah would stay late again tonight. He hadn't left for his parents' place last night until after eleven in a buggy borrowed from *Daett*. Isaiah had been back this morning to pick her up for the drive to church, which hadn't been necessary, but he had insisted. He would return to the valley tomorrow. She wanted to accompany him back, but she wasn't quite ready. Another week in Lancaster County with the wedding coming up in October would be exactly what *Mamm* and she needed to make their plans.

Esther tried to keep her mind straight as she helped serve the married men's table. Her hands were full of peanut butter bowls and red beets and slabs of margarine on flat plates. Isaiah didn't help with his constant winks in her direction. What did he want? That she spill red beets all over the tablecloth? That was going to happen soon if he didn't stop teasing her.

She finally gave in and returned his smiles, shivers running up and down her back. This was becoming embarrassing. Esther emptied her hands, and with one last smile toward Isaiah, she slipped into the kitchen and stayed there. She couldn't risk more winks and smiles. She shook her head. Here he was, a bearded minister, and she, a minister's widow, acting like teenagers.

The first round of tables was soon finished, and Esther seated herself for the second serving. There were young people left who hadn't eaten, so there would be a third round served. Back in the valley, almost everyone made it to the first two servings on Sundays, but they were a smaller community, unlike the Lancaster County districts that were bulging at the seams.

Esther gave the young girl who served their table a smile and a quick greeting when she dropped off a fresh plate of sliced bread. "Hi, Barbara."

"Looks like you have made a perfect catch in that valley of yours," Barbara said, eliciting chuckles from the women within earshot.

"I think I have," Esther agreed without blushing. Maybe she had become accustomed to the feeling of falling in love.

"Well, the best to you," Barbara told her.

Esther nodded her thanks and grinned.

The meal concluded, and Esther helped with the dishes in the kitchen. She noticed Isaiah's broad back going out the front door toward the barn, so she slipped into the living room to collect Diana, but *Mamm* waved her away.

"You go with Isaiah. I want to spend some time with my granddaughter."

Esther gave in at once.

Diana gave her a quick hug before Esther left. That Diana didn't object was *goot*. It spoke of the security and stability she found in her extended family. They were together again, and Isaiah had spent considerable time with the child last night.

Esther returned to the kitchen and made her way through the mudroom, where she collected her shawl. She was at the end of the walk by the time Isaiah had *Daett's* spare driving horse out of the barn. Rather than wait, Esther hurried over to help him. Isaiah grinned when she approached the buggy.

"You can stop teasing me now," she scolded. "You had me turning all kinds of colors all day."

"But you're the sweetest thing when you change into multiple shades of red."

"Don't you forget you're a minister," she reminded him as she fastened the tugs on her side. "You should behave yourself."

"I don't think I can ever behave myself around you," he said with another wink.

"I'm getting in the buggy before I turn bright red and purple."

Isaiah tossed her the reins before he hopped up to settle on the seat. "Where's Diana?"

"Going home with *Mamm*."

"Grandma time."

"That was a *goot* sermon you gave."

He sobered. "In all honesty, Esther, I hope I didn't embarrass you too much, but those were things I wished to speak about. I know I'm clumsy at times, and that I get embarrassed easily, like I did with Peter and Edna, but—"

"You didn't have to say them because of me."

"I wanted to say them. For my own sake and for others like me who are a little afraid of the emotions that come with love."

"You are sweet, you know, for a minister."

He laughed. "I'm glad you think so. I'm not sure sometimes myself."

"Isaiah." She touched his arm. "You have no reason to doubt yourself. I'm madly in love with you. Why else would I sit there and allow you to say such things?"

He regarded her for a moment. "I'm not glad that Mandy was taken from me, but I am glad that I am allowed to know you, Esther. It's a great honor."

"I could say the same," she said softly, leaning against his shoulder. "But stop saying such things, or I'll be reduced to tears again."

"Tears are *goot*. They mean that you love me."

"You already know that."

"I need all the confidence I can get." He sighed. "This is new territory for me."

"And for me," she said, her hand on his arm. "But I am thankful, very thankful, that we are making it, Isaiah."

His answer was a smile as he turned into *Daett*'s driveway.

"I want Bishop Beiler to officiate at our wedding in the valley," she said as they came to a stop by the barn. "Would you speak to him before you leave?"

"You want me to tell the bishop the wedding won't be here?"

"*Yah*. It will be okay. I'm sure he will be most agreeable. I could tell from the way he acted today."

"You just want me to get in trouble again."

Esther laughed. "Aren't I worth a little trouble?"

He grinned. "You have a point," he said as he climbed down from the buggy. "I'll see that the arrangements are made before I leave."

"Thank you, Isaiah." She climbed down to plant a kiss on his cheek. "But I imagine you're being accommodating until we've said the vows, and then you'll boss me around."

He winked. "I guess that's part of the risk of falling in love. You never know what will happen."

"Hmm...you are very dangerous. Maybe I shouldn't wed you after all."

He shook his finger at her. "That's not going to happen."

THIRTY-NINE

On a Thursday afternoon more than a week later, a Greyhound bus wound its way through the lower levels of the Adirondack foothills. Seated inside next to her mother, Diana peered out the window for the last mile of the drive into Little Falls. The leaves on the hardwood trees had begun to turn with the first blush of red, gold, and a deeper orange scattered among the bright evergreens.

At last the bus pulled to a stop at the familiar gas station, where Dorrine was already waving from beside her buggy. Diana waved back. Esther joined in with a sudden sting of tears in her eyes.

Diana peered up at her. "What's wrong, *Mamm*? Why are you crying? We're home."

"That's why," Esther whispered.

"When will we see Isaiah again?"

Esther gave Diana a quick hug. "I think he's coming over tonight, but I don't know for sure. Certainly by tomorrow night."

"Goody!" Diana said in a loud voice, bouncing up and down.

Several of the passengers smiled at them as Esther led the way off the bus.

"You have a well-behaved child," one of them commented. "And a happy one."

"Thank you," Esther answered, smiling back.

When they stepped into the street, Diana pulled loose from Esther's hand and raced toward Dorrine, who opened her arms wide. Diana flew into them.

"Someone's happy to be home," the bus driver said with a big grin. He already had Esther's suitcase out and ready to go.

"Thank you," Esther told him. "And thanks for the safe journey."

He tipped his hat and climbed back into the bus. Esther grabbed her suitcase and headed toward Dorrine's buggy.

"Oh, Esther!" Dorrine exclaimed, her arms open again. "You've come back."

Esther laughed and gave Dorrine a hug. "What did you expect, silly?"

"I wasn't sure there for a while!" Dorrine giggled. "It's just so *goot* to see the two of you, and to see Isaiah this past Sunday. The man preached up a storm. What did you do to him in Lancaster County?"

"Got things straightened out and began to make our wedding plans." Esther lowered her voice. "We had to work through a rough spot, but it's smooth sailing now."

Dorrine hugged herself in delight. "So will you tell me? Surely I can know when it will be?"

"*Yah*, this wedding season. The last Thursday of October."

"Oh, that's such *goot* news. No wonder he seemed reborn."

Esther laughed. "And we're having the wedding here in the valley. Isn't that extra *wunderbah*?"

"That's a little risky." Dorrine paused in her stride. "Have your parents agreed?"

"*Yah. Mamm*'s coming two weeks ahead of time, and the wedding won't be that large. After all, it's the second wedding for both of us."

Dorrine helped Diana climb into the buggy and whispered over her shoulder, "Isaiah was sure acting as if it's his first wedding this past Sunday, and look at you! You're aglow."

"The Lord has blessed us, there's no doubt about that," Esther said, hurrying around the other side of the buggy to hide her red face.

Dorrine still noticed, and said with a sigh when Esther climbed in, "Well, I'm happy for the two of you. Now, if only we could figure out what's going on with Joseph. He has me worried." Dorrine clucked to her horse, and the buggy headed up the street out of Little Falls.

"What's wrong now?" Esther asked.

"He was gone for a few days about the time Isaiah went out to see you. Did Isaiah maybe say something to you about it? I didn't dare ask him on Sunday, and John wouldn't either. He said it's none of our business, but Joseph is our neighbor, and Arlene is my cousin."

"You think it had something to do with Arlene?"

Dorrine wrinkled her brow. "Beats me. But how do you think Joseph could ever have persuaded old Peter to change his mind?"

"Maybe Joseph did something romantic," Esther said, and they laughed together at the joke.

"You know that's not the answer. So what is it?" Dorrine asked.

"I'll have to go down and ask him," Esther decided.

"Would you? And then stop in and tell me afterward. I'm so curious. I can't help myself. I mean, what if Joseph and Arlene are getting married? Wouldn't that be something?"

"*Yah*, it sure would," Esther mused, settling back on the buggy seat. A moment later a smile crept across her face. "What if Joseph somehow did convince Peter to change his mind? Why couldn't the Lord bless him the way the Lord is blessing us?"

Dorrine appeared skeptical. "But Joseph isn't Isaiah…"

"And neither am I Arlene."

Dorrine clucked her tongue in sympathy as her horse slowed for the long climb up the crest of Highway 5. Silence settled in the buggy until Diana burst out at the first sight of their house on Fords Bush Road. "There it is!"

"*Yah*, there it is," Esther agreed. "It's so *goot* to be home."

Dorrine pulled to a stop in the driveway, and Esther hopped out to lift Diana down and retrieve her suitcase.

"I'll see you later," Dorrine said. "I know you want to get settled in." She jiggled the reins to trot her horse on down the hill.

Esther watched her go for a few seconds before she took Diana's hand and entered the yard. The first hard frost had bitten the roses sometime in the past week, and the blossoms hung faded and weary. Diana let go of her mother's hand to run up to them and take a long breath, her face pressed into the petals.

"They don't smell anymore. What happened, *Mamm*?"

"Winter's coming, sweetheart. But there will be spring again and many more roses. We will always have roses in our lives. I promise you that."

Diana's countenance lifted slightly. "I like winter too, I guess. And snow."

"It's all in the Lord's plan. But come, we have many things to prepare. First of all, we need to walk down and say hello to Joseph. Would you like that?"

Diana nodded vigorously, and Esther left the suitcase on the front porch. A moment later she was heading down the road with Diana by her side. They might as well see Joseph before she became wrapped up in household duties and supper preparations.

Surely Isaiah would come over tonight. He might wish to appear restrained, but she was confident his desire to see her would win out in the end. She had told him before he left Lancaster County of her travel plans.

Diana let go of her hand to race ahead and barge into the greenhouse. As Esther drew near, Joseph appeared in the doorway with Diana by his side and a big grin on his face.

"Well, look who's back!" he called to Esther. "Welcome home."

"Greetings to you too." She glanced around. "You've been sprucing up the place."

Joseph laughed. "*Yah*, it's time."

"So what is going on, Joseph? What's the secret?"

His grin was broad. "My wedding to Arlene, Esther. Peter and Edna have relented."

"Joseph!" Esther exclaimed, rushing over to give him a quick hug. "How did you accomplish that?"

"The Lord's blessing," he said with a chuckle.

"You're not deceiving me," Esther told him. "You did something."

"Maybe," Joseph allowed. "But we'd best leave that unsaid. We don't want more rumors going around the community, do we?"

"You didn't take roses to Arlene, did you? Or worse...to Peter?"

Joseph roared with laughter. "I had to be a little more original than that, believe me."

"Well, if you won't tell me, I'll just ask Arlene."

"Arlene doesn't know. I have to maintain some secrets, you know. After I told you everything about Silvia's Rose."

"Oh, Joseph." Esther stepped closer. "I can never thank you enough for the story you told me about Silvia and your work with the roses. You changed our lives. We will never be the same."

He hung his head for a moment. "I'm not worthy of your kindness, Esther. I doubt if I would have a *frau* in a few weeks if it weren't for you, so I think we're even. Now, about the wedding...I would like you and Isaiah to serve as the witnesses on my side of the family. Can you make another trip back to Lancaster County? Please say yes. I would be greatly honored."

Esther gasped with delight. "Joseph! Of course we will. I don't even have to ask Isaiah to know that. But why...I mean..."

"Maybe I want to seal my *goot* standing in Peter and Edna's eyes with a minister as my witness at my wedding." Joseph's eyes twinkled. Then he glanced down at Diana, who had begun to pull on his arm.

"Are you coming up for supper tonight?"

Joseph patted her on the head. "I think Isaiah is coming, and I have lots of work to do. I'm getting ready for my new bride's arrival."

The little girl's disappointment showed, so he added, "But you can come over here for supper after Arlene and I are married, and Arlene and I can also come up to your place when your *mamm* invites us."

"Goody, goody," Diana chanted, hopping up and down on one foot.

"That sounds like a good plan, but now we have to go." Esther took Diana's hand. "We just wanted a quick visit, Diana. Joseph has to get back to work, and we still have to unpack."

"Looks like you'll be stopping in somewhere first," Joseph said with a grin. "I saw drapes moving across the street."

Esther hid her smile. "Dorrine should have come over and asked you what was going on herself."

"Don't be too hard on her. Not every man has his promised one hustled back home to keep her from marriage," Joseph said, his face grim. "But that's all over and settled, so we will hold no bitterness against the man."

"You have a golden heart, Joseph."

He just shook his head and remained silent.

Esther left him to hurry across Fords Bush Road. Because Dorrine had made her curiosity so plain, there was no need for discretion. Dorrine must have come to the same conclusion and rushed out to the porch to meet her.

"So, what's going on?" Dorrine asked with quick glances toward the greenhouse.

"Their wedding is on again—and soon, from the sound of things. For some reason, Joseph was able to change Peter's mind."

"Marriage!" Dorrine's eyes grew round. "I never thought that would happen. Not after the way Peter and Edna stormed out of the county."

"Well, that's the big news." Esther took Diana by the hand. "We need to get home and do some unpacking."

They said goodbye to Dorrine and made their way back up the hill. Thinking about Joseph's surprising news, Esther didn't notice the buggy parked beside the house until she was almost in the driveway. Isaiah had climbed out already and regarded her with a bemused expression on his face. "Distracted, are we?"

She let go of Diana's hand to race toward him and throw her arms around his neck. His face hovered above her, and she almost kissed him, but she remembered just in time that they were outside.

"I'll save that for later," he whispered with a wicked grin.

"Are you coming in for supper?"

"Do you want me to?"

"Stop being naughty."

"I have to go home and do my chores first, but I couldn't wait to see you and make sure you had made it back safely."

"Oh, Isaiah." She pulled him close again. "We have so much to speak about, so much of our future to plan."

"I can hardly wait."

FORTY

Back in Lancaster County on the morning of Arlene's wedding, Esther slipped into the upstairs bedroom at her parents' place on Hoover Road for a quick goodbye hug from Diana.

"Sweetheart, will you be okay staying with *Mammi* today?"

Diana nodded, her sleepy eyes barely open.

"She'll be *goot* as gold," *Mamm* assured her from the open bedroom door. "Plus she needs practice staying with us. You have your own wedding day coming up. We'll stay at your house in the valley and give you at least a few days alone with Isaiah over at his place."

Esther tried to hide her flaming face as she gave *Mamm* a quick hug and a kiss on the cheek. "Thank you. You know how to warm my heart."

"Go." *Mamm* motioned with her hand. "Enough silliness. Isaiah just drove up and is outside waiting for you."

"Aren't you happy that Joseph is getting to wed Arlene?"

"*Yah*, but I still think it's a bit strange," *Mamm* replied.

Esther didn't protest. She gave Diana one last hug before she hurried downstairs. She knew *Mamm* had no real animus against Joseph.

The first rays of the sun broke over the horizon as Esther stepped out on the front porch. *Daett* was waiting beside Isaiah's buggy, leaning on the wheel while engaged in deep conversation with the man.

Isaiah still noticed her and waved.

"*Goot* morning," she called as she strolled across the yard.

Daett moved away from the buggy as Esther approached and gave his daughter a warm smile. "Both of you have a *goot* day now. And wish the happy couple the best from us."

"We'll do that," Isaiah assured him as Esther climbed in the buggy. He gave her a shy glance. "It's *goot* to see your lovely face again this morning."

"You'll have me blushing before we even get there. You just saw me a few days ago."

"I can never see enough of you," he said as he drove out of the lane. Together they listened to the steady hoofbeats of Isaiah's borrowed horse on the pavement.

She didn't look at him. She would only blush worse. But what did it matter? With a sigh she leaned against his shoulder and slipped her hand into the crook of his arm. "I'm tired, Isaiah. I think I'll sneak a little nap."

He chuckled. "Are our wedding plans getting to you? And now this quick trip down to Lancaster County? I'm sure you were up late last night talking with your *mamm* and *daett*."

"*Yah*, I was, and what a happy time we had. I wish you could have been there."

"You know I would have been if we'd arrived earlier, but we didn't get in till close to midnight."

"At least we're traveling back together." She yawned.

"Say, did you ever find out what Joseph did to change Peter's and Edna's minds?" he asked.

"No, but I don't really care. I'm just glad it happened."

"And I'm glad you'll soon be my *frau*."

"Stop it," she said, snuggling close. "You just want a kiss."

"*Yah!*"

She complied but quickly warned him, "No more today." He laughed beside her.

"I am so happy," she whispered. "So very happy."

"I hope Joseph and Arlene are as happy was we are."

"I'm sure those two will be quite happy together, just as we will be."

She nestled against his shoulder again. The love she shared with Isaiah was special. Surely the Lord would never take him from her as He had taken Lonnie. No, they would grow old together and end up in rocking chairs.

As they turned into the Yoders' driveway, Esther sat upright on the buggy seat and smiled. Old age with Isaiah would be a pleasant experience. Diana would be grown and married by then, as would any other *kinner* the Lord might give them. She would sit on Isaiah's front porch and look out over the ridge toward the Adirondacks and give thanks that she had been given a man like Isaiah to love.

"Whoa there," Isaiah called out as they rolled up to the barn.

Several young boys hurried forward and greeted them before beginning to help unhitch.

"I see we get first-rate service this morning," Isaiah teased them.

They grinned and didn't answer, their minds obviously occupied with their duties. Behind them the lane had begun to fill with buggies. Esther navigated her way around the extended shafts and hurried up the wooden walk.

Arlene opened the front door and wrapped Esther in a hug.

"It's finally arrived, Arlene! Your wedding day!" Esther whispered excitedly in Arlene's ear.

"*Yah*, because of you and Isaiah," Arlene whispered back. "Oh, this is so *wunderbah*, Esther. So really *wunderbah*."

"*Yah*, it is," Esther agreed. "But I don't think Isaiah and I had anything to do with it."

Arlene ignored the protest and rushed on. "*Daett* and *Mamm* must have been so impressed with the idea Isaiah gave Joseph. He arrived here with a load of vegetables for *Mamm*'s canning, and *Daett* was looking at papers afterward. I'm sure those were letters Isaiah wrote along with Bishop Willis and the other ministers from the valley, all giving their approval to our wedding. *Daett* wouldn't show me what they had written, and neither would Joseph. All Joseph did was grin and say that we should be happy the problem was solved." Arlene gave Esther another hug. "I have been floating on clouds these past weeks, and today I will be a married woman. I thought this day would *never* come." Her face glowed as she gazed rapturously across the lawn. "And all these people...oh, Esther, can you believe this?" Arlene rushed into the yard to greet more of the arriving guests.

Esther sighed and waited until Isaiah came up on the front porch to join her.

"Arlene's on cloud nine," he observed with a grin.

"She thinks you caused this with your letters from the ministry in the valley."

Isaiah laughed. "Now, that's a tall one. I hope you straightened her out."

Esther motioned with her head. "Like that's possible. Look at her. No one will get a word in edgewise today."

"That's what love does, I guess," he said, faking a mournful sound. "I will forever be known as the flower minister. Bishop Beiler teased me when I arrived here this morning, so word has officially drifted down to Lancaster County."

Esther reached up to pat him on his cheek. "No doubt due to Peter. But don't worry. You'll soon be known as a married man and have a whole bench full of *kinner*. This trouble will all be forgotten."

His face brightened. "Are you prophesying, Esther?"

"Hush," she warned as Arlene bustled back onto the front porch with several visitors in tow.

They would soon both burst out laughing if they didn't stop their fun. Esther forced herself to sober up and followed Isaiah into the house with a properly bowed head and a meek look. It only made things worse when Isaiah glanced back at her. Joseph must have noticed them when he appeared in the kitchen doorway because a grin spread over his face. Esther rushed ahead of Isaiah to burst into an empty bedroom, where she closed the door and collapsed in giggles on the bed. This kind of thing was all quite unseemly for a future minister's *frau*, and she had to gain control of herself.

Esther stood and smoothed her dress with both hands. The bedroom door cracked open behind her, and Arlene peeked in. "Is everything okay?"

"*Yah*, I'll be right out," Esther managed evenly.

Arlene still stepped inside instead of going away. "You're not sick, are you?"

"I'm fine. I'm just being a little silly."

Arlene's concerned look didn't leave. "Sorry, Esther, but I'm on pins and needles that something will go wrong. I was up almost all night and couldn't eat a thing this morning. One's wedding day is one of the most important days ever in a woman's life."

"*Yah*, come." Esther took Arlene's hand. "You should be out there with Joseph as he greets your guests."

Arlene's glow returned. "You will stand with us right now, you and Isaiah?"

"Of course!" Esther led the way out into the hallway.

Joseph was busy shaking hands. He turned to greet them both with a smile. "There you are, Arlene. I was beginning to think someone had succumbed to the jitters and fled the house."

The guests joined in the laughter as Arlene blushed and took her place beside Joseph. Esther joined Isaiah on the other side of the couple. Fifteen minutes later, Peter appeared to shoo the wedding party upstairs.

"Stay out of sight," he ordered. "Where have you people learned all these newfangled ways? Greeting the guests before the service begins. Whoever heard of such a thing?"

But he had a slight smile on his face as Joseph nodded and led the wedding party up the stairs. Whatever methods Joseph had used to win Peter and Edna over to his side, he had done a permanent job. Someday she would untangle that riddle.

Isaiah leaned over to whisper in Esther's ear. "Just think. Three more weeks, and our wedding day will have arrived."

"I can't wait," she whispered as he squeezed her hand.

The murmur of voices from the small party filled the upstairs hallway, while the sounds of benches being set up in the living room below rose in the background. Peter soon reappeared at the bottom of the stairwell to motion them down. Joseph led the way again with Arlene by his side. The guests had organized themselves with Bishop Beiler seated against the wall at the head of the minister's bench. In just a few weeks he would sit on a bench in her small living room in the valley and her *wunderbah* moment would have arrived.

Esther tried to still the pounding of her heart as she seated herself across from Isaiah. The service began. The first song was sung, the signal for Joseph to stand with Arlene and follow the ministers upstairs for their final wedding counseling. Isaiah and Esther would also receive their instructions, even though they had both been married before. There were always things one could learn, and she didn't mind. But it would all be a dream when the day arrived. She'd float right through as Arlene appeared to be doing. The girl seemed lost in the clouds and maybe even a little higher. Her face absolutely glowed when the couple returned, but her happiness likely didn't come from the ministerial instructions she had heard. There was so much joy in the room that the singing seemed to almost lift the benches off the floor.

The preaching began when the ministers returned, though it appeared that neither Joseph nor Arlene was paying the least bit of attention. Their gazes were fixed on each other.

Bishop Beiler didn't preach, but he stood up at ten minutes till twelve when the last sermon concluded and said with his warmest smile, "If our brother and sister are still willing to enter into the holy vows of matrimony, will they please stand."

Thankfully, Arlene had enough sense not to bounce up. Maybe she couldn't. At the moment she appeared ready to swoon. Esther unconsciously put out her hand to steady her, but Isaiah shook his head from the seat across from her.

Esther took a deep breath and relaxed. Everything would be okay. Bishop Beiler had already asked the first question, and Joseph must have answered because Arlene's *yah* rang through the whole house.

Several of the older women hid their smiles. An overeager bride was no disgrace. Arlene's desire for a decent husband must be well known in the district. Had not Esther herself gone out to the valley in pursuit of Isaiah? She must remember, in any case, to keep her own voice down once her time came for the vows.

"And now, in the name of the God of Abraham, Isaac, and Jacob, I pronounce you man and wife," Bishop Beiler said.

They all stood while Joseph and his bride led the way out of the house toward the barn, where the meal would be served for the day.

Isaiah reached over to hold her hand and whisper, "You will soon be my *frau*, Esther."

FORTY-ONE

A week before Esther's wedding, she awoke with the blush of dawn on the horizon. She quickly dressed and fixed a cup of hot chocolate in the kitchen. With her hair hung unbound over her shoulders, Esther slipped outside on the front porch to lean on the railing. A faint light was on in the Kings' place down the hill on Fords Bush Road.

At Joseph's house, adjacent to the greenhouse, he and Arlene had become late risers now that the growing season was slowing. Still, Arlene would be up soon, puttering happily around in her kitchen. Arlene had blossomed in the weeks since her wedding, and at the Sunday service her face was aglow with happiness whenever she gazed upon Joseph's bearded face seated in the men's section.

Peter and Edna had arrived for a family visit yesterday, and they were planning on staying through the weekend. The tale of how Joseph had won over Peter and Edna still remained a mystery. When Esther's *mamm* arrived a week ago to help with her wedding preparations, Esther had asked her if anything was known about the subject back in Lancaster County.

Mamm had simply replied, "You shouldn't be so curious, Esther. If people are getting along, be happy yourself."

Which was true, but she still wanted to know.

Joseph and Arlene, along with Peter and Edna, would be up at noon for a light lunch. A supper invitation was what the occasion called for, but Esther's household was too buried in work with the wedding just a week away. Dorrine had offered the King barn for the meal after the wedding ceremony, along with John and the boys' help to clean the area. Esther had accepted the generous offer on the spot, and the cleanup was scheduled for right after breakfast today.

Inside the house, her wedding dress pattern was laid out on the unused bed upstairs, the cloth still on the bolt. She should wear her dress from her wedding to Lonnie for practical reasons, but *Mamm* had told her weeks ago in no uncertain terms, "You need a new dress. It would be indecent for you to wear the same wedding dress twice."

"*Yah, Mamm.*"

For once *Mamm* was on the side of roses and falling in love. *Mamm* had even approved when Esther had chosen a risky color for her dress. She'd wanted a light green, though here in the valley darker colors were the safest selection. Widows especially were expected to show restraint and maturity, but there went another expectation out the window. She hoped Isaiah wouldn't bring a bouquet of roses to the ceremony.

Esther suppressed a giggle, and the sound tinkled happily down the valley in the still morning air.

"You seem to be enjoying yourself," *Mamm* said from behind her. Esther jumped, sloshing the hot chocolate in her cup.

Mamm smiled. "Just teasing, dear. That hot chocolate looks good. I think I'll get a cup and join you."

"I would like nothing better," Esther told her as *Mamm* disappeared into the house. She returned a couple minutes later.

"I haven't seen many roses since I've been here," *Mamm* said. "With all that fuss I heard about, I thought I'd have to walk through whole beds of them just to arrive at your front door."

"*Mamm*, really. It wasn't that bad."

"You came rushing down to Lancaster County all teary-eyed. I think it was that bad."

"So you and *Daett* never gave each other flowers?"

Mamm laughed. "We're old-school, remember?"

"There's nothing wrong with roses. Nor with falling in love."

"You sound like you're trying to persuade yourself." *Mamm* glanced at the rising sun. "The morning's getting on. You should put your hair up. Someone on the road might see you."

"You're right. Shall we go inside?"

"I'm not trying to spoil your morning, dear."

Esther smiled warmly. "Duty first, then pleasure. I still believe that, and I'm very glad you are here."

"So am I." *Mamm* nodded. "And I'm glad you still believe in the old values."

"I'm your daughter. I'll always be that."

The two entered the house, and Esther headed toward her bedroom. She emerged ten minutes later dressed for the day. She made her way to the kitchen, where she found her mother with a second cup of hot chocolate, cooking eggs and bacon on the stove. Esther filled the oatmeal kettle with water and had it boiling by the time she had set the table for three. With the oatmeal stirred into the hot water, Esther left to dress Diana.

"What day is it?" Diana asked, still sleepy eyed.

"Thursday, and we're going down to clean out the Kings' barn this morning. That's where we'll have the meal after the wedding."

"Will I get to go to the wedding?"

"*Yah*, dear. I only went to Arlene's wedding by myself because I had to be a witness and was busy all day. You will certainly be at my wedding."

"But I have to stay with *Mammi* afterward."

Esther nodded. "Only for a few days, then *Mammi* and *Dawdy* will leave for Lancaster County again, and you will come over to Isaiah's house, where we will live from then on."

"Okay," Diana muttered as Esther dressed her and led the way out to the kitchen for breakfast.

"Hi, sleepyhead," *Mamm* teased.

Diana managed a smile and perched herself on the back bench. *Mamm* and Esther seated themselves to bow their heads in prayer for a few minutes of silence. Diana did likewise, her small hands folded on her chest.

When everyone looked up after *Mamm*'s soft amen, Esther dipped oatmeal into Diana's bowl and added milk and sugar. She did the same for her own, and they ate eggs, bacon, and toast afterward. A final silent prayer of thanks was offered before they cleaned the table and washed the dishes. Soon the party made their slow way down Fords Bush Road toward the Kings' residence.

"My, my, everybody is here bright and early," Dorrine sang out from her front porch. "I'll be with you in just a minute."

Esther led the way to the barn, where John and his three boys had begun to pull out the machines and park them under the other shelters. Dorrine appeared with brooms, and John went to find shovels. Jason brought a wheelbarrow, and the cleaning began. A tall ladder was needed to reach the cobwebs in the upper rafters. Esther climbed up halfway and stopped.

"You'd best let me to that," Jason told her with a grin. "We can't have you breaking an arm or a leg the week before your wedding."

"That wouldn't be very romantic at all," Esther agreed, retreating down the steps.

In seconds Jason was at the top of the ladder with his arms outstretched, holding the end of the broom. Esther was steadying the ladder with both hands when Isaiah's chuckle came from behind her. "A little short on one end, I would say."

"Isaiah!" Esther gasped, but she kept her grip on the ladder. "You'll have us all on the floor in a moment if you don't stop scaring people."

"I just came to help," he said, pretending to pout. "And all I get is a chewing out."

"You would get a kiss," she whispered, "if this place wasn't so public."

He laughed and stepped closer to take a firm grip on the ladder. "I think Jason should come down so I can go up. Those spiderwebs must all be banished for our wedding meal. We can't have you looking at them with worry instead of gazing at me in love."

"Isaiah!" she hissed. "There are children around!"

He grinned and asked Jason as he came down the ladder, "You didn't hear that, did you?"

Jason's wide smile was enough of an answer.

"At least you haven't brought any flowers this morning," she pretended to scold.

"I knew there was something I forgot."

"Isaiah!"

"What? I'm the epitome of innocence and decorum." He climbed up the ladder and then looked down at her. "There's nothing wrong with flowers. They are so beautiful."

"Jason, just ignore all this," Esther said, but the boy had already moved on. He and John were busy pushing the last wagon out of the barn.

Isaiah was up to something. She had been suspicious for a while. She could tell by the hint of a smile on his face at unexpected times and that twinkle in his eye. Now he had shown up to help clean the barn without telling her. *Yah*, he was definitely up to something.

"I know how Joseph persuaded Peter and Edna to change their minds," Isaiah said as he leaned forward to swat at spiderwebs.

"Careful," she warned, and then she gasped. "Wait. *What* did you say?"

He winked. "I know his secret."

Esther glanced around. "Seriously?"

He shrugged and swatted again. "Peter isn't making much effort to keep the matter quiet."

"Careful," she said again, clinging to the ladder. "I don't want you lame before the wedding next week."

"You don't want to marry a man in a cast? We would have to put the wedding off for a few weeks, I suppose."

"You are so testing your limits this morning," Esther warned. "Now tell me this great secret."

"Joseph showed Peter how prosperous his greenhouse is, and he gave him a tidy sum, it seems. Sort of like a dowry." Isaiah frowned as he spoke. "Anyway, now Peter is quite taken with his new son-in-law. He drops hints all over the place. Peter has even begun to remodel their home on Mentzer Road before the winter sets in."

"Money!" Esther made a face. "That's not very romantic."

Isaiah reached for the last cobweb. "Would you prefer a fat check instead of roses? Maybe I would stay out of trouble that way." Isaiah retreated down the ladder. "All done, sweetheart!"

"Isaiah!" Esther hissed again as John came toward them.

Isaiah turned to greet John with a big, innocent smile. "What a fine morning to clean out the barn, *yah*? Rain should be moving in tomorrow from how my cows are acting."

"Greetings." John stuck out his hand. "We have everything timed perfectly. Thanks for coming over to help. That way I can get the last of my plowing done before the rains get here."

Isaiah grinned. "You know weddings. They are always getting in the way of work and responsibilities."

John laughed. "Be careful," he said in a stage whisper. "Esther is standing right behind you."

"Is that right?"

Esther already had the broom lifted high, as if ready to bring it crashing down on Isaiah's head.

"I thought women used rolling pins." John choked back a laugh. "But I guess a broom works. It might hurt a little less."

"Is that said from experience?" Isaiah asked, pretending to scramble out of the way.

Esther couldn't help herself. She joined in their laughter. "You're coming up for lunch, John. Joseph, Arlene, and her parents are coming too."

"Ah," John said. "From broom to lunch in a heartbeat. Women! I do declare."

"*Yah*, they are something," Isaiah said. As he moved off with John, he winked over his shoulder.

Esther clutched the ladder again and hung on for a few moments.

"We could use some help over here," *Mamm* called from across the barn, so Esther headed that way.

They worked until eleven. Esther left to prepare sandwiches and set them out on the table. Joseph, Arlene, and Ben arrived at exactly twelve with Peter and Edna in tow.

Esther glared at Peter behind his back. Meanwhile, Arlene hovered over her *daett* as if afraid he would do something wrong. Peter might be happy about the prosperous business Joseph had, but his actions were an insult to both Joseph and his daughter.

Joseph must have noticed her disapproval because he stepped close when they had a moment alone in the kitchen. "What's wrong, Esther?"

"I found out your secret. Isaiah says Peter is blabbing it all over Lancaster County."

Joseph grinned. "I don't care. I just didn't want to be the one who told you."

"You're not insulted?"

"No. I got Arlene. What do I care about money?"

She sighed. "It seems so wrong."

"What's wrong?" Joseph tilted his beard forward on his chest. "Please don't worry about it. By the way, I have *goot* news from Silvia's *daett*. The judges in California gave Silvia's Rose an award. It is now official. Silvia's Rose is an All-American Rose. I got the notice yesterday."

"Oh, Joseph! That's *wunderbah* news! I'm so glad for you and Arlene."

"That's better." Joseph patted her on the arm. "And thanks for inviting us up for lunch. It means a lot to me that Peter and Edna get to know the community better."

Arlene must have heard the last line because she rushed into the kitchen to gush. "*Yah*, this is so *wunderbah*! Joseph has made me so awfully happy. I'm so...I don't know how to say it...but with *Mamm* and *Daett* here, and now you have us up for lunch with Isaiah...oh, Esther..."

Esther grinned at Joseph. Then she turned to his wife. "Come help me with lunch, Arlene."

Joseph smiled his thanks and shuffled off toward Peter and Edna, who were greeting Isaiah with broad smiles and hearty handshakes in the living room.

"So how's married life?" Esther asked Arlene.

Arlene's hands shook as she laid out the sandwiches. "I just can't say how much I love Joseph. And to think that you and Isaiah are the ones to thank..."

"Arlene, please." Esther stopped her. "No thanks is necessary if you'll help me with lunch. I'm just glad you're happy."

Arlene glowed like a kerosene lamp with the wick turned up high.

FORTY-TWO

On the evening of their wedding day, Esther took hold of Isaiah's hand under the table in the Kings' barn. The first strands of a familiar hymn rose around them: "Blest be the tie that binds, our hearts in Christian love; the fellowship of kindred minds, is like to that above."

Esther took a deep breath and gazed into Isaiah's eyes. This would be the last song, and she wanted the moment to linger. Isaiah's fingers moved in hers, and he leaned closer to whisper, "This has been a very special day, sweetheart."

"*Yah*, it has. A day we'll always remember," she replied, her face flaming at the words. But they were oh so true. Today she had promised her heart and hand to this man for the rest of her life. Bishop Beiler was now sitting across the room, smiling and singing with all his might. One would think this had been the bishop's own wedding from how much he had enjoyed the proceedings. But he had known Esther all her life. He had baptized her and officiated when she married Lonnie. He had also presided over Lonnie's funeral service. And now the bishop had made the trip all the way to the valley to join her hand in holy matrimony to Isaiah.

The third line of the song began: "We share our mutual woes, our mutual burdens bear." Esther forced herself to focus and at least pretend to sing. She couldn't get a word out at present, other than a croak perhaps, but her mouth could move. Esther kept her gaze away from Isaiah and moved her lips until the last of the words died away.

Several of the young unmarried boys leaped to their feet and made their way outside to their buggies, but everyone else lingered. Guests began to move about, and Bishop Beiler and his *frau*, Lois, were the first to come over and shake their hands.

"This occasion was well worth the trip," the bishop exclaimed. "Many congratulations to the both of you, and thanks so much for the honor and the chance to see this new community in your valley for myself."

"We thank you," Isaiah told him. "You'll be staying and preaching for us on Sunday, won't you?"

Bishop Beiler grinned. "Will there be any flower bouquets?"

Isaiah reddened considerably and seemed tongue-tied, while everyone roared with laughter. Esther squeezed Isaiah's hand, and he managed a weak smile.

"I'm so sorry," she whispered in his ear.

"Don't be," he whispered back. "This is my fault...and I'm not done yet."

Esther's face showed her horror. "You don't have bouquets hidden away somewhere, do you?"

Isaiah joined in the final notes of laughter and shook his head.

"You are mysterious," she leaned close to say.

He winked and turned to the next person in line. "Now that you have all had a *goot* laugh at my expense, maybe I'll bring along a bouquet of flowers as a thank-you gesture next Sunday."

This produced another round of laughter, and Isaiah grinned from ear to ear. He wasn't serious, but he did have plans. She had suspected that for some time. Maybe he had strewn the path leading up to the front door at his place with rose petals. The thought prompted her to lean close and ask, "Have you made a rose-strewn pathway across the living room floor for me?"

Isaiah attempted to laugh, but his face paled.

"Ah! I must be close."

Isaiah chose to ignore her. Bishop Beiler had long moved on, and Bishop Willis and Beth now stood in front of them, with Deacon Daniel and Sadie behind them in the line.

"I can't believe you only moved here this spring," Beth told Esther. "I know we spoke about Isaiah that first evening, but you did not let the grass grow under your feet. In only a few months you snagged a husband. *Goot* for you."

"Now you have me blushing," Esther said, lowering her head.

"And *I'm* the one who gives out flowers," Isaiah quipped.

Willis shook his finger at them, his face still wrinkled from his hearty laugh. "I'll have a confession from both of you at church for bringing Bishop Beiler in to marry you. We can't have things like that going on in the valley."

"Maybe a bouquet of roses would console you," Isaiah teased, and the laughter rolled again.

"There have been more flower jokes today than I've ever heard in my life." Bishop Willis gasped for air. "But I must say I haven't enjoyed myself so much in a very long time."

"I'm glad to hear that," Isaiah told him. "Maybe we can tell our grandchildren the whole story someday."

"*Yah*, and be sure and mention my role," Willis added. "Tell them I *rose* to the occasion."

Beth groaned at the joke.

"See how well my jokes work? I guess I'd better stay behind the plow rather than venture into the flower world," Willis said.

Beth consoled her husband with a pat on his arm. "I think we had best be going."

With nods all around, they moved away to make room for Daniel and Sadie.

Daniel extended his hand in greeting. "Sounds like I'd best brush up on my flower jokes first."

"Just keep them to yourself, thank you," Isaiah shot back.

Sadie pressed around the side of her husband to shake Esther's hand. "Our men are quite taken with the flower stories tonight, it seems."

"*Yah*, I've noticed," Esther said, shaking her head.

"I'm having Daniel bring me a bouquet someday just to show him how the fancy people act," Sadie said.

Esther giggled. "It was quite fun getting flowers. I think you'd like it."

"Oh, I know I would. Not every day, of course, but a few times a year."

"Maybe Isaiah has started quite the trend, I'm thinking," Esther told Sadie.

"Well, I'm wishing you and Isaiah the very best," Sadie said, sober faced now. "May the Lord give you many long years together and *kinner* as He sees fit. You have already been such a blessing to the community, so I know this will continue. Thank you, Esther, for moving here. I can never say that enough."

"Oh, hush."

"Every word is true and spoken from the bottom of my heart."

"Thank you," Esther whispered. "You're all so kind."

Sadie moved off, followed by Daniel, and next in line were Peter and Edna.

"Many blessings from the Lord," Peter said, extending his hand. "I'm glad I could be here today."

"And I'm glad you both could come," Esther told him.

Peter regarded Isaiah for a moment. "I wouldn't have predicted it, but it seems you have turned your flower fiasco into quite the charming community story. Congratulations on your skills, Isaiah. I seem to lack them myself."

"Oh, Esther's beauty did that. I only went along for the ride, but now you see why I trotted around the neighborhood with flowers in hand."

"*Yah*, I do see," Peter said with a grin. "She is a worthy woman."

Esther stood there silently, her face beet red.

"You must not mind them." Edna leaned close to shake Esther's hand. "That's men for you."

"Maybe even Peter will be bringing flowers home soon," Isaiah teased.

Edna grinned and said, "I'm thinking not, but with all the roses our son-in-law is raising, anything is possible."

Peter's face lit up. "*Yah*, it's true. Not that I approve of such nonsense, but I must say the *Englisha* people are paying outlandish prices for those roses. That sets my daughter up quite well, to say nothing for us in our old age." Peter grinned from ear to ear. "This valley seems to have a knack for turning the strangest things into proper, respectable ones. I must say I wouldn't have believed it without seeing it with my own eyes."

"Maybe you'll be moving here soon," Isaiah suggested with a smile.

Peter put his head back and laughed. "I'm thinking not. Lancaster County is the right place for two old people like us."

"Speak for yourself," Edna shot back.

"See what this valley does to people?" Peter said, faking a glare at Edna. "Even my lovely *frau* opens her mouth and expresses her opinion."

"Then you must be coming back more often," Esther told them with a smile.

Peter grunted and looked at her as if she had said something awful. "Maybe, but we should be going now. Joseph and Arlene left right after the singing ended."

"Old people hang around until late," Edna reminded Peter, and he gave her another fake glare.

"Look what you have started," Isaiah muttered once the two were out of earshot. "You stirred up marital disharmony."

"I think your flowers started it," Esther retorted, giving Isaiah a wicked smile.

The line soon thinned and their witnesses slipped out. Only *Mamm* and *Daett* remained with Diana half asleep on her *mammi's* shoulder. Esther stood up, and Isaiah followed her with a long stretch of his legs.

"*Goot* to be moving again," he said. "I'm glad I don't get married every day."

"You'd better be."

Isaiah chuckled, and she joined in. *Mamm* looked up when Esther approached, and Diana sleepily opened her eyes.

"You're going home with *Mammi* now, sweetheart. Remember? I'll see you on Sunday, and then you'll move in with Isaiah and me at Isaiah's house."

Diana nodded and closed her eyes again.

"She'll be okay," *Mamm* assured Esther. She gave her a kiss on the cheek. "You have done well, daughter, and the Lord has blessed you."

When Esther turned around, Isaiah was nowhere to be seen.

"He's gone to get his horse," *Mamm* told her. "Go now. We have everything under control."

As if to make the point, *Daett* came over for a quick hug before

Esther picked up her wrap and slipped out of the barn. A chill was in the air, and Esther pulled her shawl tight around her shoulders. Isaiah had Echo out of the barn, so she helped him hitch the horse to the buggy. He still hadn't said anything when they climbed in and drove out to Highway 5. Isaiah jiggled the reins and headed east at a steady trot.

"Talked out and laughed out?" Esther teased.

"Nah, just thinking. It's not much that I have for you at the house, and I'm wishing it was more."

"Isaiah, tell me now," she demanded, taking his arm in hers.

He frowned. "Joseph grew his *frau* a rose because of the great love he had for her. I couldn't do that, Esther, but I wished to show you how much you mean to me."

"Isaiah," she chided. "I don't mind not having roses. We keep going in circles. Soon I'll be thinking we're Joseph and Arlene attempting a conversation."

They laughed, the sound gentle in the still night air. A clear swath of bright stars hung outside the open buggy door, illuminating the valley below.

"It is a beautiful night," he said as he turned right off of Highway 5.

"You're not going to distract me. We're alone now, and you *will* tell me."

"I'll show you instead," he promised, turning into his driveway and parking beside the barn. "It's in the house."

"What is?"

Isaiah silenced her with a touch of his finger on her lips. He climbed out of the buggy, and Esther hopped down to help him unhitch. She waited while Isaiah took Echo into the barn. He returned a few minutes later to take her hand and lead the way toward the front door.

"Isaiah, you're scaring me," she whispered.

"Not worse than you have scared me."

He opened the front door, and they stepped into the dark living room. Isaiah let go of her hand to light a kerosene lamp. He motioned for her to follow and led the way into the kitchen. Esther went as far as the doorway before she peered around the frame. Isaiah was standing beside the table with his lamp held high. The light flickered on a rose set in the center of the table, its familiar white and crimson colors flowing into a deep orange. All around the pot rose petals were spread, and nestled among them was a small wrapped box with a fancy bow.

"Isaiah. What is this?"

"You've already seen the rose that Joseph created for Silvia, but this I made myself." He picked up the box. "It's for you, Esther. It's not much, but it's what I could do."

Esther stepped closer to run her hands through the mounds of rose petals. "What extravagance! And whatever is this?" She took the box from his hand.

He leaned forward to kiss her lightly on the cheek. "Just open it."

Esther did so with the crinkle of paper soft beneath her fingers. The light from the lamp revealed two bottles, both of them also wrapped in bows.

"Open the lids and take a deep breath," he said.

She did, and a beautiful aroma filled the kitchen. "What have you done, Isaiah?"

"Rose oil," he said. "With all my love."

"You *made* this?" She turned the bottles slowly under her fingers. "And all these petals on the table?"

"I didn't make those."

"But you didn't have to do all this. You're all I wanted."

"And you're all I've wanted," he said, setting the lamp on the table. "I had to do something for you after all that we've been through."

"Oh, Isaiah," she whispered as he came close and opened his arms.

The lamplight flickered gently on the orange-and-white rose petals, with the breeze from the open kitchen window moving gently across their faces.

DISCUSSION QUESTIONS

1. What were your feelings regarding Esther's move to the valley? On her chances for success with the handsome Minister Isaiah?

2. Could anyone you know make a move to a new area and be surrounded by this level of support from the community?

3. Dorrine King is also on a quest. She wants to help Arlene conquer Joseph Zook's heart. What are your feelings on that venture? Your opinions of Dorrine?

4. Are you familiar with the background story of Silvia's arrival in Lancaster County and her search for true love? If not, this story is available as a free e-book novella titled *Promising a Rose.*

5. Who benefits the other the most: Esther or Isaiah?

6. What explains Joseph's easy rapport with young Diana? Does Isaiah do as well with her at first?

7. What do you think Joseph's long-term plans are when he suggests to Arlene that they copy Esther and Isaiah's dating relationship?

8. Isaiah praises Esther in public at the barn raising. Explore your own feelings if you had been in Esther's place. Has this ever happened to you?

9. Did you expect reconciliation for both couples as they walk through their dark relationship times? What other outcomes could have occurred?

10. Do you think Joseph found true love again with Arlene?

ABOUT THE AUTHOR

Jerry Eicher's Amish fiction has sold more than 800,000 copies. After a traditional Amish childhood, Jerry taught for two terms in Amish and Mennonite schools in Ohio and Illinois. Since then he's been involved in church renewal, preaching, and teaching Bible studies. Jerry lives with his wife, Tina, in Virginia.

How to Heal a Broken Heart

Mary Yoder's life couldn't get much better. Engaged to be married, spring is in the air and love is in her heart as she looks forward to the fall wedding she's always dreamed of.

Six months later on a crisp November morning, Mary awakens in a beautiful valley near the Adirondack Mountains on what was to be her wedding day, heartbroken and alone.

Her sister, Betsy, tries to protect Mary from the romantic overtures of Stephen Overholt, a longtime Amish bachelor. Betsy is considering jumping the fence for the *Englisha* world and encourages Mary to follow.

Meanwhile, Mrs. Gabert, an elderly *Englisha* grandmother, launches her own matchmaking effort on behalf of her grandson Willard, who is a missionary to Kenya and nursing his own broken heart. She hopes that Willard and Mary can find comfort in one another despite the fact they come from two different worlds.

As Mary struggles to accept the Lord's will, she must determine whether or not one of her potential suitors can give her the future that was denied her.

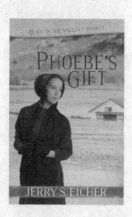

Dreams Never Die When You Believe in Them

Phoebe Lapp's grandmother was *anything* but ordinary. Before her death, the eccentric elderly woman purchased three Assateague ponies, seemingly for no reason. But after her passing, Phoebe learns of her beloved grandmother's wish to start an Amish pony farm in a lovely little valley near the Adirondack Mountains for hurting *Englisha* children. That dream now lies with Phoebe if she decides to fulfill it, but a teaching position is available as well. Which path should she choose?

Further complicating her decision, before her passing, Grandma Lapp asked a neighbor, David Fisher, to be involved in running the farm and help Phoebe. David agrees, but his sister Ruth has yet to abandon her *rumspringa*, and the only reason she hasn't left the church already is because of Grandma Lapp's kindness. Unbeknownst to Phoebe, David has secret hopes of attracting her affection, but Ruth's decision to stay or jump the fence could make things difficult for him.

Phoebe knows she has choices to make—whether or not to honor her grandmother's legacy and what to do about David's growing attentions toward her. But she's not alone. God is with her every step of the way.

To learn more about Harvest House books and
to read sample chapters, visit our website:

www.harvesthousepublishers.com

HARVEST HOUSE PUBLISHERS
EUGENE, OREGON